*N*EAL would never forget his first glimpse of Miss Delilah Mannering. She was perched upon a stile, her ragged skirts up to her knees, in one hand a half-eaten peach. A monstrously ugly dog was sprawled at her bare and very dirty feet.

Nor would he forget her first words. For after he had sprung to her defense, knocking down the strange man who would not let her go, Miss Delilah turned to him and said, "Well, you have a very handy bunch of fives, sir. It was very kind of you to draw Johann's claret for me. I'm sure I'm very grateful, because my case was growing desperate—not of course that I would have knuckled under to a curst loose fish like Johann, but there's no denying he *had* put me in a tweak—but, who the devil *are* you?"

An Eligible Connection

Maggie MacKeever

FAWCETT COVENTRY • NEW YORK

CHAPTER ONE

The hour was early, bright and cool. Mist rose from the stream by which were pitched a few shabby tents, some gaudy caravans. From behind the wagons came the low voices of men tending their livestock. In the air was the smell of wood smoke and frying bacon, the clank of cooking pots.

Within one of those caravans was imprisoned a young girl. Her name was Delilah. No tinker, this damsel, with her flaming red hair and freckles, her snub nose and large brown eyes and mouth that was a bit too wide; and no beauty, either, for all that her determined repulsion of a certain suitor's delicate attentions—a repulsion accomplished by the application of a frying pan—had led to her current incarceration. Ruefully, Delilah tossed aside the sliver of mirror in which she had been contemplating her unprepossessing features. Clearly it was not her personal beauty that had inspired such ardor in Johann.

She rose from her narrow bunk to pace the floor, an exercise made all the more difficult by the presence of a huge and hideously multicolored hound, known affectionately to his mistress as Caliban, and referred to by the tinkers in various unflattering terms, the kindest among which was "monster." Caliban opened one eye to observe Delilah's progress. Halfheartedly, he wagged his tail.

No more than herself, Delilah thought, did Caliban like this enforced inactivity. It was her fault for not dealing more tactfully with Johann. Delilah could not regret the act. The skillet, as it had connected with Johann's skull, had made a most satisfying thunking sound. It would have done him no great damage; Johann had a very thick skull. In more charitable moments, Delilah was accustomed to thinking him a perfect blockhead.

Delilah was not feeling especially charitable just then. She amused herself by compiling a list of epithets to which Johann might justifiably lay claim: mugwump, potwalloper, whopstraw. Here her inventiveness failed her; in lieu of further derogations she uttered a few good round oaths. Caliban, accustomed to such bursts of vulgarity on the part of his gently bred mistress, engaged in a huge yawn.

Delilah leaned against a battered chest of drawers and stared out the small window. She could have squeezed through it, she supposed—though generously fashioned, Delilah was both agile and petite—but it was hardly worth the effort. Johann or one of his cronies would catch her before she advanced three feet.

The morning promised to be a pleasant one; how she wished she might scamper about in the cool grass, feel the sunwarmed earth beneath her bare feet. Delilah glanced down at those appendages, which were distinctly begrimed. There was little enough in her appearance to suggest a young lady of gentle birth now. Delilah didn't in the least mind her loss of dignity; she was as little inclined toward decorum as she was toward tact. She minded very much, however, the curtailment of her freedom. Only that freedom had made this nomad existence bearable.

She moved closer to the window, pressed her little nose against the pane. Athalia would be coming soon with her breakfast. Perhaps Athalia might be persuaded to render a small favor in return for the only thing of value Delilah still possessed: her mother's wedding ring. Delilah hated to part with that item, not from sentiment—another attribute that Delilah did not claim, as had not her mother, at least in regard to that piece of jewelry—but because without it she would truly be destitute. Yet even more she would hate to marry Johann.

It was not that Johann was displeasing or deformed; among the tinkers he was considered a very handsome man. Certainly he had done his utmost to ingratiate himself. But Delilah, if

6

she had to marry, and she imagined that eventually she must, had a notion of choosing as her bridegroom a fine, straight, handsome, noble young fellow, not a swarthy and middle-aged tinker who had already buried two wives, and who would expect to be waited upon slavishly. Delilah had no intention of wedding herself to a lifetime of drudgery.

But how to avoid it? Athalia was her only hope, the only person to show her any kindness in all of Johann's entourage—and even Athalia did so with an eye to feathering her own nest. The tinkers thought of Delilah as their meal-ticket. It would be through no efforts of Delilah's if, eventually, she served as such.

The windowpane was cold, and her nose had grown numb. With a last longing glance outdoors, Delilah moved away. It was Sunday, and the village church would be filled. Easy to envision the local gentry in their leather-lined pews, the peasants in the aisles, the white-gowned girls on either side of the chancel, the rector intoning the liturgy. Perhaps the rector would offer a few pertinent remarks upon christian charity—while his congregation pondered in a most uncharit-able manner upon chickens snatched away from their coops, and newly purchased horses that were transformed over-night from prancing beauties into broken-winded nags. The most wonderful among Johann's many talents was a dazzling sleight of hand. Though they would never know it, Delilah agreed wholeheartedly with the villagers that it would be a very good thing for all of England if Johann were hanged.

Delilah was not a girl to nurse grievance long; resentment served no practical purpose. She dropped cross-legged onto the floor beside Caliban and drew the hound's huge head into her lap. Caliban, tongue lolling, gazed up at his mistress with an adoring expression. Delilah gently pulled his ears.

In this position Athalia found them when she entered with the breakfast tray. Cautiously, she eyed the hound; Caliban, who was considerably larger than his mistress, had been know in the exuberance of his greeting to knock unwary recipients over. The hound showed no inclination to stir. Athalia set down her tray.

Delilah contemplated this gift of providence, decided that Athalia was in an approachable mood. Sometimes it was difficult to determine the woman's state of mind; Athalia's dark face—a darkness not only due to the pigmentation of her skin, but also to her strong aversion to water and soap—evidenced as much emotion as a stone. Once she might have been beautiful, but now her face was very weathered, and her untidy dark hair streaked with gray. "Can you stay a minute?" asked Delilah. "I've grown very weary of my own company."

Athalia glanced behind her, then firmly closed the door. She crossed her arms beneath a bosom that once had been magnificent. "Johann is cross as crabs, and getting himself foxed. You've got yourself in a dreadful pickle, *leicheen*."

"The devil," retorted Delilah, around a slice of bacon that she was sharing with Caliban, "fly away with Johann! The mere thought of him puts me in a passion. Athalia, I have been thinking. There is only one thing I can do."

"Aye." Athalia looked sublimely unconcerned. "Marry him."

Delilah was a very astute young lady despite her tender years, which numbered a mere seventeen; and therefore was aware that Athalia's sentiments regarding Johann were extremely warm. Since it would hardly have been politic to comment that she would liefer ally herself with the devil than with the tinker, Delilah refrained. "I cannot. You will see why. I have decided, Athalia, that I must confide in you."

Athalia, leaning against the wall, did not look especially gratified. "I won't go against Johann, for all your fine words. Blow the gaff, if that's what you're wishful of, but don't be thinking to make *me* out a flat."

"Athalia!" Delilah, who intended precisely that, opened wide her eyes in what she devoutly hoped was an expression of wounded innocence. "As if I would try and make a, er, flat of someone who has so steadfastly stood my friend. You know that Johann does not love me; he wishes only to gain a fortune. But I have deceived you all! I have no fortune. It was all a sham."

There was an expression, now, on Athalia's rock-hewn features, and the expression was bewilderment. She sat down on the bunk. Encouraged, Delilah sniffled. "The worst of it is that I have made trouble for you, for it was you who convinced Johann to take me in. Truly, I am sorry for it, Athalia! I know how angry Johann will be to discover he's been duped. Pray, do not think too badly of me—I was desperate, you see, with my mistress dying, and without a ha'penny to my name.

8

If you had not happened along, I should probably have had to go upon the streets!"

Nor did this speech fail in its intent: Athalia looked, and was, aghast. "Your *mistress?*" she echoed. "You said 'twas your mother that we buried. Don't be trying to pull the wool over my eyes."

"Oh, no, dear Athalia! Never!" Delilah had learned during the past few years to tell a very convincing lie. "Perhaps if I start at the beginning it will make better sense. I was in service to the lady whom you came upon in such grievous difficulties—a sort of companion, you see. Indeed, I was at my wit's end, what with the accident, and no money with which to pay the doctor, and there was no one to whom I could apply. And then the tinkers came, and she expired, and I was in a terrible dilemma because everyone was applying to me for the money that was owed. And so," Delilah blushed bright pink, "I did a terrible thing. I lied."

Athalia hugged herself, as if fending off imaginary blows. Were this tale true, those blows would become all too real, once Johann heard of it. Johann might treat this red-haired miss with kid gloves, but others weren't similarly privileged. "You said you were heiress to a fortune," she protested. "You said Johann would be repaid his money, and much more beside."

"So I did." Delilah raised huge tearful eyes— accomplished by staring unblinking upon Caliban's marbled back for several moments—to Athalia's stricken face. "Lies, all of it. I feared no one would help me if they thought me truly penniless." She wiped her face against her sleeve. "Alas, I am no more than a rank adventuress. I must tell Johann, naturally, but first I had to acquaint you with the truth. Oh, Athalia, you look so angry! I cannot blame you for being sadly out of curl, for I have behaved abominably—but I beg you will forgive me."

Looking much more inclined toward murder than absolution, Athalia rose from the bunk and in her own turn paced the floor. Caliban opened an eye and snapped lazily at her heels. "Unless we're both to be hobbled, Johann mustn't find out. My head he'd have on a platter, and there's no telling what he'd do to you."

Even the intrepid Delilah did not care to ponder that, the

weakest spot in her schemes. "Athalia, how *can* we keep it from him?" she wailed. "He is bound to learn the truth eventually. How much simpler it would be if I could disappear!"

Athalia's thoughts had followed similar lines—to wit, that she wished she'd never seen hair nor hide of this troublesome chit; consequently, Delilah's comment stopped her in midstride. "Where would you go?" she inquired. "What would you do? A young lass like yourself, alone—I tell you, *leicheen,* it won't do."

This brusque kindness, from so unlikely a source, almost proved Delilah's downfall. Ruthlessly, she squelched her conscience. Athalia might show a passing concern for her welfare, but Athalia would also sell her own grandmother to a brothel-keeper for a quartern of gin.

"There *is* someone I could go to," Delilah said demurely. "If only I could get him word."

"Him?" Athalia regarded the girl, whose cheeks were flushed, and grinned. "So, *leicheen,* you have a gentleman friend."

Delilah grew even pinker, an embarrassment prompted not by maidenly modesty, but by the tremendous crammers that issued through her own lips. "I do—or I *would,* could I but let him know that I've turned agreeable." She fished a letter from the pocket of her shabby skirt. "I've written to tell him so, but there is no way to post this—you know how closely I am watched. If only he knew of my predicament, he would come straightaway to my rescue. But how am I to tell him? All this has put me in the pathetics! Athalia, can *you* help me?"

Athalia wished nothing more than to wash her hands of a golden goose that could lay her no more than breakfast eggs, and which had additionally caused Johann's attention to stray, but she was cautious by nature. "Well—"

"Oh, please!" Delilah did not despair, despite the uphill nature of her work. "You are my last hope! And if I do not contrive to remove myself from here, Johann will find me out. He may even think you have known the truth all along, and have pulled the wool over *his* eyes! He would not like that, I think." That Athalia agreed was obvious. "Listen, I will add a postscript to this letter, and arrange that my friend meet me somewhere. The inn, perhaps? And then I will escape—and you, knowing what time I am to leave, will provide yourself an alibi. That way I will simply disappear, and Johann will never know you had anything to do with it. What do you think?"

What Athalia thought was that she would shortly be fretting her guts to fiddlestrings, and so she remarked. Johann would no longer sit idly twiddling his thumbs while this grand plan was put into effect that a pig could take wing and fly. "And furthermore," she added, "he'd be bound to think I was in it up to my neck if you up and hopped the twig."

"Not," Delilah repeated patiently, as she simultaneously mourned the pussyfooted tendencies of her fellow conspirator and polished off the remainder of her breakfast, which had grown cold, "if you are with him when I do so. Beside, I shall throw him off the track by pretending to be smitten with him. Perhaps he'll think I've been kidnapped." Still Athalia looked doubtful. Delilah drew a deep breath. "I realize I ask you to take a risk. You will be repaid."

This promise did not sit well with Athalia, who pointed out irately that Delilah's previous promises of repayment had brought this predicament about. Delilah merely smiled and delved into the bodice of her gown. Suspiciously, Athalia regarded her outstretched hand.

"Take it," said Delilah. "If you help me, it's yours."

Greedily, Athalia contemplated the wedding ring. She was fond of such baubles, as witnessed by her countless chains, most of which had turned the skin beneath them green. Had not Delilah been such an innocent, Athalia would have had the ring from her without further ado—but it was not Athalia's way to take advantage of damp-eared infants. This was a failing which she frequently had cause to regret, as in the present instance. Were Johann to learn of this conspiracy— avarice warred with prudence, and won.

"I'll just add a couple lines to this letter," Delilah remarked cheerfully. As she did so, Athalia bit the ring. Apparently it passed muster, for she slipped it on her finger. Delilah dropped the letter into her hand. "Speed is of the essence," she said solemnly. "And secrecy."

Her decision made, Athalia grinned. "Never fret, *leicheen,* I'll see this posted. And I'll keep dubber mum'd."

"I shall be eternally grateful," Delilah replied humbly. This meekness deserted her immediately Athalia had gone. Quickly, she moved to the window. Athalia set out not toward Johann's wagon, as Delilah had half-feared, but across the field. So far, so good. It remained now to await Sir Nicholas Mannering's response to a dramatic epistle from a daughter he had not seen in five years.

CHAPTER TWO

Athalia was, after her own fashion, a woman of her word: as pledged, she posted Delilah's letter—after doubling back to her own wagon and initiating a great search, the fruits of which were a scrap of paper and a charcoal stub. Athalia could not read, but she could trace letters as well as anyone. A queer coincidence, surely, that the characters on Delilah's letter were also engraved in the golden wedding ring? Her task accomplished after monumental labor, Athalia once more set out across the field. Ah, but Delilah was a rum one. Athalia was very curious about what sort of trickery was being set in train by that carrot-headed miss.

As were certain other individuals, almost a whole week later, although those other individuals lacked Athalia's appreciation of enterprise. It was the dinner hour in the elegant Brighton residence of the duke of Knowles, an hour anticipated with no great pleasure by any member of the duke's retinue, all of whom were present in the pretty dining room, done in the Classical manner with fine stucco decorations.

This retinue, grouped around the table of mahogany,

polished to the brilliance of fine glass, which stood upon pillars and claws, with brass casters, numbered three. Seated at the duke's left hand was his cousin Edwina Childe. A woman in her fifth decade, Edwina's manner suggested a girl half that age. Her hair was an improbable shade of yellow, her eyes a trifle too close-set, her features and figure gaunt from constant dieting. On this particular occasion, which was to go down in the annals of family history as highly memorable, she wore a lovely and totally unsuitable gown of sea-green.

In direct contrast to Edwina's beribboned and beruffled finery was the attire of the lady seated to the right of the duke of Knowles. Her evening gown was of pale yellow muslin, its only claim to high fashion its Mameluke sleeves. Nor did the gown's owner aspire to modality, though she possessed an abundance of lovely chestnut-colored hair and stunning amber eyes. The hair, however, was drawn back into a severely unflattering style; and the eyes were expressionless. Still, there were those who appreciated Sibyl Baskerville's understated beauty and quietly ironic demeanor. Her cousin the duke, who was not among that number, had often taken leave to wonder aloud why she should have left so many hopeful suitors languishing on the vine while she pursued a determination to remain unwed. Spinsters who had achieved the advanced age of twenty-seven, he believed, could not afford to be so very particular in their preferences—unless they did not mind the embarrassment of being firmly on the shelf. To these taunts, Binnie always responded with her habitual goodwill; to marriage with a man whom she could not love, she preferred leading apes in hell—or, which was much the same, an existence in which she served as the duke's unacknowledged housekeeper. As usual in such confrontations, the duke was left with no adequate response—a fact that did not in any way prevent him from venting his spleen.

Seated next to Binnie, contemplating a sideboard table which exhibited a mirror with candles on each side, fixed to the brass rail rather as if it were his own coffin complete with lions' heads carved in the mahogany, was her brother Neal. A young man of twenty-two, clad in the dashing evening regimentals of the Tenth Dragoons, Neal resembled his sister to a startling degree; but where Binnie was so self-effacing as to appear almost colorless, Neal was astonishingly handsome. His chestnut hair was not cropped so short that it failed to curl, his amber eyes were most often merry and warm and sincere.

Those golden eyes held no such expression now, as they gazed upon the duke—nor did the eyes of Binnie or Edwina. All three members of the duke's retinue stared at him blankly. As usual, Binnie was the first to speak. "Gracious God, Sandor!" she murmured serenely. "Bits o' muslin, high flights— whatever can you mean?"

The duke turned his cold blue attention on Binnie, obviously without appreciation of the temerity that had prompted her to speech. Blandly, she met his regard. The duke repressed an impulse to swear, not from consideration for the delicate sensibilities of the females present at his dinner table, for the duke was not in the habit of considering anyone but himself, but because he knew it was futile to try and get a rise out of Binnie. For the fact that she neither fawned on him nor exhibited awe in his extremely overbearing presence, as did the majority of the females of his acquaintance, including those privileged to be taken under his protection, he accorded Binnie no plaudits. Indeed, he was accustomed to referring to her, among his cronies, as Miss Prunes and Prisms. The satisfaction accompanying this admittedly childish and churlish behavior was greatly lessened by the conviction that she spoke even worse of him.

"Mannering's girl," he said abruptly, and waved a singularly dirty piece of paper under Binnie's Grecian nose. "The missing heiress has come to light. In a tinkers' camp, no less. So dire are her straits that she's written to her father, begging for rescue—and in the process, I might add, scribbling a great deal of fustian."

"And since Mannering is dead, and you are his executor, the letter came at length to you?" Binnie contemplated the dinner table, strewn with the remains of an excellent meal, among which had been stewed pippins, scalloped oysters, crayfish in jelly, lobster in fricassee sauce, stewed mushrooms, and a solid syllabub in a glass dish. "You will have to do something about the girl; to ignore her plight would be shockingly remiss, and I am persuaded you would not behave

14

so shabbily. Dear me, how very tiresome! A man of rank and fashion can hardly be expected to trouble himself over a schoolroom miss—heavens, when would you have time?"

Though these remarks were delivered in the most sympathetic of manners, the duke was not deceived. Nor were the others, who were—to their sorrow—well acquainted with this long-standing enmity. "A letter!" said Edwina hastily, before the duke could utter a withering rake-down, and thusly spoil her appreciation of her apricot tart—an indulgence for which she would atone by going without her breakfast on the following day. "God bless my soul! Miraculous, is it not, how bad news always seems to catch up with one, while good news so often goes astray? And in a tinkers' camp, you say? Lud! I cannot help but think, dear cousin Sandor, that this is shockingly irregular conduct. The chit must be lacking altogether in principle. Well-brought-up young ladies simply do not *do* such things!"

"Nor do they employ vulgar expressions," remarked Binnie, who had tweaked the letter from Sandor's fingers and was perusing it with vast appreciation. "Or display an unbecoming violence of feeling. Mistress Delilah, it would appear, has little patience with ladylike things. Neal, you will enjoy reading this—do be careful with it; heaven only knows where it's been! In the coal-scuttle, from the looks of it. Sandor, do you think this girl may be an impostor, out to claim Mannering's wealth? Apropos of that, I wonder if she knows he left his entire fortune to her. She could hardly expect such generosity, after she ran away."

"Run away?" echoed Edwina, as she took a second helping of the apricot tart. "Gracious! Dear Sandor, you cannot mean to take up such a rag-mannered girl."

Until that very moment, His Grace had contemplated no such thing. It was not his habit to cater to the sentiments of his dependents, if anything the contrary; and the contretemps that would result from the introduction of a hoydenish madcap—as Miss Delilah Mannering most obviously was—into his household was a notion that afforded him marked satisfaction. The duke's sense of humor was practically nonexistent; he was dissolute and stern and selfish; he admitted scant fondness for anyone or anything, especially the cousins who dwelt beneath his roof, and who evidenced an

15

unshakable determination to cut up his peace. Therefore, he thought it would be a very good thing if they received a richly merited comeuppance. That of the three Binnie alone set herself at loggerheads with him did not occur to His Grace; and if it had, he would have thought merely that Edwina and Neal deserved to suffer for the sin of being spiritless. His Grace the duke, it becomes apparent, was a man impossible to please.

Binnie, who had from experience learned to read the expressions that flickered across the duke's attractive countenance—for the duke's countenance was a direct proof of the adage that beauty is only skin deep— awaited his next remark with no small suspense. She was not disappointed. "How can I do other than offer the girl a home?" he said, in a noble manner that Binnie found sickening. "The poor child has no living relatives of any close degree. I can hardly leave her with a band of tinkers, especially when Mannering charged me to look after her. Beside," he added, quite ruining his selfless performance, "I'm already encumbered with the lot of you; what matters one more?"

A brief silence greeted this ungentlemanly remark. Binnie, who might have responded in a manner calculated to take the wind out of His Grace's sails and simultaneously send him into a thunderous rage, was occupied in keeping her brother from reacting similarly, an act accomplished by kicking his shin. What Sandor said was true enough; they were dependent upon him and would be for three more years, until Neal came into his own inheritance, on which happy day the Baskervilles would be privileged to bid the duke go and be damned.

Edwina, who could not anticipate a similar release from Sandor's ill-tempered dominion, choked on the apricot tart that had turned into a sodden, tasteless lump in her mouth. "Tea!" she said thickly. "It is very refreshing when one is in trouble. Let us have some!"

"If you wish to curdle your insides with that stuff, do so; but don't try and inflict it on the rest of us." Sandor had missed none of the byplay, including the pained expression on Neal's face as Binnie's shoe had connected with his shin, and was as a result regaining a degree of good humor—or humor as good as was possible for him, which in a more

16

agreeable person would have been called foul. "How much trouble can be caused by a mere dab of a girl, even if she is—and she sounds to be—a pernicious brat? Don't distress yourself, Edwina! Binnie will look after her."

"To be sure I shall!" said that lady cheerfully. "I shall exert myself to bring her into fashion—we shall be as merry as crickets, I vow! In truth, I must consider this a piece of astonishingly good fortune! 'Twill be an excellent way to prevent myself falling into a lethargy." Sandor was not pleased that his deliberate provocation should be met with smiles and sweet good humor; he scowled. Binnie patted his hand. "Give it up, cousin! I shan't allow you to stir coals. You are certain in your own mind that this Delilah is who she claims to be?"

The duke jerked away his hand, and rose. "I am. Neal, you will find the chit and bring her here. Tomorrow."

Neal, who had been sorely regretting his decision to dine *en famille* instead of in the officers' mess, roused from his bitter trance. "Tomorrow I cannot. I am otherwise engaged."

"Then break the engagement!" advised the duke, callously. "If you don't show some independence now, you'll live forever under the cat's paw." He contemplated Binnie, who was fiddling with her fork. "Even more so than you do now." Binnie glanced up at him. Brilliantly she smiled. In a very nasty temper, the duke strode from the room.

He was a damnably attractive man, she thought, with his golden hair, his arrogant sun-bronzed features, his chill blue eyes; and his athletic figure showed to good advantage in evening dress. Had Sandor not been totally deficient in all the graces, he would have been nigh irresistible. Despite his various inadequacies, many women had found him so— current among them a dazzling barque of frailty named Phaedra, who had held Sandor's erratic attention longer than most of her kin. Doubtless Sandor was even then en route to an assignation with the lady, after which he would perhaps adjourn to the theater, then pass half the night at the gaming tables or possibly in company with fellow members of the innumerable societies for convivial purposes which flourished in Brighton—the Choice Spirits, or the Knights of the Moon, or the Humdrums. Sandor was popular among the gentlemen; even the prince regent was pleased to call him friend. Binnie

17

could only consider the gentlemen very undemanding in their tastes. For herself, she was grateful that the life of a gentleman of leisure involved little time spent at home.

"I knew it!" uttered Neal, as soon as the duke had passed from earshot. "Sandor means to prevent me from marrying Cressida; I suppose he thinks to keep me under *his* thumb for the next three years. Well, I shan't tolerate his cursed interference! I *shall* marry Cressida, and once I am married my inheritance will be my own."

Binnie studied her brother, whose golden eyes glittered angrily, and whose face was flushed. "Pray moderate your manner," she said quietly. "Sandor has not forbidden your marriage."

"No, but he wouldn't." Neal drank deeply from his wineglass, then set it down so firmly that it overturned. "He'd let me go on thinking that I was to escape him, then at the last minute introduce some impediment. It's my opinion that Sandor's been dipping into my money, and doesn't wish me to find out, and therefore keeps me on so damnably tight a string."

"But, dear boy!" protested Edwina, who detested strife. "Sandor *did* buy you into the prince regent's own regiment. Surely that is indication of *some*thing!"

"Yes, but what?" Abruptly, Neal pushed back his chair. "If Sandor had a grain of proper feeling, he wouldn't insist I fetch this accursed girl. How will Cressida feel, do you think, when I cry off from another engagement?" In Sandor's absence, he glared at Binnie. "I know, you will say I refine too much on it! But Cressida is all sensibility, and cannot help but be wounded by what must appear my neglect. Oh, there's no point in discussing it. Naturally I must do as I am told. But I warn you, Sandor is going to push me too far!" And on this ominous note, he exited.

Binnie propped her elbows on the table, and sighed. Perhaps she was cruelly unfeeling, as Neal obviously believed, but it was not in Binnie's nature to make a fuss about trifles. If truth be told, it was she who disliked Neal's prospective alliance with Cressida Choice-Pickerell, and not Sandor— though Binnie strongly suspected that Sandor's apparent compliance derived from his knowledge of her sentiments. To give the devil his due, he was very apt at guessing one's thoughts—and Binnie's thoughts on the matter of Cressida

Choice-Pickerell were most unsuitable for a lady of dignified appearance and mature years.

"Mercy on me!" Edwina lustfully contemplated the remainder of the apricot tart. "What a sad affair! I never heard of such a thing. Sibyl, why must you always be at daggers drawn with Sandor? Once you rubbed along together very well. You still might, were you to try and be just a little conciliating."

"Why should I?" retorted Binnie, rather irritably. "Were I to say nothing that could get up Sandor's back, I would never say anything at all—and though that might suit Sandor very well, it would not suit me. As for the other, Sandor was once a very different person than he is now."

" 'Twas with Linnet's death that he changed." Edwina's eyes filled with easy tears. "He blamed himself, for insisting that she overcome her fear of horses—which is a great piece of nonsense because he could hardly have planned that she should get her neck broken! But there it is. Her pretty neck *was* broken and with it Sandor's heart. Poor boy!"

That this was hardly an appropriate term to apply to a man of five-and-thirty years, and one who was additionally wealthy as Croesus, Binnie did not point out. Privately, she considered Sandor's legendary rudeness the result of nothing more sentimental than laziness. He had early discovered that it required less effort to be cruel than to be kind, and would see no point of expending the effort to amend a habit that the world tolerated in him. As for Linnet, Binnie remembered her very well. She had been a lovely girl, ingenious and gay—and a trifle deficient in intelligence. Had Linnet not taken her fatal tumble within a few months of her marriage, Sandor would have quickly found his ingénue bride a dead bore.

"This Mannering girl," continued Edwina, who in lieu of an audence was perfectly content talking to herself. "Sibyl, what is this story about her running away? Surely it was just Sandor's little joke and she did no such thing? Because if she did, I cannot imagine what he is about, introducing her into this household!"

Binnie picked up the letter from where it lay by Neal's plate and handed it across the table. "Read for yourself. As for what Sandor intends, it is to see me at point non plus. He will not succeed, but he must ever try."

Holding the letter gingerly, Edwina perused the contents. As she read, her eyebrows rose. "Ransom! Kidnapping! God bless my soul!" She dropped the sheet and stared at Binnie. "My dear, I wish you would consider marrying Mark, because then we could *all* leave Sandor's house, and he would have to deal with this chit himself—because I don't mind telling you she doesn't sound at all acceptable!"

"No," Binnie said flatly. "I do not intend to marry anyone. I suspect that letter is the product of a highly imaginative mind—which may be forgiven a child of seventeen. Consider, Edwina: the poor girl is an orphan, alone in the world. How unhappy she must be. It will take no great effort on our part to show her a little kindness. And the heiress to a considerable fortune can hardly be left to languish in a tinkers' camp."

"True." Edwina brightened. "Maybe *she'll* get married and we can all live with her. I do not scruple to tell you, Sibyl, that I am likely to sink into a decline if I must tolerate Sandor's brutishness for much longer! I'm sure it's not surprising if he should consider you abominably provoking, because you *are!* But I have never raised my voice to him, or offered an unkind word, and I think it very hard that he should dislike me equally!"

So little moved was Binnie by this blunt statement of Sandor's sentiments regarding herself that she plucked an apple from a pretty silver dish and polished it on her Mameluke sleeve. "Sir Nicholas Mannering, from all reports, was an odious monster of ill nature, such as in comparison would make Sandor look a veritable paragon. He so abused his wife that five years ago she fled his home—taking with her their daughter—in company with his secretary. Sir Nicholas was furious, more at the desertion of his secretary than his wife. He made no effort to find the renegades until it was brought to his attention that in lieu of his daughter his fortune would pass to a distant relative that he particularly abhorred. Sir Nicholas instigated inquiries. The secretary was tracked down without difficulty, but he had parted company with Sir Nicholas's wife some time past. Of the other two, there was no trace."

Entranced, Edwina plunged her fork into the remainder of the apricot tart. "Goodness! Then what?"

Binnie shrugged. "Then nothing, until now. Sir Nicholas left all to his daughter, perhaps believing her still alive, perhaps thinking such a tactic would tie up the estate, and consequently frustrate the distant relative for some time. It fell on Sandor to determine the whereabouts of the heiress. I believe he made some effort in that direction, even if it was not considerable. There you have it. The heiress *has* been found, due more to her own initiative than to Sandor's diligence." She smiled. "I'll wager Mistress Delilah will make a happy addition to our cozy little family."

Edwina was prepared to accept no such wager. Pondering the customary state of the duke's household, where the servants walked in awe of their sharp-tongued master, and Binnie forever irritated him, while she and Neal constantly racked their brains for avenues of escape, she emptied the tart dish. And now their daily routine was to be enlivened by a damsel who was clearly no better than she should be, and who would doubtless cause an already unbearable situation to go from bad to worse. "Angels defend us," muttered Edwina, gloomily.

CHAPTER THREE

Miss Cressida Choice-Pickerell was a young lady of remarkable competence. She was sensible, level-headed, and of unimpeachable character; she was well versed in such genteel accomplishments as playing the harp and painting on velvet; she was in every situation both well-bred and refined. Additionally, she was a beauty, with dark hair and aristocratic features and gray eyes; and only the most uncharitable of observers would claim she had deliberately set out to make herself a pattern card of respectability.

Yet there was some truth in such an observation, however uncharitable; Cressida did exhibit an awesome respect for, and adherence to, the proprieties. For this, there was good reason: Miss Choice-Pickerell's ambition was to surmount the obstacle posed to her social progress by her background, which though immensely wealthy was unfortunately tainted by trade. Her father was a prosperous city merchant. Daughters of tradesmen, no matter how successful, were barred from the drawing rooms of the Upper Ten Thousand.

To those drawing rooms Cressida aspired. In her quest she had been aided by her mother, who nourished her own ambition to rub shoulders with the *haut ton*. It was due to the combined machinations of Cressida and her mother that the Choice-Pickerells had hired for the autumn season a house on the Steine. This had not been the most fortunate choice of residences, perhaps; despite the attractions of the elegant promenades, the shops and libraries, the most prestigious residences were located not on the Steine but on the Royal Crescent, and on the Marine Parade. The Steine in August might afford much entertainment to a man of the world—for it was crowded with sportsmen and trainers, prizefighters and bookmakers and military officers, as well as females of dubious profession—but young ladies of good reputation were safer elsewhere.

Still, Cressida was in Brighton, and that was what signified. She consoled herself that the bow-fronted houses on the Royal Crescent and the Marine Parade allowed their occupants scant privacy. And after all, who needed a view over the channel? If one wished to observe a wide expanse of water, one needed only step outside.

It was not such scenic vistas that had brought Cressida to Brighton, nor even the salubrious air, breezy and bracing and good for sluggish livers and general debilitation. Nor was it the fact that Brighton was the gayest, most fashionable place in all of Europe. Cressida's presence in this pleasure spot was prompted by the simple reason that the Tenth Light Dragoons were encamped on home leave there.

Accompanied by a footman and her maidservant, Cressida was engaged in a brisk morning stroll. Personally she had little taste for morning rides and water-parties and cricket matches on the Steine, pursuits which she considered so much noise and nonsense. Aspire as she might to the heights, Cressida's soul was distinctly plebian. Even as she emulated the *ton,* and sought by means fair or foul to insert herself in the best front door, she deplored their irresponsible frivolity.

Thusly ruminating, the ambitious Miss Choice-Pickerell made a brisk inspection of shops displaying toys, rare china, lace and millinery, none of which tempted her to dip into elegant reticule. Much as she might loathe her status as the offspring of a wealthy cit, Cressida had inherited a great deal of her father's merchant-class shrewdness. She could spot a bargain at a glance—and if there was no bargain, Cressida would not buy.

Though chintz and cambrics, ribbon and fine muslin might not tempt Cressida to part with her money— Cressida, avowed her fond father, was a nipfarthing—she had, all the same, struck in Brighton precisely the sort of bargain that most appealed to her. Her father might claim that Lieutenant Neal Baskerville would never come up to scratch, would cry off before the fatal hour, but Cressida knew otherwise. Cressida understood the gentlemanly precepts of honor, as her father did not. Lieutenant Baskerville could not break off a formal betrothal without appearing the veriest coxcomb. Cressida planned to burst upon the *ton* in a very memorable style, via St. George's, Hanover Square.

Not, of course, that Neal had shown any indication of developing cold feet. Cressida flattered herself that he was absolutely enraptured with her. Certainly he was indefatigable in his attentions. Cressida would take good care that he continued to be. She was a wise young lady, far too shrewd to let either her ambition or triumph show.

At this point in her ruminations, as she proceeded toward the library on the Marine Parade, where she planned to gaze out to sea through a telescope, or perhaps peruse the London newspapers, delivered punctually each evening by coach,

23

Cressida's progress received a check. Neal himself confronted her, looking rather out of breath.

"I have been looking everywhere for you," he said. "Your mother told me you had gone this way. Cressida, I must speak with you."

"Well, you are doing so, are you not?" Cressida prided herself on her practicality. "Ought you not to be on parade? Colonel Fortescue will be very displeased that you neglect the drill. You will likely receive a severe reprimand."

Neal was not especially gratified to receive from his fiancée a gentle lecture on the perils of missing parade of a morning, though what she said was true. Lieutenant Baskerville's colonel was not enamored of him, a circumstance deriving not from Neal's deficiency in military ability, but to Neal's cousin's friendship with the colonel's dashing young wife. Neal firmly believed that Sandor had taken up with the fair Phaedra with that exact end in mind. Was he never to be freed of Sandor's cursed influence? With a lessening of anger, he gazed upon the young lady who was his current hope of escape.

She was waiting patiently for his explanation, her gray eyes fixed on his face. It occurred to Neal that he'd never glimpsed the slightest hint of passion on those exquisite features. However, passion was not an emotion with which young ladies of refinement were expected to be familiar. "My God, you're lovely, Cressida!" he uttered, rather thickly.

Miss Choice-Pickerell frowned, looking simultaneously offended and demure—to good effect had Miss Choice-Pickerell studied her attitudes before her looking glass. Obviously, she was not flattered by his ardor. Reflecting that it was a damned dull courtship when both sides conducted themselves with the utmost decorum, and further reflecting that tedium was preferable to being made Sandor's cat's-paw, Neal apologized.

Gracefully, Cressida indicated forgiveness. "You have not told me," she reproved, "what has caused you to come racing after me like the veriest schoolboy. After all, we are engaged for this afternoon."

"That's just it: we're not." Neal offered her his arm. "Sandor has bespoken me to run an errand for him. I am very sorry for it, but I must beg off from my engagement to you."

Lieutenant Baskerville, thought his fiancée, might be a

24

man of rank and fashion, a very Apollo in form, but there were numerous flaws in his character. Chief among those defects was a lack of the courage to beg leave to differ with his cousin's royal decrees. "I see," she said quietly. "What excuse has he used this time? I can only think His Grace does not approve of your association with me."

"Sandor," retorted Neal heatedly, "doesn't approve of anything. In this instance, I am to fetch Mannering's daughter to town—she will be Sandor's ward. And I don't think even her considerable fortune will make up to her for being under Sandor's thumb. In fact, I think that if I explained to her the nature of her guardian, the child would much prefer to stay where she is!"

Cressida did not receive the information that a wealthy damsel was to take up residence in His Grace's house at all philosophically. "And where might it be that she is?" she inquired. "Surely it would be more fitting if the duke himself brought the girl to Brighton, perhaps in company with your sister? To be so abruptly thrown among strangers must be frightening to a child—you did say she is a child, Neal? Surely she would benefit from feminine company."

Neal contemplated the character of the child, as revealed in her highly dramatic letter, and then the prospect of Sandor and Binnie closeted together in a carriage. Reluctantly, he smiled. "Edwina goes with me, at Sandor's decree. Lord, but it's a cat-and-dog life we lead. Cressida, *why* must we wait until spring? There is no impediment to our marriage, since Sandor approves."

This attitude, suggesting as it did that Neal regarded his upcoming nuptials as a matter of expedience, didn't recommend itself to Miss Choice-Pickerell. Although she might look at her marriage in exactly that light, it was hardly flattering that her prospective bridegroom should do likewise. Nor did it augur well for her intention to rule the roost once they were wed.

"Sandor this and Sandor that," she said bitterly. "Sometimes I think, sir, that you wish to marry me merely to escape your cousin. I dislike to be second fiddle of all things."

This remark, for it was no more than the truth, and consequently roused in its recipient a deep sense of guilt, caused Neal to stop dead in his tracks and look down upon Cressida's lovely countenance. The gathering storm that he saw there did not soothe his conscience. "Cressida, you misunderstand," he lied manfully. "I would rather forfeit my life than disturb your peace. It is merely that I fear Sandor will change his mind."

Had not Cressida suspected it would give Neal a disgust of her, she would have engaged in a tantrum. As it was, she did not think a mild display of wounded sensibility would be taken amiss. "Am I so ineligible for marriage with yourself?" she inquired dolefully. "Clearly you must think so or you would not be so concerned with what your cousin thinks. I begin to wonder, Neal, if I have been trifled with! Perhaps you do not truly wish to marry me. For if you did, I cannot see what His Grace's approval has to do with anything."

Nor was Neal flattered that his fiancée should accuse him of being a false accuser, but he sought to make amends. "This will never do!" said he. "My dear, you know I haven't sixpence to scratch with. If I run counter to Sandor, it's bellows to mend—and I've a very strong hunch that Sandor plays the hypocrite. He's a damned high stickler, and our marriage is the first thing during all the years I've been his ward of which he has approved."

Cressida pondered whether or not to take exception to the profanity that had sullied her ears and decided, this time, to let it pass. She wished to appear neither priggish nor commonplace. Furthermore, Neal gave every appearance of a young man about to fly off the hooks. Another of the traits that she lamented in him was a sad volatility. "You have never told me how you came to be his ward. Surely your sister is of an age to set up housekeeping on her own."

"Certainly she is, and I'm sure she would, could she but afford to. Binnie has even less liking for Sandor's hospitality than I." Neal turned away; they continued their idle stroll. "But no provision was made for her; I suppose our parents were sure she would marry. She is dowered, of course, but no more—and Sandor will not allow her to touch her dowry. He would not wish to short her husband, he says, in the unlikely event that she *does* wed. As to how it came about, our parents died within weeks of each other, and we were both underage. Sandor made himself responsible for us, though I cannot imagine why. Certainly not of generosity! And ever since he has contrived to see us reduced to such straits that we are brought to a standstill."

Such excess of emotion did not meet with the approval of Miss Choice-Pickerell. "His Grace has always been all that is polite, to me," she said repressively.

"Oh, Sandor can play the pretty, when it suits him." Neal's laughter was mirthless. "Take my word for it, Cressida, he's the devil incarnate. And now there's this Mannering chit, whom he will doubtless also somehow use to his advantage. A very pretty piece of business it is! I wish myself well shut of it."

So irate was Neal's demeanor, so flushed his countenance, that it caused Cressida quite a fright. "Don't put yourself in a taking," she advised, rather unwisely. "Since you are so concerned with the duke's opinion, you might reflect that he would hardly approve you making an exhibition of yourself."

Lieutenant Baskerville turned on his fiancée a countenance that was totally devoid of affection. "Moonshine!" he said roughly. "Don't *you* go ringing a peal over me, Cressida; I have quite enough of that from Sandor. And so little do I care for the high-and-mighty duke that I would rejoice to see him dead!"

"Well!" Cressida drew away and stared. "How *dare* you speak so to me! Never did I think that you would use me in this vulgar way."

Cressida's notions of vulgarity did not march with Neal's, but he did not demonstrate to her the difference. In truth, Neal was himself shocked at the fervor of which he was guilty. Too, it was hardly prudent to voice a wish for the death of a man who had countless enemies. Were the duke to be found murdered some glorious morn—a not improbable event considering, for example, the enmity in which he was regarded by one Colonel Fortescue—Neal would likely find himself among the prime suspects.

"I'm sorry." Ruefully, he ran his fingers through his chestnut hair. "The truth is that I'm sadly out of curl. I'd much rather spend my afternoon with you than set out on the trail of the Mannering chit. Say you will forgive my boorish behavior, my dear."

Cressida studied her gloved hands, of which she was very proud: small hands and feet were one of the first essentials of beauty required by the *ton*. Not for the first time, she lamented that a young lady of her innate gentility should be born into the world of commerce. She also lamented that her means of entrée into the upper spheres should be a gentleman prone to hey-go-mad humors. "In view of your mood," she responded severely, "it is perhaps for the best that our engagement for this afternoon is broken. You offer me a very poor sort of amusement, Neal."

What Neal was tempted to offer his fiancée was violence. Never had he realized so clearly that their sentiments were opposed. So far was Miss Choice-Pickerell from understanding his feelings regarding his overbearing cousin that she clearly thought him prone to brief fits of madness. "You leave me," he said stiffly, "nothing more to say."

But Cressida was a clever girl, and she knew when she'd gone too far. She laid her dainty hand on Neal's arm and gazed up at him beseechingly. "Now it is I who must offer apology," she murmured. "I have spoken hastily, and out of turn—but it is concern for you that prompted me to be so mannerless. It makes me very unhappy to think that you and your cousin have grown so estranged. The duke of Knowles is a very influential man. I wish you would be more careful in your dealings with him. Why, if you displeased him sufficiently, he could probably even have you clapped in jail!"

That this sudden concern for his well-being was an abrupt volte-face, Neal was aware; but he was not surprised that Cressida should be so inconsistent as to in one moment consider Sandor an ogre, and in the next a saint. Females were consistently inconsistent, in Neal's experience—save for his sister, and on the same subject. Too, Cressida's melting expression would have soothed the ruffled sensibilities of a far more discerning gentleman.

"You need not worry for my safety," he responded, obviously gratified that she should. "Sandor would not dare go so far—at least, I think he won't. My darling, I am a brute to harangue you in his stead; and you are an angel to put up with me."

At that moment, and by design, Cressida looked angelic indeed. "If you wish it so very much," she offered nobly, "we may be married before the spring. My mother will be disappointed, I daresay—but for myself, I don't care a rush if we are married here or in Hanover Square." Modestly, she blushed. "You are to be my husband, after all. I must learn to defer to you in all things."

Confronted with a vision of lovely and submissive femininity, Neal was positively bewitched—but not so bewitched that he failed to heed a deep pang of conscience. Also, and oddly, Cressida's sudden acquiescence roused in him a reluctance to be so abruptly wed. "No, no!" he replied quickly. "It must be as you wish. A wedding is a solemn matter." Strange how that remark roused in him unease. "I would not wish to cause you unseemly haste."

"Dear Neal." Cressida's long lashes fluttered. "You are so very good."

With this, too, Neal disagreed; at that moment he felt himself an utter varlet of insincerity. "I must go," he said abruptly. "I will call upon you tomorrow, Cressida." She suffered him to salute her hand.

She also allowed herself the pleasure of watching his handsome figure move away from her down the street. His brusque leave-taking she attributed to consideration of her sensibilities; obviously he had been laboring under strong emotion, and he would not wish to offer her further affront. All in all, and despite Neal's various misdemeanors, she was content with the interview. He would learn to be less frivolous and volatile, she believed, once she had separated him from his frippery fellow officers.

Miss Choice-Pickerell might have been less complacent had she been aware that at that very moment her fiancé was seriously questioning if there was any point on which they thought as one; but Miss Choice-Pickerell saw no reason to concern herself with what her prospective bridegroom might and might not think. Lieutenant Baskerville was, to her, no more than a means to an end. She would have preferred a title, naturally, but she knew the folly of setting her sights so high. Neal would serve her purpose very nicely; his lineage was impeccable, and no one could sneeze at a lieutenant in the Tenth Light Dragoons; he would make an unexceptionable husband, once he was properly house-trained.

With the practicality on which she prided herself, Cressida contemplated the main topic of their recent conversation, and decided that Neal was not entirely rational on the subject of the Duke of Knowles. To Cressida, the duke habitually behaved with a pretty deference that pleased her well. She was not so much a fool as to set her cap at Sandor; His Grace would no more marry a merchant's daughter than he would the dashing Phaedra Fortescue, who was already married anyway. Still, Cressida thought it would be very nice to be related to His Grace by marriage. Obviously, Neal was unaware of the advantages of relationship to such a very important man.

That reflection brought Miss Choice-Pickerell to a matter that caused her considerable discontent. Who was this Miss Mannering that Neal had gone to fetch? More important, what would she mean to Cressida's carefully laid plans? Neal was a very engaging young man, and Miss Mannering, by her presence in the duke's house, would see a great deal of him. Still, Neal had referred to her as a child—and at what age did childhood end?

At this point, Miss Choice-Pickerell's diligent footman dared to interrupt, with a diffident observation that Miss Choice-Pickerell was about to walk head-on into a military parade. "I'll brook no interference!" announced the young lady, in a tone so grim that her footman cringed.

CHAPTER FOUR

Miss Cressida Choice-Pickerell was not the only lady of note to stroll about the streets of Brighton that fine morn; although Miss Sibyl Baskerville would be the first to admit that she was no longer in her first youth, and certainly that she was far from fashionable, her passage occasioned a great deal more comment. With a plain cloth redingote worn over an unadorned muslin gown, and on her chestnut curls a bonnet so dowdy as to make her appear an impecunious governess, Binnie might justifiably have been expected to pass unnoticed. However, she did not. Miss Baskerville was no less a sight of Brighton than was the legendary Green Man—a Mr. Cope whose affectation it was to dress entirely in green, who ate nothing but green fruits and vegetables, whose rooms were painted and furnished in that color, whose gig and livery and portmanteau, gloves and whip were all green. And as did Mr. Cope, Binnie walked daily on the Steine.

Nor did her reputation suffer from this enterprise; there was not a soul in Brighton—with the possible exception of Miss Choice-Pickerell, with whom she did not stand on good terms—who would dare speak a censurious word against Miss Baskerville. It was not wholly due to the influence of her cousin the duke that this was so; in her own right, Binnie enjoyed a great popularity. She was without pretension; she was both quick-witted and kind; and if she was eccentric, which not even her dearest friends could deny, eccentricity was to be tolerated in a lady of lineage so impeccable. Too, though the duke might not especially like his cousin Sibyl, she was under his protection; and the duke was not a man to overlook a slight. Consequently, Miss Baskerville enjoyed the privilege, denied to ladies of far more exalted position than she, of going and behaving exactly as she pleased.

She did not do so unescorted; Binnie was not of the temperament that out of sheer wrongheadedness flaunted the proprieties. It was not that Binnie deliberately adhered to *les convenances,* but merely that she was innately well-bred—except, that is, in regard to her cousin the duke, in whose presence she invariably conducted herself like a fish-wife. She said as much, to the gentleman whose privilege it was to accompany her on this leisurely promenade.

"It makes me," she admitted, "very much disgusted with myself. Sandor has some justification in claiming I flaunt my presence on the stage like some vulgar character from a comedy. Although *he* is scarcely qualified to throw stones at me, for Sandor might serve as an object lesson in triumphant depravity. Oh, curse the man! Let us talk of something else. This discussion of Sandor's virtue—or the lack thereof!—is far too great a bore."

Miss Baskerville's companion acceded, gratefully. It was he who had introduced the subject, thinking to perhaps ease the strained relationship between his beloved and his friend—for he was Miss Baskerville's very ardent admirer, and the duke of Knowles's friend; and on one side was frequently regaled with ironic observations regarding the Monster of Depravity, and on the other with vituperative comments about Miss Prunes and Prisms. Quite frequently he felt as if he were caught between the devil and the deep blue sea.

Of his less than comfortable position, Binnie was aware. "Poor Mark!" She smiled up at him. "All this fuss and botheration has put me out of sorts, and it is very noble of you to take up the cudgels on Sandor's behalf. I suppose it is no wonder he has so high an opinion of himself, since the ladies were all running mad for him before he was fifteen. Myself, I think that to be sighing and dying for so foul-tempered a gentleman is ridiculous." Suddenly she laughed, a delightful, gurgling sound. "What high flights! I make it sound as if Sandor strews corpses in his wake. If truth be told, Mark, I enjoy crossing swords with him."

"He takes," her companion responded, "unfair advantage. Although, to give Sandor due credit, I don't imagine he thinks of it that way."

"Certainly not!" said Binnie. "He doesn't think of it at all! But we will speak no more of Sandor, if you please."

Through the streets they wandered, past shops displaying toys and rare china, lace and millinery. Their progress was not rapid; many other people had ventured forth this morning to partake of the salubrious air. There was Lord Petersham to be greeted, and his confidence to be received: he had adapted for his servants' liveries a certain shade of brown, his preference for the color being due to his devotion to a widow of that name; Mr. Tommy Onslow; Sir John and Lady Lade, who related a risqué tale of how Major Hanger and the regent had induced country girls to race on the Steine for the price of a new smock. It was a diversion, she believed, slightly more elevating than shooting at chimney pots. And then Sir John repaired to Raggett's, where every day thousands of pounds were won and lost; and Lady Lade adjourned to Mr. Donaldson's library, there to sit under the colonnade and watch the fashionable parade up and down the street.

Binnie contemplated her companion, who was looking a trifle severe. He did not like, she knew, her association with Letty Lade, who before her marriage to Sir John had been the mistress of a notorious highwayman known as Sixteen-string Jack, and whose speech, to say the best of it, was rather coarse. She looked away from his closed face and down the street, and saw the determined approach of a fashionably clad young lady, attended by a footman and a maidservant. "Gracious God!" uttered Binnie. "Quickly, Mark, let us walk out to the pier."

With a quizzical expression, her companion complied. In a manner suggestive of great haste, they progressed along the sea-walk, bordered by the beach, that served as an esplanade. It was a busy roadway, crowded with pedestrians, bath carriages, riders, and numerous vehicles. On the beach itself were bathing-machines and donkey rides for the children. Livery stables were interspersed with shops in the business area behind the esplanade.

Miss Baskerville was persuaded to bypass the local fishmarket, where one could purchase fish caught but an hour before, and to step onto the pier that jutted into the sea. Part of its purpose was the landing of cross-channel passengers from Dieppe, who before the construction of the pier had been disgorged in boats on the beach. "Now," said her companion, "what was all that about? Who was the young lady bearing down on us with all the determination of the Royal Fleet?"

"That," responded Binnie, with a speaking glance, "was Miss Choice-Pickerell. The holder of my brother's heart. I am not this day in a mood to tolerate Cressida. She has drawn the leading-strings about Neal very nicely, but that is no reason why *I* may not hold her at arm's length." She sighed. "This is not sour grapes, I assure you, though that is how it must sound. I hope I am not the sort of sister who will resent any female her brother means to wed. But Miss Choice-Pickerell is a very opinionated young lady, with an exalted opinion of herself; and I am convinced Neal doesn't care a straw for Cressida, nor she for him. I cannot help but think such a match can only result in misery."

Mark, who privately considered that Miss Baskerville was imposed upon not only by her cousin but also by her brother, gazed blankly out to sea. "What is it about the young lady that you so dislike?" he asked. "In appearance at least, she is unexceptionable."

This remark, concerning a damsel generally accorded a diamond of the first water, caused Binnie to smile. "In all fairness, I know nothing against her, save that her father is a wealthy cit, and that makes no difference to me. Or it *wouldn't*, if I thought Neal had a sincere attachment for her. Miss Choice-Pickerell has never to my knowledge involved the slightest censure; she adheres strictly to propriety, even in its slightest form. I cannot say why I am so deficient in good taste as to positively loathe the girl. Yet I wish that Neal would encounter someone more suited to him. I'll wager that if he did, he would find himself—as regards Miss Choice-Pickerell—heart-whole in an instant." Again she sighed. "Although, since they are formally betrothed, it would be best if he does not! Neal cannot cry off from the engagement, and Cressida certainly will not."

Her companion made no response, but merely stood gazing out at a fleet of coastal fishing boats. Binnie fell silent, listening to the pounding of the waves and, in the distance, a military band. Again she had been tactless. It was easy to forget, in her easy friendship with Mark, his unflagging devotion to her—a devotion that Binnie, despite her efforts and his own, could not bring herself to return.

Covertly, she studied him. Mark looked very elegant in his curly-brimmed beaver and drab Benjamin, his tightly fitting coat of superfine and fawn inexpressibles and Hessian boots. The face above the deep, stiff white cravat was not handsome, but such was his easy charm and grace of manner that to be handsome would have been superfluous. Mark Dennison was beloved by all of his acquaintance—and of all that acquaintance, Binnie couldn't imagine why his greatest regard was for a frump like herself. She decided he only thought he loved her, and that—like Neal—he would benefit from acquaintance with a lady more suited to him. Yet it caused her a pang to contemplate a day unbrightened by a glimpse of his delightfully homely face, his green eyes and dark hair. Unaccountably gloomy, she plucked at a loose thread on the sleeve of her redingote.

Binnie had misjudged her companion; he was contemplating

not his own wounded feelings, but her concern for her brother's plight. Mark was very well accustomed to Miss Baskerville's refusal to take him seriously. "What will you do?" he asked abruptly. "About Neal?"

"What *can* I do?" Helplessly, she spread her hands. "It is Sandor's place, is it not, to offer interference?—if interference there is to be. Truly, I think he's left it too late. But it is too fine a morning to be sunk in gloom! You will oblige me, Mark, by speaking of other things."

Mark did indeed oblige, as was his habit, with a story of an August day some years back when all of fashionable Brighton had turned out to witness on the Downs a great sham battle of seven thousand troops, which featured various jolly incidents such as the arrest of a military officer for sitting on a drum. Halfway through his narration, he became aware that the attention of his audience had strayed. Now it was she who gazed out to sea, and the bleak expression in her golden eyes aroused his compassion. "Binnie," he said quietly, and touched a chestnut curl that had escaped from beneath her bonnet. "Have you ever been in love?"

Binnie stared at him, startled not by the bluntness of the question, but at its appropriateness; she had been contemplating the disastrous nature of that emotion, and the havoc it wreaked with common sense. "I was very far gone in infatuation, once," she said doubtfully. "Not that I imagine it is the same thing. Brief though splendid it was, until I discovered that I had been sadly taken in." She grinned. "The object of my affections, as I recall, accused me of unbecoming levity."

So far was Mark from sharing her appreciation of this dénouement that his face grew grim. "My poor darling!" he said, gruffly.

Her amber eyes opened wide. "Gracious God, do you think I nourish a broken heart? Fiddlestick, Mark! Why, I haven't even thought of it for years—ten, to be precise. A long time to wear the willow, you must agree. Don't envision me some poor creature of romance, I pray. I shall be perfectly content to be a spinster aunt."

"A spinster!" he echoed, even more roughly. "You, at your last prayers! Utter fustian, my darling. Or has it escaped your attention that I have been dancing attendance on you these past several months? Oh I know this is no moment to tell you once again that I am desirous of setting in matrimony, or that my affections have become fixed—because you will only tell me once again that we shall go on more prosperously if I refrain from pitching you gammon." Mark paused for breath and regarded his beloved, who was gazing steadily at his immaculate cravat, and whose cheeks had grown quite pink. "All the same, and though you don't wish to hear it, I am offering you a love-match."

"I must count myself honored," gasped Binnie, in an agony of embarrassment. "You are a bachelor of the first stare! With everything prime about you, as Neal would say! And truly I do not mean to shatter your hopes, but you have taken a positively addlepated notion into your head, and this fixation you have about marrying me is the absolute height of absurdity!"

Perhaps because he was bemused by her flushed countenance, Mark took this blunt dismissal of his ardent courtship in very good part. Because he did not speak, Binnie peered up at him anxiously. "It is not that I am indifferent to you," she added quickly, "but believe me, Mark, we should not suit. I think Sandor must be correct in saying the man does not exist who would suit me—but that is my fault."

Mark regained his composure sufficiently to express a wish that Sandor might repair straightaway to the nether regions. Promptly, Miss Baskerville agreed. "It was very good of you to make me a candid confession of your sentiments," she continued briskly, "and you need not fear that I fail to understand that it was done for the sole purpose of elevating my spirits—which it has. But if you continue to console blue-deviled ladies by the offer of your heart and hand, you will speedily find yourself in the suds. Now I must return home and make ready for the arrival of Sandor's latest acquisition." He looked puzzled. "Good gracious, I haven't told you that Mannering's daughter has been made Sandor's ward!" She repaired the omission immediately.

In silence Mark listened, as they walked back past the fish-market and along the esplanade; he was accustomed also to Binnie's frantic evasion of serious discussions of romance. That she was not indifferent to him, he knew very well; what he did not know was whether Binnie's fondness for him was the warmth of simple friendship or something more. He did not think she herself knew the truth of it; she shied away not only from his offers of marriage, but from a closer examination of her own sentiments. She was a bit of an enigma, this lovely lady who went to such great lengths to make herself unattractive, who bristled up at professions of devotion like a huffy porcupine. Mark could only conclude that she had been very badly treated by the long-ago object of what she termed "infatuation." Himself, Mark would have called it a great deal more. He also would have very much liked to wring its object's neck.

"You are not paying attention to me," Binnie chided, as they turned in at the entrance to the Royal Crescent, where the duke owned an elegant bow-fronted house. "Or else you are very blasé, for I have just told you that Mannering's heiress is currently in residence at a tinkers' camp. You realize you must breathe a word to no one. It would hardly enhance the chit's credit were *that* to become known. And I wish the girl no ill, even if Sandor does mean her to be an apple of discord."

Mark abandoned his conjectures, which included a fervent wish that Binnie would confront her own emotions before he grew old and gray. "Mum as an oyster!" he agreed. "My love, you are very hard on your cousin. I am the first to admit Sandor has faults, but he would hardly bring this girl to Brighton merely to cause you discomfort."

"No?" Binnie paid scant heed to this observation; a sudden thought had struck her, had brought a speculative gleam to her golden eyes. The Mannering chit was a minx, on all accounts, and Neal— "Well! I see I cannot convince you that I am what is vulgarly called in for it. And perhaps—if only—but there! You will not wish to hear about *that!* Good day, my friend, and thank you for your companionship, and do forgive my sulks. We shall meet again 'ere long!" So saying, she whisked herself through the front door.

Mark stared at that nicely carved and painted item, above which was a pretty fanlight, then smiled as he turned away. Miss Baskerville was decidedly original. He admired her character, even as he mourned her cavalier conduct toward himself. For that treatment he did not blame her; Binnie was more frightened than unkind. But of what? Surely she could

37

not think that he would ever treat her as less precious than she was? A small frown upon his engaging features, Mr. Dennison strolled slowly along the Royal Crescent. There must be some manner in which to break through her awesome reserve.

Within the duke of Knowles's elegant bow-windowed house, Binnie leaned breathless against the door. She had been rude and graceless, had acted abominably, and that Mark accepted such behavior from her in no way mitigated her sin. What a fool he must think her! A missish ninnyhammer! 'Twould be far better for the both of them if he—since she lacked sufficient resolution, another circumstance which she deplored—washed his hands of her. Were he not so patient, so damnably optimistic—belatedly Binnie became aware that the butler was staring at her curiously. Her cheeks hot, she decorously mounted the stairs.

Mark she would think about some other time, she decided, and cravenly dismissed him from mind. Of more pressing importance was the problem of Neal. Absently Binnie surveyed herself in the looking glass, and noted with disfavor that her bonnet was crooked, and that there was a smudge of dirt on her chin. Ah well, her various deficiencies did not seem to weigh with Mr. Dennison. And then she reminded herself sternly that she did not mean to think of him.

Height, medium; figure, neat enough if a trifle thin; features that, if not remarkable, could neither cause offense; hair and eyes of so very exotic a texture that they caused their owner embarrassment. The effect of the hair—which when loosened tumbled in riotous curls to her waist—Binnie could and did subdue. About the eyes she could do nothing, since her wish for self-abrogation did not extend to burdening herself with quite unnecessary spectacles. Nothing in this reflected image, surely, to spark admiration in the breast of any man.

What on earth possessed her, to be going on in this mawkish way? It was not her own few assets that Binnie had meant to contemplate; she grimaced at the mirror. If only the Mannering heiress turned out to be a beauty—well, she would shortly see.

CHAPTER FIVE

Several hours after his sister had gloomily gazed into her
mirror and prayed that the Mannering heiress might turn
out to be a nonpareil, Lieutenant Neal Baskerville was gazing upon that selfsame young lady. Beauty was not among
the words that sprang into his mind.

The journey to the meeting-place named in Mistress Delilah's
highly colorful letter had not been a comfortable one. Already unaccountably depressed by his interview with his
fiancée, Neal had found his cousin Edwina's incessant chatter
very difficult to bear. She was far from the most perspicacious of traveling companions, and even had she realized that
the young lieutenant preferred to be left to uninterruptedly
pursue his own morbid thoughts—to wit, that he was about
to be leg-shackled to a female who was constitutionally incapable of sharing his point of view—she would have found it
difficult to curb her garrulousness. Since Edwina did not
realize, thought in fact that Neal's glowering expression was
prompted by Sandor's disruption of his plans for the day, she
attempted to offer consolation, and consequently was more
than usually irritating. Miss Choice-Pickerell, she observed
as Lieutenant Baskerville's neat cabriolet bowled along Church
Street, was the perfect solution to their difficulties. Cressida
was, in Edwina's opinion, a good biddable girl, and one who
would be pleased to take under her newlywed wing, and into
the residence she would share with her bridegroom, a sister
and cousin-by-law who were admirably well equipped to show

her how to go on in society. This point settled to her own satisfaction, if not to Neal's, Edwina rattled on amiably about where that hypothetical residence should be.

Neal listened to her, miserably. A kind young man, when it occurred to him to be, he could not disabuse his cousin of her extremely cockle-brained notion that Cressida would welcome the suggestion that she share her home with Edwina and Binnie. Nor did he imagine that Cressida would cherish hints about ladylike conduct. He could put his foot down, he supposed, and insist that she do both, but that notion did not endear itself to him. To say the truth, Neal had reached the point of wishing to dismiss all thought of matrimony. That he could not do so was brought home to him more strongly with each of Edwina's words. She and Binnie were no happier under Sandor's dominion than was Neal himself. That their lives should not be further blighted was dependent on him. There was no choice but marriage, even if by it he only changed jailers. Cressida's father was a shrewd old gentleman; he was not likely to relinquish control of the purse strings.

All the same, as husband to the well-heeled Miss Choice-Pickerell, Neal would be a young man of considerable financial resource. If Cressida would not extend hospitality, he imagined he could arrange that Edwina and Binnie set up housekeeping on their own, elsewhere. Nor did this solution recommend itself to him, and understandably: a young man of two-and-twenty could hardly be expected to anticipate with relish the responsibility of two separate households.

In this manner they progressed out of town, Edwina chattering gaily about the regent's Royal Pavilion, a residence she apparently thought Neal should emulate, complete with peach-blossom ceilings and walls decorated with mandarins, and fluted yellow draperies to resemble the tents of the Chinese; while Neal in a cowardly manner contemplated taking French leave. In this manner also they progressed; although Edwina, having exhausted the topic of interior decoration, switched to the broader subject of the Neighboring Monster, Napoleon. It was as she was discussing the Upstart's character, especially in regard to his wife, Josephine, whom he had callously tossed aside when it became belatedly apparent that she could not produce an heir, an act of inhumanity that appeared to be inextricably entangled in Edwina's mind with the emperor's recent and disastrous defeat in Russia, that Neal espied the appointed inn.

It was a pleasant-looking place, if not the sort generally frequented by persons of quality, a long, squat, whitewashed building with bright green shutters, crimson curtains in the lower windows, white hangings in the bedchambers above. A ruddy signpost perched up in a tree proclaimed the name of the establishment, its golden letters twinkling in the sun. Neal alit, led his horse to a trough filled with clear fresh water, the ground around it spread with fragrant hay. Sternly he instructed a rosy-cheeked urchin to care for his steed, and Edwina to remain in the cabriolet; and then set out in search of the innkeeper and a glass of ale.

Neal expected to encounter some little difficulty in tracking down the Mannering chit—indeed, he half-expected to discover he'd been sent on a wild-goose chase. It was, after all, almost a week beyond the time appointed in Delilah's letter as most suitable for a rendezvous. As matters evolved, however, the expedition had not been in vain. Along with a glass of fine old ale, the genial innkeeper provided the information that a young girl had been haunting his property for several days. "If it's the tinker's lass you're wanting, sir," he added, with a doubtful glance at Neal's well-bred figure in his superbly fashioned regimentals. "Myself I'm thinking some mistake's been made."

"Lord, *I* don't want her!" Since Neal was polishing off his ale, he did not notice the innkeeper's scandalized reaction. "Is she here now? I might as well have a look at the chit."

It was not the innkeeper's place to quarrel with the quality, no matter how depraved their attitudes might seem. With a disapproving expression, he guided his visitor—and who would have guessed that so pleasant a countenance masked a soul of infamity?—out a rear entrance. Extremely queer were the tastes of the *ton*. The innkeeper could imagine no less likely a candidate for a life of shame, as this young man certainly intended, if not on his own behalf then on the behalf of another equally sunk in vice, than the tinker's lass.

With this sentiment, had Neal but known it, he would doubtless have agreed. His first glimpse of Miss Delilah Mannering was one that would haunt him, and not in a pleasant manner, for a very long time. She was perched upon

41

a stile, her ragged skirts up to her knees, in one hand a half-eaten peach. A monstrously ugly dog was sprawled at her bare and very dirty feet. Oddly, and despite her shocking appearance, Neal didn't for an instant doubt that this raggle-taggle creature was the young lady that he sought.

Her first words confirmed that impression, and for the second time that day inspired him with a strong impulse to show the entire of his acquaintance a clear pair of heels. France was out of the question, due to the war, as was America. Perhaps Australia? 'Twas said that there a man could easily disappear.

But a gentleman, however reluctant, could not desert a damsel in distress. That Delilah did not appear aware of her peril was quite beside the point, as was the fact that she was conducting her quarrel with every evidence of great gusto.

These hostilities were being exchanged with a man of middle age, wiry stature, swarthy, and furious countenance. Neal moved closer so that he might hear.

"Furthermore," announced Miss Mannering, brandishing her peach, "I've been sneaking off for a whole week, so you are not nearly so clever as you think to have found me out! And I will *not* go back to the camp with you, because I am sick to death of listening to you talk like a nodcock!" The man muttered something beneath his breath. "*Yes*, a nodcock!" she insisted. "A damned loose-screw! And if you are thinking of laying violent hands on me again, Johann, you will regret it. Even if I *don't* have with me a frying pan!"

Johann, it seemed, had exactly that intention: he roughly grasped her shoulders. "Caliban!" shrieked Miss Mannering. The hound yawned and wagged its tail.

Neal had no choice but to intervene. He politely touched the tinker's shoulder. Cursing, Johann spun around. Setting to his task with all the strength and spirit of a prizefighter, Neal knocked him down.

"Well!" said Miss Mannering, setting her disheveled person to rights. "You have a very handy bunch of fives, sir! It was very kind of you to draw Johann's claret for me! I'm sure I'm very grateful, because my case was growing desperate—not, of course, that I would have knuckled under to a cursed loose fish like Johann, but there's no denying he *had* put me in a tweak—but who the devil *are* you?"

Neal was about to introduce himself, then recalled the innkeeper's fascinated presence, and thought he had better not. Rustics were incurable gossips. It would benefit neither of them to have this day's business noised around the countryside. "A friend," he sad repressively. "Sent on your behalf by, er, a representative of the gentleman to whom your circumstances must be of the utmost import."

"Ah!" Delilah beamed. "I had begun to despair of his interest, which was a very melancholy thought. Still, I would have somehow made a recover, even though I *was* in a sad fix. Have you come to take me away? It is very good of you to trouble yourself."

The innkeeper, at this point, was prompted by his outraged conscience to try and prevent so very young a lass from gleefully embarking upon a depraved career. He begged her to reconsider; he reminded her that she had applied to him for the post of chambermaid. During this interval Johann recovered his senses, observed himself outnumbered, and stealthily slunk away.

"That is very kind," responded Delilah, as Neal, dazed, stared. "But you must see that this gentleman's offer will suit me much better. With my fa—or this gentleman's *friend*—I shall at least have money for common necessaries, and I shall probably manage to enjoy myself. Who knows, I may even be able to form an eligible connection, and I have decided that I should like that of all things, for then perfect blocks like Johann could not behave scaly to me." She regarded Neal. "Well, sir, shall be depart?"

The innkeeper was utterly aghast at this proof of how very wrongheaded young women could be; and he was very much shocked that so very young a lady should be so deadened to virtue. He said so, most censuriously.

"What the deuce," inquired Delilah, "has prompted you to fuss? Why should you find my longing for a comfortable existence—which isn't at all surprising considering the extreme *dis*comfort of my existence for the past five years—much too dreadful to contemplate?"

The innkeeper gaped at Delilah, who looked—especially in her current rumpled condition—a great deal younger than her age. "Five years!" he echoed, faintly.

Neal, at last made aware of the innkeeper's misapprehensions, desperately strove to restrain an inclination to laugh out loud. He lost the struggle. Both the innkeeper and Delilah looked startled when he dissolved into mirth. Miss Mannering did not seem offended by so ungainly an exhibition, though the innkeeper patently considered it the ultimate demonstration of villainy.

"Come along, puss!" said Neal, when he had regained his breath. "My carriage is waiting. Have you anything that you wish to bring with you?"

Delilah anticipated battle. "Only Caliban," she retorted, a marital gleam in her eye.

Neal regarded the dog, who on hearing his name mentioned had opened both eyes, and contemplated Sandor's probable reaction to this misbegotten beast. Then he contemplated Sandor's probable reaction to his newly acquired ward. "Very well!" he said, with the utmost good cheer.

Edwina had grown very weary of waiting in the cabriolet—so weary, in fact, that she uncharitably suspected her young cousin had ignobly taken advantage of an opportunity to indulge in the gentlemanly pastime known as shooting the cat. Therefore, it was with some relief that she espied a small procession making its way toward the cabriolet.

That relief was not long-lived. Neal looked so much unlike himself—that merry expression had not been glimpsed on Neal's handsome features, now that Edwina considered it, for the past several weeks—that she thought he was in truth cast-away; but her attention was primarily for the ragamuffin who trailed along behind him, clutching to her by means of a rope a very hideous hound. Surely *this* could not be the Mannering heiress! "Merciful powers!" uttered Edwina weakly; and then, as Neal tenderly placed both the damsel and her dog in his cabriolet, "God bless my soul!" She noted that the innkeeper, who had followed along after, was staring at her as if she were the fiend incarnate. "What in the world—"

Neal sprang into the driver's seat and took up the reins. They rattled out of the courtyard. "The poor man thinks you are an abbess," he cheerfully explained. "Do not let it overset you, Edwina! Myself he considers a hardened profligate, and Miss Mannering a prime piece of Haymarket-ware."

"Oh, was *that* it?" interrupted the heiress. "No wonder he was so sadly pulled-about. I must say, sir, that you tool the

44

ribbons in prime style—you must be a top sawyer with four in hand! Considering the way you also planted Johann a facer, I must conclude that you are a perfect all-around Trojan!"

It was evident to both her auditors that Miss Mannering promised to be a handful. "Baggage!" retorted Neal, appreciatively.

"Angels defend us!" gasped Edwina.

Delilah turned her attention from the driver of the cabriolet—who she considered as fine as the carriage itself, with its two great wheels and crimson upholstery, drawn by a powerful bay—to the beruffled and beplumed lady who was regarding her with abject dismay. "Flimflam!" she explained kindly. "Mere flourishing! Johann had taken a marked fancy to me, you see—or to the money which he thought I had. Clearly that was a mistake, but at the time it was the best I could contrive. Anyway, he was desirous of fixing his interest, and I pretended to surmount my reluctance to him, because it was the only coin with which I could buy time. A wearing task it was, I assure you! To lure him into relaxing his vigilance—he had me locked up at one point, which might well have put period to *all* my plans!—and at the same time to keep him from popping the question. Well! This nice young man appeared just in the nick of time, because Johann's persistence had me all of a muck of sweat, and sent him to the roundabout!" Her little tale concluded, with what she adjudged the minimum of fuss, Delilah beamed upon Edwina, and proceeded to finish off the peach that she still clutched.

Edwina stared at this brazen and deplorably dirty miss and then at the great hound. A sound very much like a snort of laughter struck her astonished ears, its source the front of the cabriolet. "Neal!" she said, awfully.

"You must not blame him!" cried Delilah, who wished no censure to fall upon her rescuer. "In the case of Johann, gentle hints do not avail. Why, *I* was forced to fend him off with a frying pan! It was a great piece of imprudence that I did not think to bring it with me today—but then, I was in a great hurry to get away. But we have not been introduced! I am Delilah Mannering."

Faintly, Edwina presented to Miss Mannering her cousin and herself. Sibyl meant to launch this hoyden into society? Edwina wished her joy of the task. Mercifully, Delilah's debut

45

would be delayed by her period of mourning. Perhaps an acquaintance with that circumstance might deflate some of the damsel's vulgar high spirits. "My dear Miss Mannering, you must be prepared to hear some very bad news."

Delilah, pondering her great good fortune, doubted that any news could be dire enough to ruin her pleasure in this day. All the same, in view of the strenuous efforts made in her behalf by these two kind people, it behooved her to be agreeable. She composed her features in an expression of patient resignation. "Yes, ma'am."

Edwina was encouraged by this unexpected docility. "Miss Mannering, your father—and from your letter, I conclude that your mother, too—my dear, this is most difficult! You must console yourself that he cared for you very much, to the point of leaving to you all his wealth. An orphan! Such a sad affair!"

An astute young lady, Delilah had already concluded that Edwina Childe possessed more hair, and a queer color it was, than sense. She fixed her eyes on Lieutenant Baskerville's strong back. "My father is dead?"

"He is, Miss Mannering." Neal could find it in himself to pity the chit. "Your letter came to my cousin, an executor of your father's will. There has been a search underway for you."

Delilah digested this information. Anticipating maidenly megrims, Edwina extracted handkerchief and vinaigrette from her reticule. The silence was long and suspenseful. Then Delilah became aware that some response was expected from her.

"Fancy that!" she said, as she scratched Caliban's ears. "I really *was* an heiress all the time. I will admit I am relieved to hear it, for I felt very guilty about the whoppers I told Johann—and now it turns out they weren't exactly lies. My mother always said I was an incurable humbugger, and I fear it is true. But I thought she would have disapproved a mésalliance with a tinker even more than my tarradiddles, and so I persevered."

Perhaps the girl was unhinged by grief. "My poor child!" soothed Edwina. "You must not take it so to heart. In time, due to your father's foresight, you will be able to command every luxury."

"I daresay I shall enjoy that," responded Miss Mannering, with devastating frankness, "but you're all about in the head, ma'am, if you think my father left me provided for out of fondness. He didn't like me above half. Nor, for that matter, did I like him!"

The vinaigrette was put to use, but not on behalf of Delilah; Edwina had recourse to it herself. Delicately, she made known her opinion that Miss Mannering was going on a very bad way. A young lady in her lamentable position was perfectly entitled to a display of aggrieved sensibility, even to fly straight into the boughs.

"Oh." Delilah looked doubtful. "But I *have* no sensibility, ma'am—and while I admit to being an unconscionable little liar, which I *am* in spite of my efforts at curbing myself, I am not at all good at cutting a sham. And I have not thought to ask where, since my father is dead, you are taking me."

Edwina had been afflicted by a raging headache, which was not alleviated by the strong stench of dog that assaulted her fastidious nostrils, and did not trust herself to reply. She gazed unhappily upon the massive hound, whose homely head, due to the confines of the cabriolet, was resting in her lap. Caliban was grateful for this concession, even if his headrest had bony knees; he opened his mouth and panted in a friendly manner, in the process drooling on her skirt. "Neal!" Edwina moaned.

"We are taking you, Miss Mannering," offered the lieutenant, "to the home of my cousin, the duke of Knowles, who has constituted himself your guardian until you come of age. And I think it only fair to warn you that you may have good reason to wish that you had remained in the tinkers' camp."

Delilah was startled by this ungracious statement, and the brusque tone in which it was delivered; she would not have expected such churlishness from the noble Lieutenant Baskerville. Obviously the lieutenant and the duke of Knowles were not on the best of terms. She glanced at Edwina.

That lady was gazing with arrant disapproval on Caliban. "Brute!" she ejaculated.

Naturally, Delilah could not but defend her pet. She was very sorry, she said stiffly, if Caliban had messed on Miss Childe's skirt, but she thought Miss Childe had very strange priorities. In Delilah's opinion, the feelings of her dog—and

47

Caliban had had a very trying time of it lately, what with being dragged around the countryside, with never enough to eat—were a great deal more important than a piece of silk.

Edwina eyed the hound, which was eyeing her lush bonnet, trimmed with pretty flowers and ostrich plumes. Definitely, he looked hungry. "Not the dog!" she cried, jerking back her head. "Sandor!"

"The duke?" inquired Delilah. "Pooh! That he should offer me a home is strong proof of a good heart."

"Sandor," Neal offered gloomily from the front seat, "*has* no heart. He is a tyrant, Miss Mannering."

"That he is," agreed Edwina. "Devoid of all humanity."

"Poppycock!" ejaculated Miss Mannering. Edwina looked thoroughly astounded, and Delilah patted her hand. It was a gesture that Edwina might have appreciated more had not Delilah's fingers been sticky with peach juice. "You will discover for yourself that we speak the truth,'" said she. "Sandor will make of you a cat's-paw, as he has the rest of us."

Immediately, Delilah resolved to take this sadly nervous lady, and perhaps even the churlish lieutenant, firmly in rein; obviously they had let themselves fall into the habit of being ordered around. Delilah considered herself admirably well suited to show them how to go about ordering their own lives with a minimum of fuss. "You need not concern yourself with my well-being," she said cheerfully, as she considered this tantalizing prospect. What better occupation for a young lady of resource and energy? "I'll stake my—my corset-cover!—that I shall be happy as a grig."

CHAPTER SIX

Unaware of the severe doubler about to be tipped him by a quixotic fate, the duke of Knowles passed a very busy day. As a gentleman of fashion, a Corinthian, he was accustomed to such expenditures of energy; as befit his position, the duke was a devotee of the hunt, the race, the cockpit. He gambled for enormously high stakes; he attended his regent at Carlton House or the Pavilion; he followed the Fancy and even occasionally removed his exquisitely tailored coat to step into the ring with one of those professional bruisers. Furthermore, His Grace did all these things with admirable élan. If the cards were against him, he accepted the most staggering losses with an apt little quotation from Horace, and without batting an eyelash; he could drink the large majority of his acquaintances under the table; he kept his mistress, when a mistress he had in keeping, in the same splendid style as he kept his bloodstock. Nor did those ladies evince any chagrin at such treatment, which implied they were of no greater consequence than any other of His Grace's innumerable possessions. Alexander Childe, the duke of Knowles, was very popular among the pretty horsebreakers of London's Rotten Row.

Currently, no fair incognita was privileged to enjoy His Grace's generous protection. This was due to no onslaught of delayed prudery on His Grace's part, but to the fact that his current inamorata already possessed a husband who kept her in excellent style, Unfortunately, the colonel's good taste did not extend to treating the lady quite so well, and they were as a result estranged. Since the colonel was this day engaged with his Hussars in a sham battle upon the Downs—an event witnessed by most of Brighton, who were in attendance in every conceivable manner of vehicle from barouches to fish-carts; and which would result, before the day was done, in at least one broken arm and considerable confusion—the duke took it upon himself to console the colonel's wife.

He found her gracefully reclining on her chaise longue, in a most elegant morning dress. The fair Phaedra, it speedily evolved, was in a very somber frame of mind.

Fair she was, in truth, a tall and voluptuous creature with black hair, a porcelain complexion, dark eyes that alternately melted and flashed. Upon the appearance of the duke, she roused sufficiently from her abstraction—resultant from a remark made to her that the Tenth were held in some contempt, having, while other less exalted regiments suffered heavy losses in Spain, been engaged in nothing more perilous than exhibiting themselves at reviews and gracing the parties of their commander in chief—to sit coquetting with him. The duke might have more appreciated her efforts to divert him had he not recently come to suspect that only a desire to serve the colonel an ill turn prompted Phaedra to open intrigue. That she would dare involve him in her scheming did not please Sandor, who considered the mapping out of subtle plots his own province; nor did he derive any humor from the situation. Still, he would not add to the discomforts of a lady already laboring under a budget of woes. In her time, before she discovered that she was in love with a husband whose disinterest matched his jealousy, Phaedra had been very good company. Sandor took his leave of her after a scant half hour, reflecting that since the game of hearts fatigued him to death, he might be wise to consider indulging in it no more. Moreover, he decided, fair barques of frailty had bored him for some time. It was a startling realization, and one that left the duke unaccountably depressed, suggesting to him as it did that he was growing old. Next, he supposed, he would find himself abandoning his other habitual pursuits—his gaming and his bloodstock, the ring and the racetrack—for the pleasures of hearth and home.

In this vein reflecting, and reflecting also that a fireside encumbered with Miss Prunes and Prisms, as alas his was, would offer scant comfort to a man grievously stricken in years, His Grace strolled along the Steine. He derived no pleasure from the greetings of those acquaintances whom he met, nor animation from the brisk sea breeze that swept inland, carrying with it the scent of gorse on the surrounding Downs. Indeed, he quite unwittingly snubbed several of his friends. What the deuce possessed him? wondered the duke. He was in a very odd mood. He wished to do something, but he knew not what; the sham fight on the Downs held out as little allure as had Phaedra herself—and that the fair Phaedra had held out no allure was a clear indication that a man had lost possession of his senses, as the lady herself would have been first to agree.

In this frame of mind, the duke repaired to the library on the Marine Parade, in hope that the London newspapers would alleviate his ennui. The newspapers did not, nor did Miss Choice-Pickerell, whom he inadvertently interrupted at the telescope. Miss Choice-Pickerell, he was informed, was a little out of sorts, having been cut dead in the street by Miss Baskerville. Oddly, this information somewhat relieved Sandor's gloom; in a world that had grown flat, Binnie could still be depended on to irritate him.

With this point of view the duke did not acquaint Cressida. She may have been a young woman of singular character, but he did not make the mistake of thinking she would understand his admittedly singular, and eminently masculine, viewpoint. Instead, the duke offered consolation of a sort: Miss Baskerville, he said, was prone to queer flights. What signified her megrims, he inquired; it was young Lieutenant Baskerville with whose conduct Miss Choice-Pickerell need be concerned. He trusted that young Lieutenant Baskerville had given his fiancée no reason for offense.

Young Lieutenant Baskerville had not, but the same could not be said of the duke himself, as Cressida archly explained. She could only think, due to the duke's habit of interfering with Neal's plans, that he did not approve his cousin's betrothal. His Grace, who was also growing rapidly bored with Miss Choice-Pickerell, but who had his own reasons for wishing this betrothal to remain in effect, politely responded that, had he wished to scotch the affair, he would hardly have blessed the match. No longer in the mood to peruse newspapers, and definitely in no mood to further bandy words with Miss Choice-Pickerell, he took his leave of her before he succumbed to the temptation of uttering a harsh setdown that must set his good work all at naught. The duke understood Cressida perfectly. She was as selfishly single-sighted as he was himself. This circumstance roused in him no sense of kinship; Sandor thought that Neal had gotten himself betrothed in a fit of folly, so eager to gain his freedom that he would even marry in hot haste. Miss Choice-Pickerell might be at the very top of the trees, but she was not the duke's notion of a comfortable little wife.

This reflection did not, despite his cousin Edwina's views on the subject, recall to His Grace his own brief marriage. So far was he from being heartbroken by the demise of his ill-fated young wife that he had not spared her a thought for a shocking number of years. Had the duke been of a contemplative temperament, which he was not, he might have admitted that his marriage to a flighty, rather cowardly, definitely skitterwitted damsel had been a mistake. He had been fond of her, as any man might dote on a charming child; but he was a man singularly devoid of the more laudable emotions, and what few finer sentiments he possessed were not wasted on a lady so long in her grave.

In an increasingly nasty frame of mind, the duke retired to Raggett's, there to go down heavily; and then to his own home on the Royal Crescent, where he indulged in a vituperative exchange with his cousin Binnie. Since that lady was so preoccupied with her own melancholy reflections as to let him think he'd won, it was in a slightly more cheerful humor that His Grace sallied forth to join his regent in a dinner party at the Pavilion.

Edwina Childe might approve a scheme of interior decoration that incorporated such fanciful details as peach-blossom ceilings and walls decorated with mandarins and yellow draperies fluted to resemble the tents of the Chinese; the duke did not. Nor did he appreciate china fishermen that stood in alcoves, with lanterns as their catch; or tall pagodas of porcelain; or lamps shaped like tulips. He did not express his disapproval to the regent, whose feelings he learned had already been wounded by the on-dits that were circulating about him, tales of drunken feasts and gay girls in secret passages of the Pavilion itself, stories that he played the callous tyrant in his family life; but he did vent his annoyance, in most explicit terms, to Mr. Dennison.

That gentleman awarded his friend an amused glance. "You say that every time you come here, Sandor. In view of your opinion of the place, I wonder you don't simply stay away."

This reasonable observation did not endear Mr. Dennison to the duke, but, since Mark was his oldest friend, Sandor offered no rebuke. Instead he contemplated in a choleric manner the painted and carved dragons that hung from silvered ceilings, crawled down pillars, darted from overmantels. And then they were drawn into a political discussion with the duke of York, who could not distinguish in his mind the difference between a Tory and a Whig, and who consequently argued both sides of an issue at the same time.

Mark, a wary eye on the darkening countenance of the duke, took the first opportunity to extricate his friend from this confusing conversation and lead him into a corridor. "What the devil's eating you tonight, Sandor? More than a dislike for Prinny's Oriental style of decoration, I think."

His Grace gazed down the passage—which was fashioned of painted glass, decorated with flowers and insects, fruit and birds, and illuminated from the outside, the effect of which was that the unwary visitor abruptly found himself in a Chinese garden. Chinese gardens, decided the duke, were among the numerous things that did not suit his taste. Then he gazed upon his friend. "Rather I should ask you that," he retorted roughly. "I'm only cursed ill tempered; you're looking fagged to death."

Due to his long acquaintance with the duke, Mark was aware that this impertinent remark was in the nature of an apology. He smiled. "It's nothing to signify."

Once Sandor's interest was aroused, it was not so easily deflected. "Miss Prunes and Prisms, I conjecture. It has me in quite a puzzle why you should be so smitten with so contumacious a female. She's turned you down again? Yet another hairsbreadth escape!"

Demonstrably the duke was in a foul temper; he did not often venture so very far beyond the bounds of common decency. So Mark dared observe. He also stated his own curios-

53

ity as to what had prompted his old friend's descent from rudeness to outright vulgarity. Since Mark's own sense of ill-usage had grown apace with each word, he then expressed extreme displeasure that the duke should have dared imply that the lovely Miss Baskerville was an old-cattish antidote, and issued an invitation to meet with pistols at dawn.

Sandor could not explain the source of his discontent, being unaware of it, and he had no desire to rise from his bed so early to engage in a duel with his oldest friend. He let the challenge pass. "What maggot have you taken into your head?" he inquired, not unkindly. "*I* didn't say Sibyl was bracket-faced; you did. I only said she was a hornet."

Mark was not assuaged. He was seriously angry with the duke for abusing his cousin. He said so, heatedly. He also said that Miss Baskerville was first-rate, the very woman calculated to suit his taste.

His Grace took leave to wonder, privately, what caused Mark to think that, in his long-standing feud with his cousin, it was he who offered the greatest abuse. As he recalled, Binnie had had his head for washing far more often than he'd had hers. Obviously it was midsummer moon with Mark. Mr. Dennison was not ordinarily prone to romantical high flights. Romance again! thought the duke, with profound distaste. A cursed nuisance was this love, which turned the most amiable men touchy and difficult.

"I know my cousin is lovely," he said, with an effort at restoring the peace. "You don't have to tell me that; I live with her!" He was then inspired by a natural impatience to undo his good efforts. "A pity her personality isn't as pleasing as her person! Good God, Mark, I told you she'd send you to the rightabout."

So he had. Since he had also told his friend that by rejection he would be blessed, Mark had not especially appreciated the advice. "This dislike in which you have taken Miss Baskerville," he uttered wrathfully, "is unspeakably odious. She is—"

"Lay all these bristles!" advised the duke, rather dangerously. "I believe I may know even better than yourself what my cousin is and is not. For the record, it is not Sibyl I dislike, but her manners. If you want her, you may have her, with my blessing! Moreover, you would be doing me the greatest of favors if you would sweep her off her feet and out of my house! Shall I forbid her to marry you? Because you may be certain that if I did, she would!"

Briefly, Mark contemplated this ignoble manipulation of his beloved's habit of running counter to the wishes of her cousin the duke. Reluctantly, he pushed temptation aside. "I congratulate you, Mark," said His Grace, who had been observing his friend's expressive features sardonically. "You are ever honorable."

If hostilities were not to be resumed, Mr. Dennison decided, the subject of his beloved had best be set aside. "You are not without honor yourself. Witness the example of Miss Mannering."

Sandor quirked an arrogant golden brow. "It is ever your habit to attribute to others a nobility of character that only you possess. Acquit yourself of the notion that my interest in Miss Mannering is at all honorable."

"No?" inquired Mark, as the gentlemen proceeded back along the passage to the supper rooms. "You lust after her fortune, I suppose."

"Dear Mark," murmured the duke, as his pained gaze rested upon great panels of lacquer, red and black and gold, before which sat gilded and silvered sofas with dragon motifs. "You know me so well."

Further conversation was nigh impossible, due to the very loud music provided by the regent's German band in an adjoining room. The effect was deafening to all but the prince, whose habit it was, when inspired by an infectious rhythm, to add to it himself by beating out a little percussion on the dinner gong. Mark, at least, was almost grateful for the din. With the oldest of his friends, he was sadly out of charity.

Still, he would have liked to ask the duke about the infatuation Binnie claimed to have nourished long ago, and which seemed to have had so adverse an effect. Sandor doubtless knew the whole of it; it was precisely the sort of thing he *would* know. No sense of human kindness, no sympathy for the frailties of his fellow beings, prompted the duke's keen attention to such details; but an inbred hankering after power. Sandor was the puppet-master. Lesser beings could but dance to his deft hands on the strings.

Stolidly, Mr. Dennison worked his way through pâtés and

curries, soufflés and such. Again he questioned why the duke had taken on the guardianship of Miss Mannering. Sandor's claim that he coveted her wealth, Mark dismissed out of hand—and then he paused. For a gentleman who disliked to put himself out on behalf of anyone, the duke had evinced a startling eagerness to take on additional responsibility. Miss Mannering was wealthy; Neal's inheritance was considerable; Binnie's dowry, as Mark could not help but know, was very handsome. Yet Sandor would not allow Binnie to touch her money, despite his stated conviction that she would never wed; and Neal he kept on a very small allowance. Moreover, the duke had been suffering heavy losses at the gambling tables of late.

Could Sandor be dipping into the funds entrusted to his care? *Was* that the reason he had taken on the responsibility of Miss Mannering? The duke of Knowles was a rich man, one whose fortune was legendary on the Stock Exchange—but other wealthy men had come face-to-face with ruin over the board of green cloth. Mark tried to convince himself that, even faced with disaster, the duke would not be so dastardly as to play ducks and drakes with monies not his own. He tried, and failed. Sandor was totally without conscience. To feather his nest at someone else's expense would not be out of character.

Unaware that his oldest friend was, along with supper, dissecting his own character, the duke was accounting for a large quantity of wine. All the world was at the Pavilion this night, and there was not half enough room for them. The room was warm, the wind instruments that predominated in the regent's German band abominably shrill, the evening one of the stupidest possible. As soon as he could, the duke approached his host, explained that he must journey homeward to arrange for the comfort of a houseguest, and once more took to his heels.

Since he had given as the reason for his departure the arrival of Miss Mannering, and since he could think of no other destination any more interesting, His Grace directed his footsteps toward the Royal Crescent. Those footsteps were none too steady; perhaps due to the heated atmosphere of the regent's crowded apartments, the wine had taken an unusual effect. In short, the duke was a trifle bosky. It was a lowering reflection for a three-bottle man and Corinthian;

a perfectly wretched ending to a perfectly wretched day.

Unsteady though his footsteps were, they led him unerringly toward the Royal Crescent, through his own front door, up the staircase. Voices issued from the first floor drawing room. He followed them.

First of the occupants of that elegant chamber to fall under his cold blue gaze was no less than the lady customarily known to His Grace as Miss Prunes and Prisms. As if by some sixth sense made aware of his presence, Binnie cast him a quick look compounded of merriment and an odd dread. The duke, in whom unaccustomed inebriation had induced a maudlin turn of mood, was put strongly in mind of a long-past day when he and his cousin had existed on terms of much greater amiability. Briefly, his cold expression softened. "Oh, Binnie," said he.

Miss Baskerville was very well accustomed to the queer fancies taken by gentlemen in their cups; though she had never before seen the duke in such a lamentable condition, she had quite frequently been called upon to deal with a brother who was three parts disguised. "Sandor," she murmured, laughter in her voice, "let me make you known to Miss Mannering."

Sandor would much rather have pursued the source of Sibyl's amusement. With immeasurable dignity, he raised his quizzing-glass.

Before him, at a small mahogany table laden with a dinner tray, sat a young lady with freckles and flaming red hair. She was distinctly grubby; she was consuming her food with much more enthusiasm than was seemly; she was staring at him in a positively vulgar way. Furthermore, her feet were bare.

A noise, which sounded suspiciously like stifled laughter, caused the duke's attention to stray to the other occupants of his drawing room. He took leave to wonder why Lieutenant Baskerville was clinging for dear life to a singularly ugly hound.

"Because Neal doesn't wish Caliban to knock you down!" offered Miss Baskerville, who was inspired by the duke's deplorable condition to unprecedented amiability. "Caliban is very strong and he is capable of quite remarkable displays of exuberance. Sandor, you have not made your bow to Miss Mannering."

Once more His Grace gazed upon that young lady. Sympathetically, she regarded him. "The devil!" she said cheerfully. "I don't expect it! The gentleman is foxed, you see."

"Foxed, am I?" the duke inquired wrathfully. Then he fell silent. It had occurred to him that he could hardly rip up at so very young a damsel, and in the very moment of her arrival, for stating what was no more than the truth.

Miss Baskerville was uncharacteristically quiet, and he glanced at her. Had Binnie come to a belated recognition of the folly of her conduct as concerned himself, to regret her countless harsh and hasty words? Was she tolerantly disposed to gentlemen in the throes of intoxication? He would not have expected it of her.

Nor should he have. *"Touché!"* murmured Miss Prunes and Prisms, ironically.

CHAPTER SEVEN

"Mercy on us!" wailed Edwina, on the following morn. "I nearly swooned from the shock! A giddy manner, flippant wit! If Miss Mannering means to go on in the way she has begun, the consequences will be incalculable!" She frowned at Binnie, who was peering with a look of great concentration into her coffee cup. "Has the cat got your tongue, Sibyl? I am telling you I understand perfectly why Miss Mannering's father made so feeble an effort to get her back! The thought of what she next may say or do has me in agonies. I vow I am absolutely sick with dread!"

Binnie, who had passed a restless night, due to an attack of what she sternly called indigestion—even while admitting to herself that it was the brief moment of accord with her cousin the duke which had left her afflicted with something like a sickness of the heart—raised shadowed eyes to Edwina's sulky face. "You are very hard on the child. She must have been exhausted by her round of talk and travel, and relieved at the discovery she was not to be abandoned, as she surely feared. We must make allowances."

"God bless my soul! Allowances, for an impertinent, pushing chit!" Edwina stared at her cousin, who wore a morning dress of white French lawn. "Sibyl, you are looking burnt to the socket. If you are weary now, when the girl has just arrived, you will have recourse to nervous medicines and laudanum before you have her half-ready to be seen!"

This blunt remark, suggesting as it did that Miss Delilah Mannering was to be her sole responsibility, caused Binnie to lower her gaze once more to her coffee cup. Briefly, on the previous evening, she had rejoiced in the knowledge that Sandor had at last overstepped himself, Speedily, it was being made clear to her that if the duke was up the proverbial creek without a paddle, it was she who must somehow ensure that they safely reach shore. Again, and without the least appreciable effort, he had turned her topsy-turvy. It was an abominable situation. So fatigued was Binnie that she thought she would rather sink than even try and swim.

Edwina, having firmly expressed her intention to have nothing to do with the Mannering chit, glanced around the morning room. It was a pretty chamber, with rosewood furniture and sofas upholstered in striped silk, a patterned Wilton carpet, a segmental barrel-vaulted ceiling. In one corner stood a harp. Then she again studied Binnie. "Tell him you won't do it!" she advised. "The girl is Sandor's charge; let him deal with her."

Binnie shoved aside her coffee cup and with it her fit of the blue devils. "Do you wish me to suffer one of Sandor's rakedowns? Just the other day, Edwina, you were begging me to say nothing that would set up his back."

Her cousin had the grace to look discomfited. If truth be told, Edwina didn't care in the least if Binnie brought down Sandor's wrath, so long as she herself was out of earshot. It occurred to her that the duke was a great deal easier to live with when Binnie wasn't around.

It occurred to her also that young Lieutenant Baskerville had appeared quite taken with Delilah, a circumstance that prompted her to seriously doubt his intelligence. Nor did she think his fiancée would take to Miss Mannering. Edwina rather admired Miss Choice-Pickerell. Sibyl, she knew, did not agree, which clearly demonstrated that Sibyl was also deficient in common sense. She was also exceedingly kind-hearted. Otherwise she would have understood, as had Edwina on first glance, that Delilah was a sly and scheming minx.

Just then Miss Mannering herself walked into the morning room, trailed by the faithful Caliban, both of whom had been greatly improved in appearance by thorough scrubbings. Delilah wore, Edwina noted, a pretty walking dress with a waistcoat bosom and puffed sleeves and a flounced skirt. It was typical of Sibyl to have had the most fashionable item in her wardrobe altered for the chit.

If Delilah was aware that Edwina was gazing askance at her, she gave no sign. "Good morning!" she said brightly. "I didn't mean to eavesdrop, but I couldn't help but overhear—does His Grace frequently fly off the hooks?"

This innocent question roused Binnie from her brown study, even as it cast Edwina smack into the dumps. "He does," responded Miss Baskerville.

"I thought he might." Delilah seated herself beside Binnie on a sofa, and Caliban sprawled panting at their feet. The hound so approved these new surroundings that he had grown positively frisky. Already that morning he had raided the larder, had caused the cook hysterics by accounting for a side of beef and a ham. He belched, blissfully.

Miss Mannering ignored this display of ill manners by her pet. "His Grace has the look about him of a man accustomed to having his own way. There is a royal assurance in his manner. Odd, is it not, that men visibly used up by dissipation often excite awe? As if undisguised profligacy were something to admire! Still I suppose the duke must have *some* good qualities, despite his vagaries."

"You're wrong," said Binnie unsteadily, as with horror Edwina stared. "Sandor has none. However, for all his shortcomings, Sandor is not a libertine."

"No?" Miss Mannering looked disappointed. "A pity; I have always wished to meet a rakehell. It all sounds so romantic; bold Corsairs and paroxysms of intemperance—not that *I* should care for it."

Binnie had begun to think that the instruction of Delilah

in the social graces might not be without its small rewards, no matter how quelling the prospect. Already she had experienced a lightening of the spirits. "You relieve me," she said drily. "Just what sort of gentleman *should* you care for, Miss Mannering?"

Delilah looked surprised. "I don't know. I wouldn't, would I, until I met him? Certainly I do not mean to fall in love after the briefest acquaintance and throw my hat over the windmill, like my mother did! Nor will I be fool enough to love a man who is running mad over another woman, which she also did, and which very often seems to be the case. People are very perverse, I think, always wanting what they can't have, and underrating what they *do!*"

This rational viewpoint struck Binnie very strongly, as did the air of worldly wisdom that sat so oddly on Delilah's young face. She chuckled.

"You are quizzing me," Delilah said reproachfully. "I don't mind! You do not know me, so I cannot blame you for not realizing that I am a downy one. Beside, you are quite lovely when you smile." Speculatively she eyed Binnie, who was struggling valiantly to contain her mirth. "I'll lay a monkey you could cut quite a dash, if you wanted to!"

"But I don't want to!" gasped Binnie. She explained that she had had several seasons, but did not take; that at length she had relinquished the arena to younger damsels. If truth be told, said Miss Baskerville, she was an ape-leader.

"Stuff!" Delilah's eyes held a glint of curiosity. "You had all those other ladies beaten to flinders, or could have had—I'll stake my reputation on it."

"Reputation!" uttered Edwina, scandalized, as Binnie burst into an immoderate fit of loud laughter. Since Sibyl obviously did not intend to impose a check on these unbecoming high spirits, Edwina was forced to act. "Miss Mannering, if I may give you a word of advice, and I feel I must: you are behaving in a way open to very unfavorable interpretations. If you go on in this manner you will soon be sunk quite below reproach. Young ladies of breeding do not employ vulgar expressions, or display such indelicacy of principle."

"They don't?" Miss Mannering appeared less dismayed by this accusation of boldness than intrigued.

"They don't!" Edwina strove for self-control. In the most

61

decidedly unequivocal terms she listed Miss Mannering's various sins. A well-bred young lady would never pry, nor make vulgarly personal remarks, as Delilah had to Binnie; she would never treat a gentleman whom she'd just met with easy camaraderie, as she had Neal; she would never take the gross liberty of accusing a gentleman of inebriation. His Grace, Edwina pointed out sternly, was Miss Mannering's guardian, and as such was due her unflagging respect and obedience.

"Even," Delilah inquired doubtfully, "when he's cast-away?"

"Especially then! Don't interrupt! A well-bred young lady, Miss Mannering, wouldn't recognize if a gentleman was, er, cast-away!" Additionally, Edwina continued, while both Delilah and Binnie looked increasingly glum, a young lady should know nothing of the irregularities habitual to gentlemen, let alone speak of them. Nor would she encourage the pretensions of persons of lowly station, to such good effect that she was then forced to discourage them by means of a frying pan. "But Sibyl can tell you more about that!" she concluded, as she rose. "You will excuse me; I must go lie down!"

In silence, the ladies watched her depart. Then they contemplated each other. "I can't, you know," said Binnie. "Tell you more about that. *I* have never been in the position of repulsing a suitor with a frying pan."

Delilah giggled. "I didn't think that was what she meant. Does Miss Childe often go off in such odd humors and talk such skimble-skamble stuff? She was evidently in a state of great perspiration. I suppose she doesn't like me very much."

"My dear." Binnie was simultaneously sorry for her newly acquired protégée and appalled by her. "I'm afraid, in spite of the unfortunate way she did so, that Edwina only spoke the truth."

"Oh, I can perfectly see *that*." Miss Mannering looked wise. "I know I must mend my tongue if I am to live in the highest style. I fear I must start from scratch, since I was only twelve when my mother ran away, but I *do* wish to learn how to go on properly. I am a quick study, I assure you! Already I have concluded that I must not be getting into scrapes, or telling Canterbury tales—or swear like ten thousand troopers, which

I *can!*—or speak of such things as the shameful lewdness of the London streets at night."

"That," responded Binnie, rather faintly, "is very perspicacious, Miss Mannering."

"Pooh! You must call me Delilah, since the task of my reformation has obviously fallen into your lap." There was a worried expression on Miss Mannering's face. "Truly I do not mean to be a charge on you, or to cause you to fret yourself to flinders—because I can see that something is already prying on your mind. And I'll be hanged if I add to your anxiety! So if you will only tell me what is required, I will do it, upon the square! I mean, honestly!"

Only the greatest beast in nature could have remained unmoved by this earnest speech, which was delivered with such fervor that its utterer's cheeks were pink; and Binnie was not impervious. Indeed, so pleased was Binnie by the sincerity of her protégée that she decided a gentle stroll around Brighton would not be amiss. Therefore she provided Miss Mannering with one of her bonnets, and an Indian shawl of worsted with a pine pattern; and accompanied at a discreet distance by a footman, the ladies set out. Caliban went with them, held firmly on a leash.

Delilah was delighted with all that she saw, from the city beaux who sported their carriages on the Downs and their persons on the Steine to the roof work of the Royal Stables and Riding Houses that had been completed a few years previously. The Stables, with their eighty-foot cupola, sixty-five feet high, she found especially memorable; although she was a little doubtful about the Moslem Indian style of architecture. Miss Baskerville, herself delighted to have so appreciative a pupil, broadened their tour. Delilah was presented to Phoebe Hessel, who sold gingerbread and apples from a basket at her side, and who in her youth had served for five years as a soldier without discovery of her sex; and was privileged to view a scar on the old woman's elbow, result of a bayonet wound. In very good spirits, the ladies then proceeded to the beach, there to observe the distant fishing fleet. They sailed at sunset, explained Miss Baskerville, and returned laden with fish in the early morn. Awaiting their return would be the London fish-merchants. Providing one rose early enough, one could observe the fish being packed into carts for the market at Billingsgate.

Not by a muscle's twitch did Delilah betray that she did not consider the viewing of cartloads of dead fish any particular treat. Determined to be conciliatory, Delilah explained in turn how one might catch a trout by tickling its fins. "Johann showed me," she said, then looked guilty. "I should not have said that, since young ladies certainly can have nothing to do with tinkers in the ordinary way of things. Forgive me, please!"

Binnie contemplated her charge, whose cheeks again were pink, a circumstance that she put down to maidenly embarrassment. Blissfully unaware that Delilah blushed only when embarked upon devilment, Binnie considered her encouragingly eager to please. She also considered it a great pity that such youthful high spirits should be so peremptorily squelched. Abruptly, she dismissed the footman.

When that young man had presented to Delilah the leash that restrained her pet and had taken his reluctant leave—he was in the process of developing a severe case of calf love for the volatile Miss Mannering—Binnie turned to her charge. "I think that when we are private," she said kindly, "we may speak without roundaboutation. I am not apt to be either shocked or take offense, and to be forever carefully choosing your words must be very wearying."

Delilah gazed upon her benefactress as if she were an angel, and nobly refrained from admitting a yen for nude sea-bathing, and from speculation upon the gay doings of the girls in town with the lads from the nearby defense camps. Miss Mannering, alas, was nigh incorrigible. Still, she had determined—among other things—to straighten out the tangled lives of the residents of the duke of Knowles's home on the Royal Crescent, and this could hardly be accomplished if the household was set on its ear. It amazed Delilah that people could acquire the habit of obeisance to a tyrannical personality. Miss Baskerville, especially, appeared to allow herself to be sadly manipulated. Delilah found in the situation a most salutary moral. Binnie was a high-minded lady, without a ha'porth of spirit—and how much less happy was she than Delilah, who was wild to a fault.

"My dear, what is it?" inquired Binnie, recipient of an

unwavering stare. "Have I made it sound a dreadful task, this learning propriety? Truly, it will not be so dreadful."

"Oh, no!" Delilah fed the remainder of her gingerbread to the faithful Caliban. "I was merely thinking about—things. I'll catch the hang of it soon enough; you'll see! Why, it was no time at all before I adapted to life in the tinkers' camp."

"You poor girl!" uttered Binnie.

"Why?" Delilah's eyes were wide. "Except for Johann, it was all very interesting. I learned how to catch a chicken with a horsewhip—from a distance you flick the whip around the chicken's neck and it can't even squawk. I even know how to ring the changes—the tinkers' word for it is *glad'herin*. You go into a shop and ask for change for a sovereign, then purchase some trifling article. Then you change your mind and bewilder the shopkeeper so that you can cheat him." She sighed. "No woman who cannot make ten shillings a day by *glad'herin* is fit to be a tinker's wife."

"Gracious God!" ejaculated Binnie. "Delilah, did you *wish* to marry him?"

"Who?" Miss Mannering inquired blankly. "Oh, Johann! Of course not. Do you know how the tinkers marry, ma'am? They call it 'jumping over the budget.' The bride and groom hop over a string or some other symbolic thing—though what it's symbolic of, I do not know!"

Miss Baskerville was not unaware that her delicate inquiry into the state of Delilah's sentiments had been delicately turned aside. Binnie was familiar with the contemplative expression that Delilah had briefly worn; though she had never glimpsed it in her own mirror, for which she was grateful, she had often enough seen it on the faces of females of her acquaintance. For a moment, Miss Mannering had looked very much like a young lady in love.

But with whom? Binnie pondered this profitless question as they strolled along the beach. She could not imagine that Delilah had, in her nomad existence of the past several years, encountered a gentleman even vaguely eligible. She could only hope that, in light of the girl's extreme youth, any such fancy would quickly pass.

"Delilah," she said abruptly. "You are, or will be, a very wealthy young lady. As such, you will come to the notice of people who are not so scrupulous as one might wish. If someone should urge you to do something that you do not feel is right—such as an elopement, or a situation that might leave you compromised—I beg that you will come and tell me."

Delilah paused in the game of fetch that she was engaged in with her hound. "Compromised?"

Again was brought home to Binnie the enormity of her task. Delilah was simultaneously worldy and naive. "You must not allow yourself to be closeted alone with a gentleman, for people are apt to draw conclusions that are both distasteful and untrue. It would ruin your credit with the world, and might leave you no choice but marriage to the gentleman."

"Fortune hunters!" Delilah's face was rosy. "The devil—I mean, oh, my! It makes very good sense, of course, but I have never thought—I mean, *me?*"

Binnie could not help herself; she smiled. Miss Mannering was far from a beauty, but she had a fresh and wholesome look about her, and her ingenuous manner could not help but appeal. Thought of ingenuity recalled to Binnie another young lady, these many years deceased. Once the duke of Knowles had succumbed to precisely this sort of volatility. Gentlemen nearing the dangerous age of forty were notoriously susceptible to May and December romance. Surely Sandor would not—but Delilah was very wealthy. She frowned.

"Have I said something I should not?" the young lady demanded. "I did not mean to. Pray forgive me!"

"Nothing of the sort." As Binnie surveyed the vivid little face turned so anxiously to her, she suffered another queer little ache in her breast. Delilah was so young, so fresh, so curiously unspoiled, despite her tendency to utter the most shocking remarks. "You will be going into society to some extent, though you are not quite of an age to be presented formally, and moreover are in mourning." She paused, searching for an appropriate phrase. "My dear, people are not always kind. I think that it would be best if in the future you spoke no more of Johann. The walls themselves have ears."

Delilah contemplated the great hound who had taken, to its detriment, the corner of her shawl into his mouth. "Not even to Miss Childe, or the duke, or your brother?"

Though she could not have explained it, Binnie instinctively responded in the negative. "There is no point," she said profoundly, "in crying over spilled milk." It was a remark reeking of hypocrisy—Binnie had in no wise managed to bear her own losses so well. She fell silent.

Though her motives may not have been of the most laudable, Delilah very much wished to please the kindly Miss Baskerville. She also longed ardently to be made a lady, even if it did sound a deuced dreary process; and she was grateful to Binnie for providing the means by which to fashion a silk purse out of a sow's ear. "Very well! I shall be silent as the grave."

Binnie said nothing. Delilah cast a quick glance at her shuttered face as she tried, without success, to wrest from Caliban the shawl. "Are you concerned with my reputation? This is all fudge, you know! No one involved will speak of the tinkers, unless it's Johann himself—and what could *he* say to the purpose? Nothing at all!"

With effort, Miss Baskerville roused from her reflections, which had been of a most somber nature, and which had been totally unrelated to her protégée. "You are correct. We need not concern ourselves with Johann. Let us discuss instead the new wardrobe Sandor has decreed I must provide for you."

Delilah was nothing loath: she had a young girl's love of finery, as well as a very shrewd notion of how such finery might best be put to use. With that notion she did not deem it prudent to acquaint her mentor. Therefore it was in excellent charity with one another that the ladies continued their perambulations along the waterfront.

CHAPTER EIGHT

As it evolved, both Miss Sibyl Baskerville and her protégée were very far off the mark. Johann had a great deal to say, and all of it to the purpose. The unhappy target of his remarks was Athalia. Due to their serious differences of opinion— Johann accused Athalia of nabbing the rust and cursed her up hill and down dale; Athalia responded that Johann must be dicked in the nob to think she would ride grub—they were quite literally at daggers drawn. The conversation was conducted primarily in Shelta, tinkers' talk, a language composed mainly of Old Irish, sweetened with some Romany and thieves' slang. Liberally interspersed throughout were such terms as *strépuck* and *luthrums' gothlin*, vulgar references to ladies of easy virtue and the offspring thereof.

Not only Athalia did Johann denounce as bachelor's fare, but also the young lady who had recently and ungratefully departed the shelter of his camp. For the former assertion Johann may have had good reason; for the latter he had none at all. The local innkeeper insisted that the lass had gone off cheerfully to embark upon a life of sin; but Johann—despite Miss Mannering's firmly stated conviction that he was a nodcock and a loose-screw—was not so easily taken in. The reason for his conviction that Miss Mannering was not, as the innkeeper so unwaveringly avowed, a straw damsel was simple: no man so beguiling as himself could be turned down by a right-thinking Paphian girl. Since Miss Mannering had sent him to the rightabout, and emphatically, Johann could only conclude that her character was unblemished, and her tastes very queer:

Also, he concluded that it was not without assistance that Delilah had hopped the twig. Only one person in the camp would have dared render that assistance. Strongly he informed Athalia of an intention to use her guts for fiddle strings.

This intention, and the fact that Johann was clutching a very nasty-looking shiv, struck Athalia with a distinct thrill of horror. She suggested that, were Johann to put his knife away, they might engage in a discussion of mutual benefit. She had indeed run rusty, she admitted, but not for the reason Johann might think. He must not conclude, she warned, that she had meant to betray him. And if he did slit her gullet, as he looked like he wished to do, he would in effect be doing himself in. Athalia had gathered some very interesting information during her couple days' absence from the camp. She did not think that Johann wished to whistle a fortune down the wind.

Certainly Johann wished to do no such thing. Regarding Athalia suspiciously, he put down the knife.

This acrimonious exchange took place outside Johann's low round tent, reminiscent of a beehive, through the top of which rose a thin spiral of smoke. Smoke rose, too, from the stove where Johann had been, before the outbreak of hostilities, soldering a tin disk. As did many others of his breed, Johann had an aptitude for rough metal work. He made a living of sorts by mending pots and pans, enlivening the camp with the sound of his hammer's tapping and the clang of tin. Johann, however, was rather more skilled at other pursuits. He was a born trickster, adept, for example, at such ploys as passing off an old horse for young by picking out the hollows of the crows of the teeth and filling them with tar. "Inside," said Athalia, and jerked her head toward the tent.

Still wary, Johann allowed her to precede him. No window illuminiated the tent; what little light there was gained admittance through myriad rips and rents. Johann closed the flap, leaving them in darkness broken only by the glowing embers of the fire. It was a diabolic scene.

Athalia dropped onto a lumpy pallet spread on the ground. She was very tired, not only as a result of a day spent trudging about the countryside laden down with baskets, household goods, toys, and cheap ornaments which she attempted with wily endeavor to sell to unsuspecting householders. When they did not buy, she turned to fortune-telling, at which she was skilled; Athalia could read palms and crystal balls, tea leaves and egg whites. If none of the preceding availed, she usually resorted to begging. Athalia was weary of it all, of sleeping under hedges and tramping in the rain, of a life of grinding, ceaseless poverty. Not much longer, she thought triumphantly, would she cower in a smoky, ragged tent.

Johann was not a patient man, nor was he familiar with introspective moods. Bluntly, he demanded an explanation of Athalia's remarks. Nor, he advised, would it be prudent of Athalia to try and make a cake of him.

Athalia was prudent by instinct: she did not remark that Johann had need of no assistance from herself to play the part of fool. Athalia was, on this matter, of a mind with Miss Mannering. Johann was a perfect block. All the same, he was *her* block, and she had need of him. She adapted a lachrymose expression and confessed that she'd been soundly taken in.

"Damn your eyes!" said Johann. "Don't go nabbing the bib."

This was encouraging; his temper had cooled sufficiently that he did not want to see her cry. "I'm mortal afraid to tell you," confessed Athalia, "what a rare mull I've made of it. You were right about Delilah all along. I would have believe you had I not been bacon-brained."

Johann was surprised by none of these remarks. Naturally he had been right about Delilah; assuredly Athalia was bacon-brained. Still, he required further enlightenment. Therefore he demanded that Athalia open her budget. Of what had she made a mull? He pledged himself to refrain from cutting up stiff.

Athalia was relieved to hear this; Johann's displays of temper gave one a nasty turn. At the moment he appeared amenable. She flattered herself that though she was no longer in her grass-time, she still knew how to put the dark eye on a man.

He was growing impatient. "She was telling us the truth," Athalia said quickly. "She really *is* an heiress. But then she fobbed me off with a tale about it being her mistress who died, and her having not a ha'penny to her name. I never guessed the little twit would play the concave suit! So I helped her." Her confession was briefly interrupted by Johann's hands around her throat. "I knew you were hankering after her!" gasped Athalia. "I was devoured with jealousy. That's why I tumbled for her hoax."

This seemed reasonable to Johann, who could envision no more fitting reason for an attack by the green-eyed monster of envy than himself. His grip loosened. "We may yet be plump in the pocket!" said Athalia, hoarsely. "Listen, Johann: I know where she's gone, and more. What I don't know about Miss Delilah Mannering isn't worth the knowing." She explained about Delilah's letter, the address of which she'd noted down. "Her father was a downy gager; he left her all his rhino. Moreover, I can see our way clear to getting our dabbers onto some of it."

But Johann, as is the way with gentlemen, even gentlemen of lowly station, had suddenly turned perverse. "That won't fadge!" he said irritably. "I don't aim to get my neck cricked. I'm no boman prig, to end up in Rumbo or on the Nubbing Cheat!"

Patiently Athalia took it upon herself to convince him that the scheme she had evolved would see them neither to the gallows nor in prison. She had no intention of kidnapping the heiress, merely of engaging in a little blackmail. The quality, as everyone knew, were very cautious of their good names. Miss Mannering would be ruined were her sojourn in the tinkers' camp to be known. A great piece of nonsense, of course; Miss Mannering had probably been better chaperoned among the tinkers, due to the sharp eye kept on her by Athalia, than in her own drawing room; but there it was. Were the affair handled properly, they would stand in no danger of being caught.

Again, Johann balked. He did not care, he said indignantly, to act the part of prattle-bag. Athalia might be a gabble-grinder, females often were; he might be a lowly tinker, but he was not without honor. Men of honorable nature did not go blabbing scandalous tidbits about the countryside.

"But you *wouldn't* be," Athalia pointed out reasonably, "because you would have been very well paid to keep your trap shut! The girl's guardian is a person of rank. He won't like having the screws put to him, but he'd like even less being dunked in the scandal-broth. He'll want the matter wrapped up in clean linen. To accomplish that, he'll pay through the nose."

Johann was not prone to quick decisions, being of a certain slowness of mind. Chewing on his lower lip, he ruminated.

Athalia allowed him to do so uninterrupted. She was certain of her ability to bring him to her viewpoint. In truth, she needed him not for the accomplishment of her plan. She did, however, in case of mishap, require a handy scapegoat. The practice of blackmail was not quite so devoid of peril as she had made out. Of course she did not *plan* that Johann should dance the sheriff's waltz. Yet, if push came to shove, better his neck be placed in the noose than her own.

Absently, she rubbed that item, sore from Johann's recent assault. That had been a perilous moment, had unnerved her so much that she'd almost abandoned her schemes. Fortunately, she had made a recover. More than a wish for money motivated Athalia. Delilah had diddled her royally. Athalia wanted revenge.

Her relationship with that young lady she passed in quick review, as well as the various things she'd learned. When Athalia had claimed to know all that was worth knowing about the heiress, she had spoken no more than truth. She'd heard the tale of Lady Mannering's flight from a cruel cold spouse, a flight for which Athalia dubbed Lady Mannering a pea-brain. Events had borne out that opinion. Sir Nicholas had provided his wife with the elegancies of life, if not with affection. Lady Mannering's flight had resulted in a miserable existence, and at length a pauper's grave. In Athalia's mind a command of the elegancies of life was worth the endurance of any cruelty.

For Delilah, who had shared her mother's miserable existence, and who might have been expected to have suffered similarly, Athalia spared no sympathy. Any kindness she'd once felt for the girl had been killed by the gross advantage Delilah had taken of it. Furthermore, Athalia could imagine no one less worn down by circumstance than the resourceful Miss Mannering.

Angry as Athalia was with the lass, she could not deny

Delilah's resourcefulness. She wondered how Delilah would deal with the difficulties that fate, in the guise of Athalia herself, had in store.

"A well-heeled cove, you say?" inquired Johann. "The guardian?"

"Rich as Croesus," Athalia replied promptly. "And deuced high in the instep." In suspense, she awaited his next comment.

It was not long in coming. "I knew as soon as I clapped my glaziers on the lass," Johann remarked smugly, "that she wasn't any pig in a poke. Mighty peevy you are, Athalia! It's a damned rum lay."

That's put the cat among the pigeons! Athalia thought smugly. She murmured her gratitude for Johann's approval of her plan and suggested they set out straightaway for Brighton. It lay not many miles distant. With luck they might arrive within a couple days.

Johann was agreeable, so much so that he permitted Athalia to bask in his unaccustomed praise. Athalia's schemes were excellent, as he had said; but Johann wasn't quite the chowderhead that Athalia thought him. Even the best of plans could be improved upon, and he had not abandoned his intention to avail himself not only of the heiress's fortune, but of the heiress herself. Naturally, he would not acquaint Athalia with this intention, lest she thrust another spoke in his wheel. It was obvious to Johann that Athalia nourished a grudge against Miss Mannering for the gammon that she'd pitched. Johann rather admired the lass. Few could make Athalia out a flat—but Athalia had risen to Delilah's bait, hook, line, and sinker, like any hungry fish.

Nor would it be politic, at this point, to reveal that he meant to take the enactment of Athalia's schemes out of her own hands. Time enough for her to learn that later, when he had contrived a way to remove himself from her reach. Athalia, when enraged, utilized utensils far more deadly than frying pans.

Amiably Johann suggested the celebration of this potentially lucrative partnership with a flash of lightning. It was no heavenly display of fireworks to which he referred, but a mundane glass of gin.

Promptly, Athalia agreed. At last Johann had come to

appreciate her. Flown with visions of wealth and luxury—which to Athalia meant no more than a proper bed to sleep in, and four square meals a day—she set out to fetch the refreshment.

CHAPTER NINE

Such great strides was Miss Mannering making toward her avowed intention of making a silk purse out of a sow's ear that even Edwina Childe was impressed by her progress. She had misjudged the girl, she decided, as she observed Delilah, seated across from her at the mahogany dining table. At least her company manners were unexceptionable.

As was her dress, an exquisitely simple creation of plain black silk, cut rather more décolleté than was usual for so young a lady, but to distinct advantage. Whatever nefarious use the heiress meant to make of her new finery, one thing was certain: Miss Mannering had no need to pad out her bodice with handkerchiefs.

Thus far the meal had gone off without a hitch. The food had been excellent, from salmon and fried smelts and veal patties through minced veal garnished with fried crumbs, potatoes in a form and stewed mushrooms to, currently, cheesecakes. Sibyl had been the model of decorum, as befit a lady to whom the role of bear leader had fallen, and even Sandor appeared preoccupied. Perhaps this once Edwina might be permitted to get through an entire seven-course dinner without being subjected to the hostilities to which she was constitutionally unsuited. Hopefully, she grasped her fork.

Miss Mannering approved of the dining room, with its fine

74

stucco decorations, its elegant mahogany furnishings. If she had any complaint, it was merely that young Lieutenant Baskerville had chosen to dine in the officers' mess. Delilah was curious about Neal, of whom she had seen little since he'd come to her rescue; though he stayed frequently at this house, he was required to be at parade by eight o'clock of the morning, and was gone before she emerged from her bedchamber. Delilah wondered what sort of female was this Miss Choice-Pickerell to whom he was betrothed, and of whom Edwina spoke with such enthusiasm, and Binnie in such repressive tones. Miss Mannering was a young lady with a superior understanding. She was aware that Binnie didn't like Miss Choice-Pickerell above half.

Delilah was also curious about her guardian, on whom she had not before this meal laid eyes since the infamous occasion on which she had accused him of being foxed. He had not thus far addressed above two words to her, though he did the honors of the table with infinite, if absentminded, grace. The duke, thought Delilah, would do everything with princely magnificence. "I believe I owe you an apology, sir," she said prettily. "It was very impudent in me to accuse you of being cast-away."

His Grace roused sufficiently from his abstraction—into which he had been plunged by several startling and highly provocative remarks made him by the fair Phaedra, during their most recent tête-à-tête—to eye his ward. Edwina, her fork suspended halfway to her mouth, held her breath. Binnie too waited, prepared if necessary to conduct herself like a tigress in defense of her cub. She had grown very fond of Miss Mannering, fonder than she would have thought possible during the space of a few days.

The duke decided to be amused. "No apology is necessary," he replied, with unprecedented tolerance. "I *was* cast-away."

"I know that," retorted Delilah, "but it was unbecoming of me to remark on it. I do not wish to run counter to conventional behavior, sir. And for me to comment on your addiction to the bottle was altogether displeasing conduct. It cannot help but have given you a very low opinion of me."

The duke took an even closer glance at his newest responsibility. She looked the veriest urchin, he decided, with her freckles and flaming hair. She was regarding him rather anxiously, with cheeks that were pink. "Don't regard it!" he said kindly. "*I* do not! Tell me, how do you like Brighton, Miss Mannering?"

"Oh! Very well!" Delilah plunged headlong into a discussion of the town and the local wonders that she had been privileged to view. The air was unusually bracing, she believed; the waves that pounded at the soft white cliffs were beautiful to watch, and one soon grew accustomed to the absence of trees. The fogs, of course, were dangerous; one must choose with care the time of day when one went walking by the sea. And in line with walking, Miss Mannering had recently witnessed the poet Byron limping along the Steine.

This artless outburst might expressly have been designed to inspire a worldly gentleman with unendurable tedium. Edwina's appetite abruptly deserted her. Anticipating that Sandor would give the volatile Miss Mannering a sharp setdown, she contemplated her fork.

His Grace had suffered a momentary impulse to do precisely that, but so animated was Delilah's manner, so vivid her freckled countenance, that he could not bring himself to give her a trimming. He was not a cruel man, merely selfish. In tones of utter disinterest, he remarked that the regent himself was often to be glimpsed parading on the Steine.

"Oh, I've seen him," replied Delilah, disapproval in her voice. "I cannot think he set a good example when he appointed a Tory as prime minister, after all those years of raising the hopes of the Whigs. He deserved to have the Whigs denounce his ingratitude and perfidy. Surely princes of all people should act like gentlemen! And then there was Mrs. Fitzherbert—well! I can perfectly understand why Tom Moore wrote *Intercepted Letters*, and why he published it anonymously. Not that he remained anonymous long! Everyone must surely know he wrote those sharp articles."

"They do," Binnie said quickly; the duke was not only an intimate of the regent, he was also an ardent Tory. "It has gained him notoriety, and ruined his prospects. By that brutal piece of folly, Moore is put quite beyond the pale."

"Oh." Delilah looked thoughtful. "I suppose he must be glad that he did not go to prison for it, as other detractors of royalty have done."

Conversation faltered as the duke pondered whether it was

worth the effort to take offense on the part of his friend and regent. He decided it was not. The intrepid Miss Mannering had said nothing that was not true, and in so doing had revealed an intelligence far more acute that he would have expected from so very young a miss. Wondering what other surprises she might hold in store, he decided to further draw her out. The prince was preparing a phantasmagoria at the Pavilion, he explained; was busily concerned with his apparatus for the production of a storm of thunder and lightning and rain, during which he intended to make a personal appearance as a ghostly phantom. Edwina, immensely cheered by this indication that Sandor was in an exceptionally genial mood, plunged her fork with gusto into the cheesecake.

Binnie was a great deal less happy that the duke had taken so marked a fancy to Delilah's company. Few young ladies received from His Grace such flattering overtures; she could not recall a single young lady on whom His Grace's approving glance had been seen to fall, with the single ill-fated exception of His Grace's young wife. In point of fact, Delilah reminded Binnie of Linnet. There was no physical resemblance; Delilah was neither cowardly nor scatterbrained; but despite the great differences the outcome was the same. Delilah acted with sublime unconcern, Linnet had been prompted by innate foolishness—but both rushed in where angels feared to tread.

And the duke was reacting to Delilah just as he had to his young wife. Obviously Sandor had serious intentions; why else would he have begun to pay Delilah immediate court? Perhaps, unusual as such a thing would be in him, Sandor was merely being polite. In any case, Binnie could only hope Delilah was keen enough of wit to realize that Sandor was old enough to be her father, and of irascible temperament beside, and would not make a desirable spouse. Binnie studied her cousin. It was very unlikely, she concluded, that so very green a damsel would prove the exception to His Grace's legendary success with the fairer sex. Countless were the casualties of that insolent, seductive glance.

Completely unaware that her benefactress cherished such a lowly and unfounded notion of her character—Delilah was not one to be flattered by being drawn into conversation with a gentleman, even with a duke—she rattled on happily. From the regent they progressed to Napoleon, and the fear held by many Englishmen earlier in the year that the emperor of Austria, the Corsican Upstart's father-in-law, would hesitate to take up arms against his daughter's husband. Utter nonsense! said Miss Mannering. Such doubts did Francis II great injustice. Never had he placed his daughter's well-being above his own.

"Perhaps I should not say so!" she continued. "I have come to think young ladies are not supposed to have *opinions*. And it is a matter of considerable import that I acquire townbronze."

The duke eyed her curiously. "Why?"

"Because I wish to form an eligible connection! Perhaps I should not have said *that* either; I can see how it might be a little off-putting. Still, there it is! I have decided that marriage is the perfect vocation for me."

"Oh?" The duke decided that he had been seeking diversion in all the wrong places. Were it amusement he required, he should have looked not to fair barques of frailty but to damsels who sojourned in tinkers' camps. "Have you in mind a candidate?"

"Well, yes," Delilah said slowly. "I rather think I do."

Horrified, Binnie interrupted. "A young man, of course," she remarked judiciously. "One of respectable background and lineage. Bear in mind, Delilah, that you will not want to subdue your spirits, or curtail your activities, as must be the case with an older gentleman. I think that thirty years of age must be the absolute outside, and you would do much better to choose a prospective bridegroom closer to twenty-five!"

Rather startled, Delilah glanced at her mentor, and discovered that Binnie looked very worried. "Do not trouble yourself, ma'am! I do not mean to be imprudent. And I am very much obliged to you for showing me how to go on."

Delilah's ingenuous remarks, and Binnie's pointed ones, had diverted Sandor's attention to his cousin. It occurred to him that he had not crossed swords with Binnie for almost two days. She was looking rather worn-down, but her pallor could have been caused by her ugly dress. Even Aphrodite, in that hideously drab creation, would have looked pale.

"If you expect Sibyl to guide you among the pitfalls of romance," he remarked, proceeding with a vengeance to make

78

up for his previous neglect, "you are very likely to come a cropper. Sibyl is far more likely to teach you how to arrive at your last prayers. I can't begin to enumerate the gentlemen whom she has brought to the sticking-point, only to rebuff them." He had the satisfaction of seeing his cousin flush. "I only thought it fair," he added, "that I drop a hint or two. Gentlemen who dance attendance on Sibyl, Miss Mannering, are invariably left at point non plus. I would not wish you to develop my cousin's habit of reducing your beaux to mere shadows of their former selves."

"Gracious God, Sandor!" uttered the much-maligned Miss Baskerville. Edwina, resigned to yet another skirmish, dropped her fork. "What have I done to set up your back?"

"Nothing!" he responded promptly. "That is the problem! It's naught to me if you are so fearful of having to repent of your choice that you make no choice at all, but it is hardly fair to Mark to keep him dangling."

There was some basis for this accusation; Binnie had employed her protégée as an excuse for avoiding her most persistent swain. Thought of her protégée recalled to her the presence of that young lady, whose manners she was obliged to reform.

Very much aware of the indefensible position in which he'd placed his cousin, and totally devoid of any scruples that would have demanded he refrain from taking advantage of that position, the duke quirked a brow. "I would not mind so much," he continued, "if Mark was not in the habit of discussing your megrims. It is a subject with which I already possess considerable experience, and consequently I find Mark's loquacity a dead bore. It is scant wonder, Sibyl, that you are left upon the shelf. You have only yourself to blame."

Considering this too much to bear, even for a lady of self-effacing manner, one to whom an untutored young damsel looked for good advice, the duke leaned back in his chair and waited for Miss Baskerville to lose her temper. She would roundly denounce him, he decided, would say that for him to criticize her conduct was for the pot to call the kettle black. And when she paused for breath he would scold her for uttering such great incivilities, and warn Miss Mannering to beware lest she dwindle into a similarly fubsy-faced old maid.

But Binnie was aware of what was expected of her by her

cousin the duke. "Why, Sandor!" she said sweetly. "I did not know you wished me to marry Mark. You should have said so sooner; I would have gone on quite differently. I thought you would not want me to marry anyone, for it would mean you must exert yourself to find a new housekeeper—and I know how very much you dislike to exert yourself."

"The devil!" said the duke, with every evidence of great shock. "You *have* played fast and loose with Mark. If you have led him to cherish hopes that you do not mean to fulfill—shame, Sibyl! I had thought you a woman of *principle!*"

This provocation Binnie also ignored. "Indeed I am! Why should you think me indifferent to Mark? *Do* you wish me to marry him? If so, I must seriously consider it. Naturally it is my duty to oblige you, Sandor."

The duke eyed Miss Prunes and Prisms and wondered what she'd do if he called her bluff. Meanwhile, Edwina regarded them both gloomily. She knew that Binnie would be happy to immediately remove herself from this house—Binnie believed a wish for that removal prompted Sandor's harassment of herself, and Edwina usually agreed—if only he would give over her dowry into her own hands. Since Sandor refused to make Sibyl a present of her money, and since Sibyl refused to marry to please anyone but herself, they had for several years been at an impasse. Edwina was heartily sick of it. Quietly, she nudged Delilah, who was so fascinated by the proceedings that she'd propped her elbows on the table, all the better to miss not a single word.

"Is it?" the duke inquired ruminatively. "Your duty, Sibyl?"

Unflinchingly, Binnie met his cold gaze. That she'd painted herself into a corner she knew very well. Oddly, the realization did not trouble her. *Did* she love Mark? It might explain her strange moods of late. "Are you grown deaf, Sandor? I just said so. Witness me eager to do your bidding in all things."

The duke decided that it would be unchivalrous of him to take further advantage of the indefensible position in which his cousin had placed herself. He had no wish to trick her into marrying Mark, when all was said and done. Without the acerbic tongue of Miss Prunes and Prisms, he suddenly realized, life on the Royal Crescent would be decidedly flat.

However, he could not deny himself one last taunt. "Trying

it on much too rare and thick, Sibyl! Take care that I do not put your professed willingness to the test."

This sounded very much like a challenge. Binnie did not, strong as was the temptation, look away. "We will go on much more prosperously, Sandor, if you will refrain from pitching straws."

Whether His Grace might have heeded this good advice remains unknown—although it is safe to conjecture that he would not have, since good advice had as little effect on him as water on a duck, and furthermore there was a distinct glint in his cold eye. Miss Mannering had followed the preceding remarks with an ever-increasing contemplativeness. She had decided that the duke was a very vexatious gentleman, and deliberately so; she further concluded that Miss Baskerville was sublimely incapable of managing her own affairs. "How queer!" she said. "Now I understand that while it is improper for me to be impertinent, it is acceptable behavior in gentlemen. It is all of a piece with everything else, is it not? For it is definitely a man's world. Take mistresses, for example. One never hears of a kept *man!*" Edwina, who had hoped that with Delilah's interruption some degree of tranquility might be restored, moaned.

There was a profound silence, broken only by Caliban's distant howls. The hound, whose mealtime presence had proven distinctly disruptive—it being difficult to restrain so large and enthusiastic a beast from sampling every dish—had been confined for the duration in his mistress's bedroom. Miss Baskerville, observing the duke's brooding expression, was with all her might battling an untimely impulse to fall into the whoops; Edwina, expecting from His Grace an annihilating outburst, had closed her eyes to pray.

As it turns out, His Grace was unaware that the irrepressible Miss Mannering had delivered a Parthian shot; he was not even thinking of her. Mention of mistresses had recalled to him the fair Phaedra, and the revelations she had made when he expressed an intention to end a relationship that had endured several years. *Could* what she claimed be true? Sandor feared it could. He recalled the interval when Phaedra had been absent from her usual haunts, ruralizing at some unknown destination, for a period of months. At the time he had thought little of it. Now it appeared he should have been a great deal more interested.

Why wait so long to tell him? Because one thing could be verified didn't mean the rest were true. The reason for her silence was explained easily enough: Phaedra had seen the wisdom of adding a second string to her bow.

She had frankly admitted she meant to keep him dangling, not out of any affection, but because Sandor's apparent devotion kept her husband interested in her, if hostile. The duke cursed the day he'd become involved with a lady who ran with the hare and hunted with the hounds. Were her startling claims factual, were the colonel to suspect—Sandor shuddered. He was in the most damnable dilemma possible. What he could do to extricate himself, he did not know. Phaedra had withheld the most pertinent information of all.

"Are you quite speechless with anger?" inquired Miss Mannering, with interest. "In that case you must be *very* furious. Truly I do not mind if you scold me, because I *have* been impertinent. I thought, you see, that you might not be aware that you were behaving scaly. But I am sorry if you took it amiss!"

Blankly, the duke looked at her. What the devil was the chit nattering on about? "Do not regard it," he said, for the second time that evening, a circumstance that caused Delilah to reflect that her bear leaders had a queer notion of ladylike behavior if they accepted her outbursts so calmly. And then he set out to amuse her with a description of the King's Head in West Street, where during the Restoration Charles II was said to have slept.

Relieved beyond description, Edwina returned her attention to the cheesecake. She now understood that Miss Mannering was an excellent creature who improved amazingly upon acquaintance. Any young lady who could deal so well with Sandor had Edwina's unqualified blessing. Linnet had dealt similarly well, as Edwina recalled. Clearly Sandor preferred very young ladies.

And why not? Definitely it was a solution. Delilah wished to form an eligible connection, and no one was more eligible than the duke of Knowles. What signified an age difference of a paltry eighteen years? Delilah was a mellowing influence.

Binnie's thoughts followed similar lines, but they inspired

her with no similar enthusiasm. What was wrong with her? she wondered. Why should she care if her cousin entered into yet another disastrous marriage? With Delilah she need not be concerned; Delilah could demonstrably handle Sandor very well.

This conclusion brought Binnie neither amusement nor relief. Perhaps she was in her dotage. But surely ladies were not prone to turn touchy and difficult until somewhat more advanced in years?

Delilah, for all her youth, had not been born yesterday; she knew it was due to no efforts of her own that the duke had undergone a rapid change of mood. A very knowing one, Delilah pondered the implications of the scene which had just been enacted before her. Surreptitiously she glanced at Binnie, who appeared to be engaged in silent communication with her empty plate; and at Edwina, who beamed a blessing. Unaware of what prompted this friendliness, Delilah returned the smile. No victim of false modesty, she congratulated herself on an excellent evening's enterprise.

CHAPTER TEN

Had Miss Mannering been privy to a conversation that took place between Lieutenant Neal Baskerville and his fiancée later that same day, she might have been even more intrigued. It was not the nature of the conversation that was cause for conjecture—alas, the conversation of Miss Choice-Pickerell roused scant interest even in its object—but the manner by which her discourse glaringly illuminated their prospective relationship. Cressida very clearly intended—or so Neal deduced from her remarks—that her bridegroom would dwell under the hen's foot.

She did not say so, naturally; Cressida was far too refined to utter any statement that smacked so strongly of vulgarity. Nor, to give her all due credit, had Cressida considered the matter in that particular light. All the same, had the manner in which her marriage would be conducted been broached to her, and had she deemed it prudent to respond, she might have stated an intention to firmly hold the reins. Leisured young men were notoriously unable to manage for themselves. Consider how many of them had gotten themselves in deep water (Cressida was an avid reader of the gossip columns), if not worse! Neal would come to be grateful for her firm hand at the helm.

They were engaged that evening at a private soirée, an affair so very crowded that no visitor of rank would arrive to find the staircase empty and consequently drive away from the door. The highest accolade had been bestowed upon the proceedings: it was a shocking squeeze. Therefore, the guests went about looking languid, the better to mask gratification at being present at so fashionable and successful an affair; and the hosts strove with equal vigor to avoid looking very smug. All enjoyed themselves immensely, except Lieutenant Baskerville. By the thought that he might be—*would* be—engaged with Miss Choice-Pickerell for all the remaining evenings of his life, the lieutenant was extremely depressed.

Cressida was unaware of the cause of his abstraction, though she could not help but realize he was holding himself at a distance. Neal's behavior did not especially bother her; she already knew him prey to strange humors. In comparison to the unbecoming fervor of which he was occasionally guilty, she preferred to see him subdued. Indeed, she meant to see the feckless lieutenant continually subdued, once the knot was tied.

Those rapidly approaching nuptials were the topic of Cressida's discourse. She chattered on, under the mistaken assumption that her husband-to-be cherished an interest in such topics as her choice of bride-clothes. She conducted an animated discussion as to where they would reside—not in Bloomsbury among such rich merchants as her father; she thought Neal would rather dwell among the *ton*; she was sure

84

he would be pleased to learn her father was on the lookout for a suitable house. Neal was not, though he forebore to explain that he would much rather have chosen his own home. In short, Cressida was to the last degree tiresome in examining all the details of their alliance and asking questions without end.

To those questions, she received only vague replies. Briefly perplexed by his lack of enthusiasm, Cressida decided that the lieutenant was discomfited by her frank discussion of such details. She chided him for it. She was aware, Cressida stated, that the Upper Ten Thousand—of whom Lieutenant Baskerville by birth was one—considered certain subjects taboo; but she could only consider it very silly if a young man could not discuss his own marital arrangements without embarrassment. It was not as if she asked him to wear his heart upon his sleeve.

Fortunate that she did not, reflected Neal, as he murmured a meaningless response. Startling as it was in a man on the verge of marriage, Neal was eminently heart-whole. Sternly, he berated himself for wishing that by some miracle he might be released from his appointed fate of becoming leg-shackled to a tiresome, prosy, managing female. He had responsibilities. Escape was past praying for.

Cressida wondered what among Neal's frippery pursuits was of sufficient import to have caused him to become so glum. She achieved, or so she thought, enlightenment. "Ah!" she murmured. "Colonel Fortescue."

"Eh?" Neal realized that she'd provided him the perfect excuse. "The colonel, yes. I have so aroused his displeasure that he read me a severe reprimand. If I again misbehave, he said, he will act in a way to disgust me with the army altogether. He added, with the greatest insincerity, that he should regret my going out of the regiment."

"Good gracious!" Although Cressida had no high opinion of the Tenth—the officers whereof were incurably frivolous, associating with no one but their own corps, being more concerned with their blood horses and curricles and little amusements than in the defenses of their country in time of war, an example set them by their commander in chief, the regent—she was too wise to let her boredom show. "Neal, what have you done?"

85

"To incur his displeasure?" Neal gazed around the crowded room. "I requested leave to pass a week in town. It is to Sandor that I owe thanks for drubbing, not to any act of mine."

Cressida was rapidly growing out of patience with her fiancé, who was displaying a great deal more interest in their fellow guests than in herself. She attempted to arouse the lieutenant's compassion by relating the occasion on which his sister had cut her in the streets.

"Never was I so snubbed!" she concluded. "I cannot conceive what possessed Miss Baskerville to turn a cold shoulder on me. The duke was very shocked when I told him of it. He said I was not to regard your sister's crotchets, which I thought very pretty in him." Here she paused; Neal had turned on her an enraged countenance.

"You told *Sandor?*"

"Of course I told His Grace!" Cressida replied indignantly. "Why should I not have? I am to become one of the family! *He*, at least, thought very poorly of your sister's behavior to me."

Obviously Miss Choice-Pickerell was chagrined that her fiancé did not think likewise. Equally obvious were her unflagging efforts to puff up her own consequence. With effort, Neal refrained from comment.

The lieutenant was in a reckless humor, decided Miss Choice-Pickerell, eyeing him. He wore an expression so forbidding that it alarmed her not a little, suggesting as it did that he might wish to declare off altogether from his betrothal. This was a most distressing thought, not because of the vile scandal in which such a step would involve Neal, but because of the embarrassment it would cause herself. How tiresome of him to be so difficult! She set out most artfully to bring him back to heel.

"You are angry with me," she uttered sadly. "I am sorry for it. Had I known you would take the part of your sister before my own, I would never have brought the incident to your attention—or to the attention of the duke. I hope he did not scold her for it. Truly, Neal, I did not mean to cause Miss Baskerville any discomfort. I quite like your sister, and can only regret that she does not feel similarly to me."

It occurred to Neal that he was displaying no more conduct than the rawest schoolboy, a fact that he did not hesitate to lay at his cousin the duke's door. Now that Neal considered it, all his problems stemmed from that source. Fervently he wished that Sandor might be made to pay for his sins.

Furthermore, he realized that to Miss Choice-Pickerell he had been less than polite. He had not meant to ignore her, it was merely that so many insoluble problems preyed on his mind. Handsomely, he offered her apology.

Cressida permitted several moments to pass in gallantries, a pursuit which she privately considered a tedious waste of time, before indicating pleasantly that romantical effusions must end. "Why did you," she inquired, removing her hand from the lieutenant's grasp, "ask leave to pass a week in town?"

"The heiress," Neal replied. Had Cressida been more interested in such matters, she might have realized his avowals had had a very hollow ring. There were advantages, he supposed, in having a fiancée as cold as an icicle; she was never likely to suspect his courtship was no more than a matter of form. Neal might do so with reluctance, but he would persevere on his chosen course. The die was cast. Edwina and Binnie and Cressida herself depended on him to conduct himself with dignity. "I thought Binnie might need some help with Miss Mannering."

Cressida's glance was sharp. "I had forgotten her. You brought the girl to Brighton, Neal: what is she like?"

"Oh, the most complete romp." Neal's tone was utterly indifferent. "Not the sort of chit that you would take to, Cressida."

Miss Choice-Pickerell thought this an odd comment, and so she observed; her alliance with Neal required her involvement in family affairs. In none of her new duties, she explained, did she intend to be remiss. Perhaps, in lieu of Neal, she might provide Miss Baskerville assistance. She fancied that help as rendered by herself was nothing to cavil at. Cressida might not by birth be absolutely top drawer, but she was very conversant with the restrictions imposed on young ladies of the first consideration. "You have not told me," she added, "how old the girl is."

"Seventeen," Neal replied, greatly abstracted. "A thoroughly rag-mannered chit."

Then it was one o'clock, time to descend to the ground floor supper room for a cold collation, an endeavor accomplished not without a great deal of pushing and shoving on the staircase. The remainder of the evening passed without further incidents worthy of comment, save for an encounter between Neal and his prospective father-in-law, who announced his belief that he knew the lieutenant too well to stand on ceremony with him, and bluntly inquired if after his marriage Neal would be in a position to be beforehand with the world, a piece of presumption that Neal considered beyond everything—until the elderly Choice-Pickerell stated firmly that Neal must sell out his commission. He did not fancy a son-in-law who looked like an ornamental monkey in his dress uniform of red breeches with gold fringe and yellow boots, he explained. Nor did he see much point in a regiment that was eternally stationed on home leave.

To these blunt observations, Neal responded noncommittally. The hour was very late when he finally escaped. Since his rooms at the barracks held out no more allure than did his chamber in Sandor's house, he repaired to Raggett's, there to plunge more deeply than he could afford, and to imbibe more freely of the brandy bottle than was advisable. Then he adjourned to the Cider Cellar, an underground resort off the Steine, and continued the process of drinking himself insensible. His awareness of his progress grew rather hazy after that, but at length he found himself walking by the sea. The night had grown foggy, and Neal's facilities were additionally obscured by brandy fumes. When a large shape loomed up out of the mist, he thought at first that he was being attacked by some aquatic monster. It knocked him down.

The lieutenant defended himself valiantly—or as valiantly as could be expected of a young man upon whose chest rested a heavy weight, and whose reflexes had been dulled by an overindulgence in the grape. Due to the dullness of those reflexes, it was several moments before he realized that he was not being devoured alive, but thoroughly washed by a large, wet, affectionate tongue. Not only was that caress familiar, but also the tones that fell upon his ear.

They were feminine, and cross. "Do come away, Caliban! What must the poor man think?" Hands patted him anxiously. "I do hope nothing is broken, sir! Caliban didn't mean any harm, though I don't expect you to believe *that*. Pray try and sit up! Because if you cannot then I must run and fetch help for you—and a dreadful fuss that would make, though it's no more than I deserve for giving everyone the slip. How I'm to form an eligible connection after making a byword of myself, I don't know! Still, I shall think of something. Do speak to me, sir!"

Neal checked his various limbs and found all intact. "What the deuce?" said he.

"Why, Lieutenant Baskerville! This *is* a piece of luck! Or it is if you don't rat on me. I should have known you were no stranger, because Caliban is not ordinarily so enthusiastic about people he hasn't met. Do come away, you wretched beast, and let the lieutenant get up!"

The weight, accompanied by various grunts and groans from its owner, was removed from Neal's chest. He sat up. Before him were Delilah and her dog, both looking disheveled and breathless. Delilah had a firm grip on the collar of her pet.

Neal rose and brushed ineffectively at the sand which clung to his dress uniform. "What are *you* doing here?"

"Caliban needed some excercise," Delilah responded promptly and blushed. "And so did I! I don't know if you can understand, but it is very wearying to be always confined, and thinking about behaving *properly*. Quite naturally I must do so, if I am to settle in matrimony, but sometimes I simply *have* to cut a wheedle. It is a sad failing in me! And so I wait till the household is asleep and then slip away to come out here where it is very peaceful, and Caliban and I have a romp. Since no one knows, it can't give anyone a disgust of me." She paused, anxiously. "Talking won't pay toll, will it? Now I'm truly in the suds! Unless I can convince you *not* to snitch on me?"

"Baggage!" Neal grasped Caliban's collar. Considering this an overture of friendship, the hound responded exuberantly. "Never fear, I'll stand buff."

"You *are* a regular Trojan!" Delilah beamed. "Since you are here, Lieutenant Baskerville, would you care to join Caliban and me on our walk? The fog is not so very bad, and one is perfectly safe so long as one watches one's step."

To stroll along the beach in the midst of a damp, chill fog was the perfect exercise for a gentleman with many worries preying on his mind. Neal wondered why he hadn't thought of it himself. "I should be delighted, Miss Mannering."

"You used to call me Delilah." She squinted up at him. "Why have you become so formal? Or is this one of the compromising positions that your sister warned me against? Surely she could not have meant that I should not be alone with you! You aren't dangling after a fortune. And since you are already betrothed to somebody else, you cannot be conniving to marry me!"

Neal dared not speak, lest he laugh himself into stitches. "I see what it is," Delilah said unhappily. "I'm being vulgarly inquisitive again. Sometimes I wonder if I shall ever be up to snuff!"

That Miss Mannering should be cast into the dumps by any action of the lieutenant's would have been unbearable. He set himself to soothe her, explained that he was certain his sister's strictures had not been meant to apply to himself, assured her she might be as inquisitive as she wished without causing him to take offense. "That's a relief!" she responded, with an air of bonhomie. "Because I'm aware that all this is dashed irregular. Tell me, sir, if you don't mind—is not the duke of Knowles a bachelor of the very first stare?"

"Sandor?" Neal was startled by this abrupt turn of conversation. "I guess so. He's generally held to be very near perfection."

"A man of immense fortune?" Delilah persevered.

Neal kept private his doubts on that score. "At least a man in very easy circumstances. Why?"

"Such a man," murmured Delilah, "would have no need of sconcing the reckoning. How very fortunate it is that I am not hampered by delicate principles!"

These remarks inspired Neal with misgivings. Delilah mentioned an ambition to settle in matrimony; surely she did not think to lure *Sandor* into parson's moustrap? The top-lofty duke of Knowles to take a tumble for a mere dab of a girl who was wild to a fault? Nemesis, with a freckled face? It was an absurd notion, and it delighted him. Diffidently, he inquired how she meant to go about the thing.

"Oh, very carefully!" Delilah tripped and Neal took her

arm. "I do not think it must be so very difficult to fix one's interest with a gentleman, especially when the gentleman has already exhibited a definite partiality. He is not aware of it yet, but I shall contrive—because, though I should not say so, I am up to all the rigs!"

Neal doubted this blithe statement not an instant. He even thought Delilah's enterprise might meet with success. She had no lack of bottom, already having exhibited remarkable courage and staying power. So pleased was Neal with the vision of his high-handed cousin falling prey to Cupid's sting, in the person of Miss Mannering, that he failed to wonder why Delilah should be interested in the duke's fortune when she had a respectable fortune of her own. Yet, much as Sandor deserved to receive his comeuppance, Neal could not help a twinge of conscience on the part of Miss Mannering. "Wouldn't you," he inquired cautiously, "prefer a younger man?"

"Younger? Oh, no!" Lost in her scheming, Delilah took scant notice of her choice of words. "Only the duke will serve my purpose. But perhaps I should not have laid my cards on the table and admitted to playing the concave suit! I'm afraid, if truth be told, that I shall never be quite the thing."

Nor would she, though Neal would have cut out his own tongue before admitting it. To a young man so recently exposed to his fiancée's awesome refinement, Delilah's lack of sensibility came as a great relief. "You have in these schemes of yours made no mention of happiness. Does that not weigh with you?"

"Happiness?" She sounded puzzled. "Of course it does. I shall contrive that also, I daresay, once I figure how to rid myself of the impediment—but first things first! Before I concern myself with that, I must pull off my coup."

By impediment, she naturally meant the fair Phaedra, of whose existence she should not have been aware. Delilah appeared aware of a great many things she should not have been—including, it seemed, the exact means by which to lure the duke into her net. It struck Neal that they had accepted Delilah on face value, had made no effort to obtain proofs of her identity. Easy enough for an impostor to step into the heiress's shoes. Could Delilah be an adventuress, grasping at an opportunity to feather her own nest? Certainly she was like no well-bred young lady he'd hitherto known. Slyly, he said so.

"Oh, I'm a rank deceiver!" Delilah said gaily, and with unnerving pertinency. "Surely you had guessed."

That she might have meant merely that she was by nature unsuited to the rôle of lady, Neal did not consider; nor that an adventuress embarked on a bold masquerade would hardly have confessed it so freely. Neal was entirely occupied with the tantalizing prospect of his detested cousin the duke being repaid in one fell stroke for *all* his sins. He stated that it was a lucky thing that Sandor wasn't in the habit of looking gift horses in the mouth.

"Yes, isn't it?" agreed Delilah. "Otherwise, I'd speedily find myself dished. I'm sure he'd try and stop me if he knew what I was about—which would be a shame, because it's for the best." A horrible thought struck her. "You won't tell him, will you, sir? It would ruin everything."

"Devil a bit, puss!" This was hardly a proper way in which to address a young lady, but it must be remembered that Neal was still suffering the effects of overindulgence in the grape. Too, Neal was laboring under the delusion, as had a certain innkeeper, that he was holding converse with a damsel who was no better than she should be. He peered down at her. She looked much more like a street urchin than an adventuress. Appearances, he decided wisely, were not to be trusted. "I'll even help you! Just tell me what to do."

Delilah had not expected such a large degree of helpfulness, even if her plan was indirectly to the lieutenant's benefit. "How very good you are, sir!"

"Moonshine! Call me Neal! After all, you have just made me recipient of deepest confidences."

Delilah had done anything but that, but she let his misapprehension pass. "Have I gone beyond the line of being pleasing *again?*"

"Not at all! You have expressed yourself with the greatest propriety."

That was an obvious clanker. The lieutenant was as great a humbugger as Delilah herself. She paused to look at him, thoughtfully.

Neal also paused—Delilah still clutched his arm—and studied the little face turned up to him. Her red hair was curling wildly in the damp air, her huge brown eyes were opened wide. Delilah noticed his rather owlish expression, and grinned. It was an enchanting face, Neal decided abruptly, for all its absence of beauty, the nose that was retroussé, the large, laughing mouth.

Definitely, the lieutenant had taken too much brandy; he had almost wished he was sufficiently plump in the pocket that this scheming minx might try and lure him into her snares. Amused by the ridiculous notion, he dropped a brotherly kiss on the tip of her nose.

CHAPTER ELEVEN

Not a bit wearied by her late-night adventures, Miss Mannering arose betimes the next day. She obtained breakfast for her hound and herself, then engaged in some profound meditation in the morning room. There Edwina Childe found her, and perscribed the application of a freckle wash of dilute hydrochloric acid; or perhaps Roman Balsam, a paste consisting of an ounce of bitter almonds and an ounce of barley flour, mixed with honey, which was left on overnight. If these sovereign remedies failed, they could try Grape Lotion, or Dr. Withering's Cosmetic Lotion. As a last resort, there was always Edwina's own remedy, which she had for years been wanting to try out. One scraped a quantity of horseradish into a teacupful of cold soured milk and let it stand twelve hours, she explained to her reluctant laboratory specimen, then strained the mixture and applied it to the affected parts two or three times daily.

Though Delilah did not think her pursuit of an eligible

connection would be aided by the aroma of horseradish and sour milk, she was too good-hearted to burst Edwina's air bubble. She wondered what had inspired Edwina to make such efforts on her behalf. Since Delilah did not ask this question aloud, she did not obtain enlightenment. It would have surprised Miss Mannering very much to learn that Edwina envisioned her the next duchess of Knowles.

She was rescued from Edwina—just in the nick of time, Delilah thought; Edwina had been making vaguely threatening noises concerning Caliban, whose wretchedly low-born appearance she did not consider suitable to a lady of prospective rank—by Binnie. The ladies were promised to go shopping that day.

Nowhere, decided Delilah, could compare with Brighton in its display of vehicles. She saw sedan chairs and heavy coaches, phaetons and curricles, gigs and buggies, and every other kind of open carriage imaginable. Almost as diversified were the people sauntering everywhere in the streets.

Past booksellers the ladies strolled, dealers in toys and knickknacks, rare china and tea. Briefly, Delilah was distracted by a bird-stuffer's shop which displayed parrots, birds of paradise, hummingbirds with gorgeous plumage. With difficulty, Miss Baskerville persuaded her that the duke would not appreciate the introduction of a stuffed bird into his drawing room. And then they embarked upon a whirlwind tour of the shops that specialized in lace and ribbons and similar folderols and furbelows so dear to the feminine heart.

Muslin and cambric and bombazine they inspected, jaconet and sarcenet and crepe. Silk turbans received their attention, bonnets trimmed with flowers, ruches, lace. The advantages of a silken Norwich shawl with a Kashmir pattern were discussed, as opposed to a large Indian shawl that wrapped around the figure. The ladies were unanimously in favor of tippets with long hanging ends, made of lawn or lace or swansdown, for day or evening wear; and opposed to the Apollo, a sort of underdress or corset worn to make the waist look slender, which Delilah compared unflatteringly to a coat of chain mail. She approved wholeheartedly, however, the daring French fashion of pantalets of flesh-colored satin, made to be worn in place of a petticoat. And she dissolved in helpless giggles at the sight of an artificial bosom made of wax.

"Cotton, I think, might be more practical," she said, as they exited to the shopkeeper's relief. The young lady had been outspoken, and the modiste had not appreciated comments on shoddy workmanship and inferior goods. "Binnie, do look! That man is trying to steal Caliban!"

Miss Baskerville obeyed, not out of concern for the hound they'd left in the care of the footman, but in hope that the would-be dognapper might succeed. No desperate ruffian confronted her, but an all-too-familiar figure in excellently cut morning garb. "Mark!" she said faintly.

Delilah was rather surprised that Binnie should number among her acquaintance a hopeful dognapper; she took a closer look. It was not the gentleman who had hold of the dog but vice versa: Caliban had rendered the gentleman immobile by clamping his teeth around a once-immaculate sleeve. "Oh, no! Caliban, release that poor man instantly!"

Caliban knew that tone, and it boded him no good. A hard row to hoe was a dog's life. He groveled dejected in the street.

"Mark, has he hurt you?" Her embarrassment forgotten in concern, Binnie hurried forward.

So this was Mark, whom the duke had accused Binnie of treating badly? Delilah regarded him curiously.

Mark, recipient of that freckled stare, returned the compliment, and decided that he saw nothing at all to admire in such a brazen chit. Made aware of this staring-match, Binnie hastily performed introductions. "No, I'm not hurt," Mark said belatedly. "I recognized your footman and thought I'd wait for you, and this beastly hound made sure of it."

"You must have tried to pet him," Delilah said disapprovingly. This high-minded gentleman was dancing attendance on Binnie? Fortunate that Binnie's affections had not become fixed. "Caliban doesn't permit strangers to pet him. He probably thought you were trying to steal him, in which case he acted very properly!" She bent to pat the dog. "And in that case, he certainly didn't deserve a scold."

That anyone should wish to steal such an ugly and ill-tempered beast was beyond Mark's imagining. Diplomatically, he kept private that viewpoint. "Binnie, I've the strangest feeling that you've been avoiding me."

Though this remark was murmured, and intended only for Binnie's ears, Delilah could not fail to overhear. Nor did she fail to note that her benefactress was looking very uncomfortable. "Oh, you must blame me!" she said brightly. "I am a selfish creature, and I've been taking up all of Binnie's time. It is no easy thing, sir, this preparation of a young lady to be launched into society!"

Again Mark refrained from comment, this time to the effect that the preparation of the irrepressible Miss Mannering for her debut would be little short of a Herculean feat. Instead, he asked if the ladies had further errands to execute, and offered his escort. "You will be very bored," said Binnie.

"Nonsense!" interjected Delilah. "If we find it amusing, why should he not? He may even learn something."

In this prediction, Miss Mannering was correct. What Mark learned—as the ladies inspected gloves of York tan and Limerick, evening gloves of white kid, French gloves trimmed with ruching around the top—was that he had a distinct and most ungentlemanly aversion to Miss Mannering. It was not only her monopolization of Binnie that prompted this dislike; Mark was put off by the freakish and the bizarre. Delilah was bold as a brass-faced monkey, he decided, as the ladies pondered the relative merits of reticules, lozenge-shaped and circular, on silver or gilt frames, knitted with beads, embroidery, appliquéd, painted. Her conduct was altogether displeasing.

Binnie was aware of Mark's opinion of her protégée, nor could she blame him for it; the usually amiable Delilah was going on in a thoroughly abominable way. In fact, she was acting like the rawest country miss, without the least notion of acceptable behavior. Binnie cast her charge a reproachful glance.

Delilah was truly sorry that she had put her mentor to the blush, but there was no help for it. She would make it up to Binnie later. *Much* later, she might even explain. At the moment she was wholly concerned with making the so-proper Mr. Dennison think her the kind of chit who took all sorts of encroaching fancies.

In that endeavor, Delilah met with very great success. Mr. Dennison was on the verge of soundly depressing her pretensions when fate, this day in the guise of Miss Choice-Pickerell, intervened.

"Good morning!" said that lady, who was in an excellent frame of mind. Binnie, in front of such an audience, would not dare cut her cold. Expectantly, she eyed Binnie's companions. "How lucky is this meeting! I have been wishing to speak with you, Miss Baskerville."

Binnie had no choice but to perform further introductions, though it seemed to Mark's suddenly critical eye that she did so with scant grace. Cressida's gray glance fixed immediately on Delilah. "So this is our little heiress!" she said, with a fine condescension that set Binnie's teeth on edge. "Well, she's not a beauty, but with such a fortune she still may take. That was what I wished to speak to you about, Miss Baskerville. I meant to offer you my services—since I am soon to be one of the family."

This speech, delivered with all the lack of consideration for the feelings of lesser mortals of a *très grande dame*, inspired Binnie with a strong wish to throttle her cousin the duke, who had permitted Neal to embark upon a piece of folly that could only make his life miserable. As well as her own, Binnie added silently. Unless she severed connections with her brother, she could not avoid his wife.

Further disturbed by the hostile silence maintained by the charmer of his heart and soul, Mark stepped into the breach. It was very thoughtful of Miss Choice-Pickerell, he averred, to so concern herself. Cressida, put on her mettle by her future sister-in-law's glaring lack of gratitude, confessed modestly that she was the highest of sticklers. Since she was so conversant with the laws of conduct ruling polite society, she would consider it very remiss in herself to fail and offer assistance in what could only be a wearing task.

Apparently Cressida did not believe that Binnie's knowledge of those laws was on a par with her own. Binnie could not fault Miss Choice-Pickerell for that conclusion; she was acting as rag-mannered as Delilah herself. It occurred to her that Delilah was very meekly accepting Cressida's unflattering comments. The reason for that forebearance soon became apparent: Delilah was gone.

Frantically Binnie looked around, an act that inspired Cressida with burning curiosity. "Miss Baskerville, whatever is wrong? You are gone quite white! And where is Miss Mannering?" And then Cressida glimpsed the heiress, on the opposite side of the street, engaged in conversation with a gaudy raggle-taggle creature with countless tawdry chains around her neck and arms and gray-streaked dark hair. With unconquerable horror, Cressida stared. "This passes belief!" she gasped. "A young lady of breeding—imprudent—unmaidenly!"

"You refine too much on it," Binnie retorted, though without conviction. "I'm sure there's some explanation."

If Miss Baskerville saw no harm in her charge's public conversation with an obviously depraved female, thought Cressida, then she shared the Baskerville lack of stability with her brother Neal. Never had Cressida known such a wrong-thinking pair. This was an opinion unwittingly shared with Mr. Dennison who, though he was not thinking of Neal, was very definitely thinking that Binnie displayed a startling want of conduct. First she cut an unexceptionable young lady like Miss Choice-Pickerell dead in the streets, and now she came to the defense of a chit to whom Mark took very strong exception indeed. Surely Binnie could not be blind to Delilah's faults? In Mark's opinion, Delilah should have been left in the tinkers' camp. Obviously it was a way of life to which she had been perfectly suited. With deep disapproval he watched her skip back across the street.

Delilah was frowning as she rejoined the group. Becoming aware of their combined censure, she looked innocent and blushed. "Have I behaved badly? I do hope not! But I saw a—a gypsy, and wished to have my fortune told. Just fancy, I shall take a journey, and meet a handsome gentleman, and have a brood of children! She swore it to me, lest her eyes fall from her head. And I have already taken the journey, have I not? So now I may look forward to the handsome gentleman and the children!"

Association with Miss Mannering was having an adverse effect on her benefactress; faced with Delilah's patent but cheerful wrongheadedness, Binnie was less censorious than amused. "One hopes," she said, with mock severity, "that somewhere between those two events you will take time out to be wed."

"Oh, I shall!" Delilah grinned. "You needn't fret your guts to fiddle strings on *that* head!"

Cressida, stricken dumb by the heiress's outrageous antics,

regained her powers of speech. As would be quickly demonstrated, Cressida had no patience whatsoever with wrongheadedness. "Gracious! I am surprised at you, Miss Baskerville! Surely you must be concerned that Miss Mannering has sullied her reputation, has engaged in the most undesirable behavior."

"I have?" Delilah looked intrigued.

"You have." Cressida's regal bearing indicated a consciousness of her superior standing: she looked down her patrician nose. "This eagerness to converse with persons of low station can only bring you under the gravest censure, Miss Mannering."

"You have," said Delilah, with the air of one making an important discovery, "a strong sense of propriety."

"I do." Cressida preened. "I trust you will not take it adversely, Miss Baskerville, but Miss Mannering is likely to sink herself quite below reproach if you do not intervene. But perhaps," and she cast Mark an arch look, "you would prefer to otherwise pass your time. In which case, I will be happy, as I have said previously, to lend a hand."

Never had Cressida expected her magnanimous offer to be turned down. She was very much surprised when the object of her benevolence uttered an emphatic negative.

"No," said Delilah, in the tone of one who will brook no argument. "You are a great deal too nice in your notions, ma'am, and I do not like to be pinched at or patronized or moralized over. Beside, I already have Binnie to play gooseberry, and *we* rub together very well."

Nor had Cressida ever received so sharp a setdown. She gaped. "I dislike your manner, miss!"

Binnie regarded her prospective sister-in-law's indignant countenance, and her protégée's stubborn one, and leapt into the fray. "And I think very poorly of *your* manners, Miss Choice-Pickerell! Whatever your aspirations, you are not yet a member of the family. In attempting to meddle where you have no place, you are guilty of presumption."

"Well!" ejaculated Cressida. "Of all the unjust things to say!"

"Unpalatable, perhaps," retorted Binnie, with immense satisfaction, "but not at all unjust. And now, Miss Mannering and I must bid you good-day!"

Cressida stared after them, pale with outrage. It was a few

moments before she realized that Mr. Dennison had not escorted the ladies, but had stayed with her. She gazed appealingly at him.

Every bit the gentleman, and also feeling that Miss Choice-Pickerell had been grievously abused, Mark set out to soothe her. He couldn't imagine why Binnie had flown into the boughs. Miss Choice-Pickerell might have phrased her observations a trifle more tactfully, perhaps, but she had spoken only the truth. There was no sense to be made of Binnie's rudeness. Perhaps the duke had not been guilty of gross exaggeration when he nicknamed his cousin Miss Prunes and Prisms.

Meanwhile, Miss Prunes and Prisms and her protégée had taken refuge in a shop. Delilah, poking through a pile of flesh-colored knitted vests, gave it as her opinion that her benefactress had dealt the odious Miss Choice-Pickerell a crushing blow.

"Would that I had! That tiresome creature! But I'm afraid she's uncrushable."

It was clear to Delilah, from the gloomy manner in which Binnie was contemplating an extremely light and transparent chemise, that Miss Baskerville was already repenting her hasty words. "Make yourself easy!" she said kindly. "Miss Choice-Pickerell isn't likely to tell your brother you sent her off with a flea in her ear; it shows her in too bad a light! It has me quite in a puzzle why he should be hankering after her."

Binnie struggled with her conscience—for in no wise should she have been discussing her brother's fiancée with Miss Mannering—and lost. "To own the truth, I feel the same way! I cannot think them at all suited, and I fear Neal will be miserably unhappy."

Delilah ruminated. "I'll tell you what it is!" she said, after a moment. "He must've been a little bosky at the time. I'll wager he's already regretting asking her to marry him, but doesn't know how to cry off. Silly cawker! We must *help* him, Binnie!"

Miss Baskerville eyed her protégée with something very close to awe. "But how?" she asked. "I have been wracking my brain, but to no avail. The only solution I can think of is to *murder* her." Delilah looked contemplative. "Gracious God! I was only funning, child."

Murder, then, was out; Delilah had no wish to overset her kindly and long-suffering benefactress. She eyed a selection of stockings, cotton and angora and silk, black and white and fashionable pink. "I own I don't immediately see how it is to be done, but I mean to think *very* particularly about it. Dear Binnie, do trust me!"

Oddly, Binnie did. She had no doubt that the enterprising and unscrupulous Miss Mannering could, if she put her clever mind to it, devise a means by which to throw a spanner in the works. She had less faith, however, in Delilah's ability to do so without landing them in briars. But what mattered a little discomfort if by it a beloved brother was spared a lifetime of bitter discontent? Binnie steeled herself.

Wise she was to do so. So concerned was Binnie with Neal's difficulties that she'd forgotten Delilah's encounter with the raggle-taggle gypsy, precisely as Delilah had intended she should. Miss Mannering did not think the spirits of her benefactress would be elevated by the revelation that a certain tinker intended blackmail.

CHAPTER TWELVE

On the subject of blackmail, the duke of Knowles was not long kept in ignorance. That afternoon found him not plunging deep at Raggett's, nor strolling along the Steine, nor attending a grand military review. Though a pleasing lack of solemnity marked reviews conducted under Prinny's auspices, the duke was in no humor to appreciate such larks as a regiment of donkeys, mounted by beaux and belles, led by a gentleman of great bulk whose large and brightly gleaming spurs hung level with the hoofs of his steed. The duke was barricaded in his study, having given his staff explicit warning that he was not to be interrupted on pain of death.

The duke's study was in effect a library, a rectangular room designed not only for displaying books, but for entertaining. At each end an apse was fronted by a screen of Corinthian columns. The ceiling was shallowly barrel-vaulted and decorated with low relief stucco and painted oval panels. The rosewood and mahogany furnishings incorporated a great deal of brass inlay, lines and stars and clover leaves, as well as brass paw feet.

The duke sat at a writing table of slender proportions. A tambour shutter had been pushed back to reveal pigeonholes and drawers which rose and fell on a spring fitting. It was obvious from the duke's appearance—his golden hair was wildly disheveled, as if he'd run impatient fingers through it; his posture slouched—that he was engaged in intensive cerebral activity.

It was not, alas, accomplishing him much, unless it could be considered an accomplishment to work oneself into a fever of the brain. Sandor could see no way out of the dilemma presented him by the fair Phaedra. The situation was galling. Sandor was unaccustomed to dancing to some other piper's tune. And what the devil did Phaedra think to accomplish? She could not keep him on tenterhooks indefinitely. Or so Sandor hoped. He had a vision of himself ancient and infirm, still acting the cicisbeo, while Phaedra still dangled that piece of withheld information like a carrot in front of his nose.

Brighton! he thought bitterly, as he slammed down the tambour shutter. That he only barely missed smashing his own fingers did not improve his mood. Brighton, where the sea-waters were beneficial to asthma and cancer and consumption, deafness and rheumatism and ruptures, madness and impotence. Would that he had stayed in London, where if he was to go to the devil, it was at least with his own hands on the reins.

Came a tapping at the door; the duke cursed. Said the butler, quaking in his shoes: "Beg pardon, m'lord, but there is a person wishing to speak to you, and he refuses to leave."

The duke took leave to wonder why the retainers whom he

employed at so generous a wage, and to whom he was the soul of benevolence, were incapable of turning away undesirable parties from his doorstep. The butler trembled; His Grace's words pealed like the crack of doom. He closed his eyes and awaited the inevitable which, judging by His Grace's temper, would be either decapitation or dismemberment.

A silence fell. Of too nervous a temperament to blindly await his doom, the butler cautiously opened one eye. To his relief, the duke was looking a trifle more amiable. He stated a decision to see this unknown caller. Reprieved, the butler fled.

It was not compassion for his underlings that had prompted Sandor's change of mind—had he ever been taxed with mistreatment of his servants, he would have responded that they were paid to put up with his whims, and beside he had never yet actually manhandled any one of them—but a suspicion that the person of whom the butler had spoken with such grave distaste might be able to shed some light on Phaedra's little mystery. This suspicion was confirmed when the visitor strolled into the room. Unkempt, obviously a man without the least pretension to gentility—but handsome for all that. None knew better than the duke that Phaedra had a predilection for handsome men.

Johann—for the visitor was he—in his turn, saw the most tremendous swell. A gager in truth, as Athalia had said, for none but the richest of men could live in this best possible of styles. A very nacky notion it had been to persuade this modern-day Midas to part with some of his ridge. Johann seated himself in a chair with saber legs and scroll back.

The duke was not impressed by this studied nonchalance. "Pray tell me the object of your visit!" he uttered impatiently.

So His Grace was of a choleric temper? "I knew as soon as I cast my winkers over you, cull," Johann approved, "that you was a right-thinking one! 'Twill be a rare pleasure to do business with such a knaggy cove."

Business? This sounded ominous. "I do not see," Sandor said coolly, "what business I could possibly have with someone like yourself."

On his high ropes was the gentleman? Johann would bring him down off them soon enough. He chuckled. Then he launched into an explanation which, since it was couched in such phrases as "wrap it up in clean linen" and "get my dabbers onto some rhino," offered the duke scant enlightenment. Quite properly, the duke had no desire to see his dirty linen laundered in public; of course this unwelcome visitor would wish recompense for keeping his trap shut. But about what could he be tale-pitching? Surely the man didn't think Sandor a pigeon for his plucking? If so, he was mistaken. Sandor didn't care a straw if Phaedra's indiscretions were published to the world.

"Phaedra?" echoed Johann, when the duke made known this sentiment. "Damned if I haven't been taken in! Because the wench gave me an altogether different name!"

"She would, wouldn't she?" inquired the duke, who was rapidly growing bored. "You see you have been misled. It is Phaedra you should speak to. Here, I will give you her direction!"

Johann did not intend to be outjockeyed by any rum swell. "Nay, that won't wash! Don't be trying to tip *me* a doubler! I know good and well that the lass—by whatever name you call her!—is in this very house."

The brief euphoria attendant upon serving his ladylove an ill turn abruptly deserted Sandor. He was a man of keen intelligence, when inspired to utilize it: therefore, the revelation that this uncouth caller could only be Miss Mannering's tinker. He raised his quizzing-glass. Miss Mannering had come within aim's ace of marrying this vagabond? And the vagabond had come within aim's ace of getting his very dirty hands on the Mannering fortune? "Good God!" he said.

Johann did not appreciate being inspected as if he were some rare insect under glass. In a belligerent manner, he announced that it was time they got down to brass tacks. Johann was a busy man and he had other fish to fry. In a nutshell, Johann expected to be very well reimbursed for keeping to himself information of a nature that would put Miss Mannering beyond the pale. Johann might not be one of the nobs, but he was wide-awake enough to know that no lass who hobnobbed with tinkers would be looked upon as eligible to rub shoulders with the quality. He would even go further, Johann promised: were the duke to fail and buy his silence, he would put it about that Miss Mannering had lived a debauched life.

"Be damned to your impudence!" uttered the duke, irritably. "You'll find no easy pickings here, man. Be off with you!"

Johann had not expected immediate capitulation, not from what must be the highest bred man in England; he considered the duke's annoyance a very proper sentiment. He also considered that the duke had not thought the matter through to its logical outcome. No young lady could benefit from the rumor that she persevered in loose morality. To this end, he gave a gentle hint. The duke heard him out with a countenance of dreadfully gathering rage. "I'll warrant," Johann concluded cheerfully, "you wouldn't like that above half. As they say, guv'nor, play and pay."

But Johann had underestimated his prey, as he discovered when the duke's hands fastened themselves on his shirt-collar and heaved him upright. "I'd as soon see you quietened first!" growled His Grace. "Defend yourself, fool!"

Johann made haste to do so. He was no stranger to the noble art of self-defense, though he played by very different rules than the swells, bring an adherent of those ignoble tactics known inexplicably to the initiates of such sport as "not playing the game." Sandor was not dismayed, however; he displayed to good advantage, as might be expected of one whose usual sparring partner was no less than the noted pugilist, Gentleman Jackson. They feinted and parried, sweated and swore. It soon became clear to the unhappy Johann that his antagonist was well up to the mark, with an extremely handy bunch of fives. Even clearer was the fact that, unless he accomplished some very low blow, it would be bellows to mend with him.

The door swung open; on the threshold, Binnie stared. She had been drawn by the sounds of struggle, but never had she expected to enter Sandor's study and discover that he and a distinctly seedy-looking stranger had come to cuffs. "Peagoose!" snapped the duke. "Close the door!"

Hastily, Binnie did so. If she had been shocked by this vulgar display, the servants would be aghast. She set herself to watch the fisticuffs with no small curiosity, such spectacles not generally coming in her way.

It was over soon enough—too soon, in fact, to suit Binnie, who had discovered in herself a positive bloodthirst—or, to be precise, a strong desire to see Sandor get his claret drawn. That pleasure was denied her. The duke planted Johann a facer—tipped the tinker a doubler, in truth. Binnie gazed dispassionately upon the fallen man, and pointed out that he was bleeding all over the Wilton carpet. Then she inquired, should the duke not mind her asking, just who this stranger was.

"The tinker!" Sandor was delighted to have stricken Miss Prunes and Prisms all aheap, as obviously he had; she looked positively stunned. "Come to try and indulge in a bit of blackmail. He threatened to blacken Miss Mannering's reputation unless I bought his silence."

Reflecting that Miss Mannering was quite capable of blackening her own reputation without assistance, Binnie sat down abruptly in the sabre-legged, scroll-backed chair. "Gracious God!" she uttered faintly. "What will you do, Sandor?"

The duke shrugged. "Nothing. He's had a sharp enough lesson. We'll hear no more from him."

Binnie doubted strongly that an individual so resourceful as Johann appeared to be would so speedily turn tail, but she knew the futility of arguing with her cousin the duke. Thoughtfully she regarded him. "Sandor! You're hurt!"

"It's nothing." Gingerly, he touched his lip. Johann had not gone down to defeat without getting in a few of his own blows. "Don't fuss, Sibyl."

Binnie had no intention of so doing, and certainly not over a gentleman so high-handed and short-tempered as her cousin the duke. Apparently he was very fond of Delilah. It was not at all like Sandor to rush so nobly to a young lady's defense. She regarded the unconscious Johann rather gloomily.

As did the duke, though Binnie did not know it, similarly regard her. The duke's retinue, he decided, was acting very queer. Edwina was continually dropping hints so subtle that he hadn't the faintest notion what she was jawing about; Neal was in the sullens; Binnie avoided him like the plague. Only Miss Mannering was behaving with the least degree or normalcy, and that was not circumstance for which to render up praise. Miss Mannering was a thorough minx. Still, she was no problem of his, and he had no objection if she played off her countless tricks. After all, he had intended that she serve as an apple of discord. Rather violently, he yanked at the bellpull. The butler appeared. The duke requested, indifferently, that the recumbent body of his visitor be dumped in the street.

Silently, Binnie watched the removal of Johann. Then she contemplated her cousin the duke. "I hope you may not find yourself with the devil to pay over this business."

His Grace paid scant heed to this wish for his well-being, which had been delivered in what he could only think a tone of patent insincerity. He applied a handkerchief to his battered mouth. "Rather, you hope I *do*. Sorry as I am to disappoint you, Sibyl, I think that I shall not."

"Odious creature! You cannot deny yourself any opportunity to try and put me in the wrong. Here, let me: you are making a sorry botch of that."

With little grace, His Grace submitted to the ministrations of Miss Prunes and Prisms. Binnie withdrew a handkerchief from her sleeve, poured brandy on it, then applied it firmly to his cut lip. Sandor winced. She smiled. "Before you accuse me of unwonted cruelty, I will point out that the tinker was hardly a model of cleanliness. I shouldn't wish you to expire of some dread disease."

"No?" Sandor grasped her wrist. "You surprise me. I should have thought you wanted that very thing."

His sudden action had so unnerved Binnie that she dropped the handkerchief. "Unhand me, Sandor."

But the duke was not an obliging sort of man. "No. Not until you tell me what has caused you to look burned to the socket. Is Delilah plaguing you? Shall I send the chit away?"

Binnie considered this kind offer only further proof of Sandor's basic villainy; he would not seriously consider banishing a damsel at whom he'd made a dead set. "Don't be ridiculous!" She glared at the strong fingers that encircled her wrist. "I am very fond of Delilah. And don't be trying to provoke me, Sandor, by calling me an antidote!"

"You are absurd." Had Miss Prunes and Prisms raised her eyes to her cousin's face, she might have noted that his cold features were unusually kind. "No matter how angry I am with you—and I admit to being frequently angry with you, which can only be what you want, since you provoke me to it!—I should never call you platter-faced. Or at least not with any degree of truth!"

Binnie was not at all assuaged by this flattering declaration; such was the agitation of the moment that she wished to scream. "Let me go."

Sandor did release her wrist, the better to grasp her shoulders and give her an ungentle shake. Binnie glared at him and raised hands that were none too steady to try and smooth her hair, which with Sandor's assault had come unpinned. He pushed her hands away. "Tell me."

Binnie wondered uncharitably if during his fracas with Johann, Sandor had received a blow to the head. "As if you didn't know! When it is all your doing! And I wish you would cease laying violent hands on me!"

This request the duke quite sensibly ignored. In point of fact, the duke did not hear it clearly, being caught up in bemused contemplation of Miss Prunes and Prisms's lovely, angry face, her sparkling, amber eyes, her clouds of chestnut hair. "Binnie, I haven't the least notion what you mean."

"How *can* you be so perverse!" The glitter in Binnie's eyes was not due entirely to anger; she was perilously close to tears. "You must be playing for high stakes indeed! Don't come the innocent with me, Sandor! Because I know it was to spite me that you allowed Neal to become betrothed to Miss Choice-Pickerell."

"What a coxcomb you would have me." With difficulty, Sandor refrained from burying his fingers in her hair. "It was only *partially* to spite you. I knew, you see, that if I didn't give my consent, Neal would marry her out of hand."

This reasonable explanation did not impress Miss Baskerville, who didn't believe a word of it, as her expression indicated. "Is *that* what's plaguing you?" Sandor inquired, surprised.

Perhaps the shaking she'd received had disordered her faculties; Binnie was feeling oddly light-headed. She fixed her eyes on Sandor's chin. "Surely even you must see such a marriage will be disastrous."

The duke, conveniently forgetting his own ill-fated nuptial enterprise, wondered why Miss Prunes and Prisms should think him so shortsighted. He refrained from commenting upon her lack of experience in matters matrimonial. He also refrained from explaining that he had never intended this particular marriage should actually take place. "If that's what's fretting you to flinders," he said generously, "I'll see the thing's called off."

Binnie in her own turn refrained from expressing strong curiosity about why her cousin the duke should suddenly wish to turn her up sweet. "I doubt that the breaking off of this affair is within your capabilities. Miss Choice-Pickerell will not easily give up her hopes of cutting a dash in the best society."

"I did not say it would be *easy*," Sandor rebuked. "I said merely that I would see it done. But for my efforts there is a fee."

Naturally there would be. Binnie scowled. "What an ungrateful creature you are," Sandor said. "If you continue to grimace at me in that extraordinary manner, you are like to truly become bracket-faced, which would be a great shame. Which brings me to the matter of my repayment for efforts undertaken in Neal's behalf: I wish that we should call a truce."

Binnie looked bewildered. "A truce?"

"A cease-fire." Sandor enlightened her. "A cessation of hostilities."

Binnie contemplated this proposal, which in execution would doubtless prove damnably difficult. Almost, she refused. But it was her brother's happiness which hung in the balance, and for that happiness any devoted sister must be prepared to make great sacrifice. "Very well," she said unenthusiastically.

Sandor did release her then and solemnly shook her hand. Quickly, Binnie withdrew from his grasp and sped toward the door. On the threshold she turned. Although Binnie had pledged peace, she had not promised to deny herself the last word. "Someday, Sandor," she said grimly, "you will be called to a rendering of accounts." The door closed behind her, emphatically.

Wearing a very severe expression, His Grace stared after his cousin. He remembered that she had accused him of playing for high stakes. And so he was, though she could have no notion of what those stakes were. If any accounts were to be settled, they would be her own.

What a hobble! thought the duke, as he touched his mangled mouth. Surely it was only a temporary aberration, this sudden desire to win a smile from Miss Prunes and Prisms.

Binnie, in the hallway, had leaned against the wall. What was wrong with her that she should be so weak-kneed? It could only be the result of Sandor's bullying. What an unfeeling man he was, to exploit her concern for Neal. That Sandor meant to amuse himself at her expense was obvious; he would taunt her in his heartless manner and derive great satisfaction from the fact that she could not in good conscience, without endangering Neal's future happiness, retaliate in kind. Well, the Machiavellian duke would soon learn he could not bring *her* so readily to heel! Slowly, engrossed in diabolic plots for the duke's downfall, Binnie trudged up the stair.

CHAPTER THIRTEEN

It was two days later when Mr. Dennison—having endured a rigorous course of steam bath and "shampoo" after the Turkish fashion, which included vigorous plummeting and slapping, in the Oriental baths established by an Indian, in the vestibule of which hung the crutches of former martyrs to rheumatism, sciatica, and lumbago; not that Mr. Dennison suffered those particular complaints, feeling only a trifle out of sorts—found himself sufficiently composed to besiege Lord Knowles's bow-fronted house on the Royal Crescent. Not the duke drew Mark there, but Miss Sibyl Baskerville, to whom he had a great deal to say.

She was in the morning room, plucking absentmindedly

and inexpertly at the strings of the harp which once Sandor's young duchess had played. Judging from the unmelodious twangs which Binnie's fingers produced, the harp had not been tuned since Linnet's day. And judging from Binnie's appearance—her golden eyes were shadowed, as if from sleeplessness; her chestnut hair piled atop her head every which way; her dowdy gown a horrible example of how very far in the wrong direction a misguided modiste could go—Binnie was in a similarly bad way. An odd aroma assailed Mark's nostrils. His nose twitched.

"Horseradish and sour milk," Binnie said gloomily, as she abandoned the harp for a sofa upholstered in striped silk. "Edwina's freckle remedy."

Mark chose a rather rigid chair. He wondered if the charmer of his heart and soul had grown quite addlebrained. "But you don't *have* freckles, my dear," he pointed out gently.

Where once Binnie would have been amused by this misunderstanding, now she was further depressed. Binnie was deep in the grip of the blue devils. The source of this dejection was, as might be expected, her cousin the duke, who was holding in a most tenacious manner to the terms of their truce. He was all that was civil and kind, politeness personified—and Binnie, aware that he was mocking her, was very hard pressed to take his unexceptionable utterances in good part. Equally hard to swallow were Edwina's raptures. Edwina considered Sandor's reformation further proof of his infatuation with Delilah, and the mellowing influence thereof. Binnie was further disheartened by the odd humors to which she had lately fallen prey. And she could not even find relief for her affliction in administering the bane of her existence a stinging rebuke.

She became aware that Mark was regarding her with concern. "Forgive me, I wasn't paying heed. What did you say?"

"That you do not have freckles," Mark repeated patiently.

"Of course I do not," said Binnie with some bewilderment, before she recalled the subject of their conversation. "Oh! It is Delilah to whom Edwina has administered her antidote. She was here with me until just a few moments ago."

For Delilah's absence, Mark rendered thanks. What he had to say to Binnie was of a private nature, and not for the ears of an irrepressible madcap. He thought Binnie might have suffered a revulsion of feeling for the girl, so melancholy had been her tone. "My dear, if I may say so, you look as if you have been racketing yourself to pieces. I fear that by entrusting Miss Mannering to your care, your cousin has put you to a great deal of inconvenience."

Inconvenience wasn't the half of it, though Binnie lacked the energy to explain. Nor did she feel it necessary to remark that the most strenuous of her recent undertakings had been a game of loo, a sort of card-sweepstakes in which the subscribers were limited to eight, and the outcome determined by the dice. It was not Delilah, or even Sandor, who was worrying Binnie to death. Always she had recognized in herself a strong streak of eccentricity and stubbornness. Now she had begun to wonder, so inexplicable were her megrims, if that eccentricity verged on madness.

She made an effort to rouse from her despondency sufficiently to entertain Mark, and thus acquainted him with the latest episode of the adventures of Miss Mannering—to wit, the arrival of the tinker Johann with the purpose of blackmail. "The greatest blackguard alive," she remarked. "Threatening to spread stories of the most compromising nature about Delilah. But Sandor dealt with him admirably." Then she smiled. "Delilah, at least, exhibited not the least horror upon learning he'd offered to bandy her name about. As I recall, she said that he was a perfect block."

Mark decided, in light of his ladylove's obviously misguided attachment to Miss Mannering, that it behooved him to tread warily. "Binnie, I hesitate to say this, but have you considered that there may be some basis for the man's claims? I mean, what do you actually *know* about the girl?"

"Gracious God, Mark!" she responded irritably. "Don't make a piece of work of it. If Sandor accepts Delilah, and he does, you can hardly do less!"

Certainly Mark accepted the chit, as a great affliction to all whose paths she crossed. He did not say so, lest he inspire Binnie to further distempered freaks. Instead he offered the information that he had seen Sandor the previous evening, at the local theater, in attendance on the fair Phaedra Fortescue.

As a conversational gambit, this fell flat. Mark therefore remarked that he had fallen into talk with the fair Phaedra's husband, at Raggett's. "Colonel Fortescue does not seem to be happy with Neal."

"How could he be?" snapped Binnie. "When Neal's cousin is dangling after the colonel's wife? I tell you, this is a dreadful coil, and Sandor is to blame for all of it. It is no wonder my spirits are positively *sunk!*"

So distressed was Mark by Binnie's downcast manner that he moved to sit beside her on the sofa. "Pray don't do violence to your feelings, my dear! I dislike intensely to see you so disturbed. What has your cousin done now to cut up your peace?"

Heartily ashamed of her vaporings, Binnie smiled weakly at him. "Pay me no mind. I am merely indulging in vagaries." Privately she wished very much that might be the case. In such crowing spirits had Delilah heard out an account of Johann's endeavors that Binnie feared the tinker might in truth be the source of that damsel's calf love. But if so, why had Delilah gone to such effort to escape him? Perhaps she had doubted the sincerity of his affection—and events had borne out the validity of such a doubt. Yet Delilah had evinced none of the chagrin of a young lady confronted with proof that her fortune was more desirable than herself. The only explanation Binnie could evolve was that Delilah had windmills in her brain.

After due reflection, Mark decided to share his suspicions of the duke. "Perhaps not," he said judiciously. "I have myself wondered—Binnie, your cousin has been suffering considerable losses of late. Oh, nothing to signify in a man of his supposed wealth—but in view of his control of your brother's inheritance, and his refusal to allow you access to your funds, and now his odd guardianship of Miss Mannering, it begins to look strange. I wonder what he is about."

With these disclosures, he earned Binnie's full attention, which was horrified. "Mark! You don't think—"

"I don't know *what* to think!" Mark grasped her hands. "Yet from something he let drop, I harbor grave doubts about Sandor's intentions toward Miss Mannering. A child under his own protection! It argues a great insensibility."

It argued more than that, thought Binnie, who was not happy to have her own suspicions confirmed. She had hoped her doubts about her cousin were no more than the product of an overactive imagination—even if one disliked a member of one's family, one could hardly relish proof that he *was* a Monster of Depravity. Were Sandor in desperate need of money, it would explain his tolerance of Delilah: even though she was his ward, he meant to marry her. No wonder he had dealt so harshly with Johann! He already looked upon the Mannering fortune as his own.

"Mark!" Binnie wailed. "We cannot allow this to happen. Delilah, married to a man of such diabolic disposition, forced to endure his inconstancy, to watch him dissipate her fortune as he has his own—and maybe even Neal's! Oh, *what* are we to do?"

Thus applied to, Mark was forced to confess he did not know. Binnie, realizing that by his offered truce Sandor had made a fool of her, envisioning her entire family perishing in Sandor's foul intrigues, reacted as would any lady of good birth and sadly shattered sensibilities: she burst into tears. Mark, confronted with the spectacle of the holder of his heart and soul suffering such agonies, reacted in an equally fit and proper manner: he drew her into his arms and rained kisses on her brow.

In these respective pastimes they continued for some time, both having found them rather enjoyable. Then Binnie sat up and tried to set herself to rights. "I must look a fright," she said morosely.

Mark was not a gentleman who admired watery eyes or reddened noses or disarranged coiffures; but he was far too much the gentleman to admit that his ladylove's estimation of her appearance was correct. "Fustian!" he said kindly. "As always, you are without peer."

Never before had Binnie realized how very *good* was her most devoted swain. He would not rip up at a lady, or try and goad her into flying off the hooks. Always, Mark would conduct himself in a manner so as not to disturb a lady's peace of mind. So she informed him, rather incoherently.

Mark's nature was not so honorable that he felt compelled to inform his tearful ladylove that he had called in the Royal Crescent for the express intention of hauling her—in a dignified manner, naturally—over the coals. Obviously this was not the moment in which to embark upon a discussion of his ladylove's shoddy treatment of Miss Choice-Pickerell. Mur-

muring soothingly, he applied his handkerchief to Binnie's damp face.

Binnie found it very comforting to be thusly soothed. Still, it accomplished little, and solved none of her problems. Neal remained on the verge of a disastrous mésalliance, and clearly Sandor would make no effort to prevent it. If Sandor stood in such grave need of funds, he would welcome a connection with a wealthy mercantile family. No doubt it was with an eye to the Choice-Pickerell pocketbook that Sandor had agreed to the match in the first place. His promise to scotch the affair would have been intended to throw Binnie off the scent. And were Neal, upon his marriage, to discover his inheritance amounted to mere pennies, what could they do? Sandor would have some excuse, perhaps say he had invested unwisely on Neal's behalf in that mysterious institution, the 'Change.

Nor could Delilah be depended on. That Binnie had ever had faith in that young lady's ingenuity was clear proof of the delusions to which she was lately prone. Thinking clearly now, for the first time in days, Binnie realized how eager she had been to clutch at straws. Delilah was a mere child, and one so lacking in common sense as to cherish a passion for a most ineligible *parti*. Generous as might be her offers of assistance, brave as might be her efforts at escape, Delilah was caught as firmly as any of them in Sandor's web.

Were there to be any hope of winning free of Sandor's toils, Binnie could rely on no one but herself. But what could *she* do, a fubsy-faced old maid without fortune or influence? Had she either, she could remove herself and her family from beneath Sandor's roof, from under Sandor's thumb. Perhaps she could arrange that Neal's inheritance be given over into, if not his own, then her keeping. Perhaps she could even arrange to take on the responsibility of Miss Mannering. Alas, these roseate visions were no more than pipe dreams. If only there was some way—

And then a plan burst full-blown into Binnie's decidedly overheated brain, the result of all the agitation and foreboding to which she had recently been prey, and the result also of the fact that Mark was, as usual, trying to alleviate her gloomy spirits with an offer of his hand and heart. Were she to marry Mark, *he* could take over Neal's affairs—who better to do so than Neal's brother-in-law? So stricken was Binnie by this admirable solution to her difficulties that she failed to take into consideration any number of things, such as the fact that Mr. Dennison, approving as he did of Miss Choice-Pickerell, was not likely to attempt to thwart Neal's marriage; and that Mr. Dennison, disapproving wholeheartedly of Miss Mannering, was not likely to take that damsel under his wing. She stared at him.

Mark, who had made declarations so often to Miss Baskerville that it had become a matter of rote, and who additionally had not the most distant reason to believe he was at all favorite in that quarter, wondered why Miss Baskerville should be regarding him in a manner that could best be described as predatory. Her lips were pursed, her eyes narrowed speculatively. Moreover, the intensity of her regard struck him with a distinct unease. "Binnie, what—?"

"Do you really mean that, Mark?" She clutched his arm. "About wanting to marry me?"

"Of course I do." Mark spoke absently; he was doubting whether even his skillful valet would be able to remove the creases from his sleeve. "Why do you ask? Have I not told you countless times that my affections have become fixed? That I should be the happiest man in the world were you to favor me?"

Binnie released him and drew a deep breath. Surreptitiously, Mark smoothed his sleeve. "I am truly sensible of the honor you do me," she said. "I am very much obliged to you."

Mark was paying a great deal less attention to these remarks than he should, anticipating that Miss Baskerville, as was her habit, would now try to convince him that a wish to marry her was the greatest nonsense in the world. Once, in the beginning, he had argued with her. Now he had begun to think she was correct, especially after her bizarre behavior during the past several days. Considering the queer fits and starts Binnie had been prey to ever since the advent of Miss Mannering, Mark could only be grateful for Binnie's marked determination to hold him at arm's length. Indeed, now that he considered it, he'd had a hairsbreadth escape. *Had* Binnie accepted his hand and heart, he would then have been forced to deal with the matter of Neal and Sandor, perhaps even Miss Mannering. Heroically, he repressed a shudder. Though he was no coward, he was grateful to be spared efforts so strenuous.

To cut Binnie altogether would be ungentlemanly, of course. Too, though he now saw clearly that they would not suit, he still admired her. A gradual lessening of attention was the ticket, he mused; a subtle indication that his ardor had cooled.

Very belatedly, he became aware that Binnie had been speaking to him, had fallen silent and was regarding him rather ironically, "Beg pardon. What did you say?"

Binnie thought it odd that her decision to take matters into her own hands had left her feeling *triste*. Yet what other choice had she? Rather than let her cousin the duke do it for her, Binnie was prepared to dig her own grave.

And this was further foolishness. Mark was devoted to her, as he had amply proven in the past. That he would make her a good husband, she knew. It was utterly ridiculous to compare him unfavorably with the other gentleman she had wished to marry, so long in the past. Even more ridiculous was the vow she'd taken to, if denied the object of her affection, never settle for second best. It was time she conduct herself like a mature woman instead of a moonstruck miss.

Holding to that stern resolution—which, if truth be told, was much more indicative of a mooncalf than a rational adult; but whatever may be said of Binnie at this moment in her progress, it is not that she was in any degree rational—she looked square at Mark. "I have hesitated in forming my decision," she said quietly, "for reasons that I think you understand. However, to keep you waiting longer for your answer would be exceedingly unfair."

Convinced that Miss Baskerville was about to give him his *congé*, which he could only think a piece of admirable good sense on Miss Baskerville's part, Mark took her hand. "My dear, you need say no more. I understand perfectly."

What a *very* good man he was, Binnie thought again, as she smiled at him mistily. Mark was prepared to gracefully accept from her even the fatal blow, the crushing of his hopes. At least she could console herself that, even if she didn't love him, she had spared him that ultimate heartbreak. "No, you don't understand, Mark. You know that I have a great regard for you. I count myself very honored that you should wish to settle with me in matrimony."

So she had said before, countless times, and it would have taken a very dull-witted man to fail to comprehend her meaning. Mark said nothing, wondering what birdbrained notion Miss Baskerville had now taken into her head.

Binnie regarded her suitor's blank expression and decided that he dared not believe his ears. She must speak more plainly. "Mark, I have decided that I would like very much to marry you." And then, because this was a lie the magnitude of which she had never before told, she lowered her gaze.

There was a silence. Binnie looked up to find that Mr. Dennison was staring at the woman by whom he had been favored with abject dismay. Dismay? Surely not! Merely, he was so stunned by his astonishing good fortune that he found it hard to believe his luck. "Heavens, Mark!" Binnie's playful tone grated on her own ears. "Have you nothing to say?"

Mark, had he not been of an honorable nature, might have made any number of comments about this very unexpected and unpleasant event. But gentlemen of honorable natures did not inform the objects of their affection that they had tumbled out of love as abruptly as they'd tumbled into it. However, it was clearly incumbent upon him to make some expression of his sentiments concerning this memorable occasion. "The devil!" he said.

CHAPTER FOURTEEN

"A perfect block!" Delilah repeated firmly. "Upon my word of honor! Why, he made so violent an attack of my virtue that I was forced to defend myself with a frying pan!" She eyed her companion. "Of course you will not use this information but in the *most* discreet manner. Will you, Jem?"

The young footman, for it was he to whom Delilah spoke, vowed silence. May he be stricken down, he said, may his whole family be subject to plagues of caterpillars and locusts if he breathed so much as a word. Delilah professed herself quite satisfied with these assurances. The footman then begged leave to ask how Miss Mannering had come to find herself in a tinkers' camp in the first place, such a circumstance being beyond his limited comprehension.

"Oh, don't let that bother you! I have come to the conclusion that among important people, brains as such are rather despised." Delilah looked thoughtful. "At least they are in young ladies. I don't know about footmen." Here Jem dared remark, respectfully, that in his opinion Miss Mannering was quite top of the boughs. Not that it was his place to say so, and he begged pardon for overstepping the mark.

"Moonshine!" responded Miss Mannering, cheerfully. "I don't regard it! And it is very kind of you to say so, but you are *not* an important person, Jem. In general, that is! You are *very* important to me! What were we talking about? Ah, yes! I was going to tell you how I met Johann."

And so she did, as they proceeded out of the city proper. This was not the first excursion Miss Mannering had undertaken in company with the young footman Jem, who had with considerable subterfuge arranged to be available each time Miss Mannering wished to take the air. It was not that Jem harbored any unsuitable aspirations regarding the object of his adoration; he was content merely to admire her from a very proper distance. Too, Jem had young sisters of his own, and he was well acquainted with the mischief that could be gotten into by frivolous fizgigs. Naturally, he would never have been so presumptuous as to offer Miss Mannering a word of advice, even in situations, such as the present, when Miss Mannering was engaged upon expeditions that would hardly have met with approval from her guardians. In Jem's opinion, those guardians kept Miss Mannering on much too loose a rein. Apparently they were not aware that she was the most complete hand.

Not that their little expeditions did anyone harm; if anything, the contrary. It was very beneficial for Miss Mannering—and for that matter, for Jem himself—to occasionally escape the oppressive atmosphere of the duke of Knowles's bow-fronted house on the Royal Crescent. The duke, however, could not be expected to see the matter in such a light. The duke, in Jem's opinion, was a pernickety, cantankerous crosspatch. Jem hoped that the duke would not find out about these little excursions, lest he require his youngest footman's head on a platter or, even worse, turn him off without a character.

Delilah was engaged in an animated and varied conversation of a worldly, gossiping nature, which clearly demonstrated an excellent understanding of any matter of diverse topics—including Napoleon's strategy in the Peninsular campaign, the renovation of the regent's Royal Pavilion as envisioned by the architect Wyatt, the unhappy situation that had existed between her parents, prior to her mother's taking French leave. As she talked, they walked over the hilly downs that were covered with short turf. Occasionally she paused to sniff the fresh, brisk air scented with gorse and the sea.

This day's excursion was somewhat less innocuous than had been its predecessors, which had included such rural delights as a visit to the remains of a Saxon camp; and most memorable among which had been the occasion when Delilah had climbed to the top of a windmill in order to see the whole panorama of Brighton spread out below with the assistance of a telescope fished out of a flour bin by the miller's lad. Jem, feet firmly on the ground, had watched the entire building rocking like a ship with the force of the wind in the windmill sails, had envisioned disaster, and had prayed. Due to his awareness of their destination, he was currently engaged similarly.

They attained the top of one of the numerous hills that surrounded Brighton, this one unblessed by a windmill. In the distance lay the town, and beyond it the sea. Much closer—and it was this fact that inspired Jem to beg assistance of his Maker—was a caravan and a grazing horse. Nearby a woman bent over a cookfire. "Athalia!" muttered Delilah, then picked up her skirts and ran.

The woman, Jem decided, appeared neither surprised nor especially pleased to see Miss Mannering. His impression was confirmed by the woman's first words. She told Miss Mannering, in terms so explicit that they caused Jem exquisite embarrassment, to go away.

But Miss Mannering was a young lady who could swear like ten thousand troopers when the occasion warranted, and consequently was not inspired to maidenly vaporings by simple, unimaginative vulgarity. "Fiend seize you, Athalia!" she retorted. "I must say I think *very* poorly of you for ratting on me."

Athalia didn't pause in her efforts to build up the fire, which she'd started with coarse stalks of grass, and around which she'd refrained from placing stones which in the heat could break, cracking like rifle shots. "You're a fine one to talk about nabbing the rust, *leicheen!* After feeding me a Canterbury story. And if you don't keep your voice down, you'll wake Johann. He's in the vardo, snoring like a pig, having thoroughly filled himself with salt beef and carrots, washed down with God knows how many pints of beer." She cast Delilah a triumphant glance. "Reckon you're in the basket now, miss! Johann don't have any love for your high-and-mighty guardian."

Having judiciously contemplated the matter, Delilah had decided how best to take the field. "I'm sure I cannot blame him," she said sadly. "The duke of Knowles is the greatest beast in nature, and it is just like him to have treated Johann in that shabby way. After all Johann has done for me! I'm sure a *true* gentleman would have offered to repay Johann— and you!—for all your efforts on my behalf. But not the duke! I think *very* poorly of his conduct in this affair."

Athalia, in whom separation from Miss Mannering had inspired a forgetfulness concerning Miss Mannering's propensity for humbugging, looked startled. "And to top it off," said Delilah, indignantly, "he told me the most outrageous clankers! He said Johann threatened to spread the most horrid tales about me, to feather his nest at my expense. Not that I should care if I *were* under a cloud, you understand, but to think that my *friends* should serve me such an ill turn—it is much too dreadful to contemplate!"

So bemused was Athalia by these artful disclosures that she quite forgot the fire and was forced to leap back abruptly to avoid being singed. She gave it as her opinion that it was Miss Mannering who served friends an ill turn.

"How can you say so?" Delilah wailed. "Whatever have I done to warrant such cruelty from you? Oh! You mean my fortune! But truly I did not know I *had* one, until the duke told me so! Had I known, I would naturally have wished to share—not that I am ever likely to have the opportunity, because the duke will not let me *touch* it." She sniffled. "I can only think he means to keep it for himself."

This didn't seem unreasonable to Athalia, who would have in the duke's position meant to do the very same thing. Suspiciously, she averred that she wouldn't again be led up the garden path. Were Miss Mannering as openhanded as she professed, she wouldn't have sloped off to avoid snacking the bit.

Delilah interpreted this colorful remark, correctly, to mean that Athalia was miffed that the heiress had run away instead of sharing her windfall. "I have told you," she said reproachfully, "that I didn't *know!* Once I found out, it was too late. I am kept a virtual prisoner! If not for the help of my friend Jem, I would never have been able to slip away today."

Athalia cast a wary glance at that young man, who remained studiously expressionless, despite his dislike of being in such close company with a draggletail. He was flabbergasted that Miss Mannering should seek out such a creature, and simultaneously full of admiration for the talent of Miss Mannering in this daring attempt to bamboozle her, an attempt in which he didn't for an instant doubt that Miss Mannering would succeed.

Nor did Delilah, though Athalia was proving a trifle more adamant than she'd anticipated, and there was the ever-present danger that Johann might awaken from his drunken stupor. Johann was, as she well knew, inclined strongly toward violence when three parts disguised. Haste was imperative. Sorrowfully, she gazed upon Athalia. "And I gave you my mother's wedding ring."

Athalia closed dirty fingers around that item, which fit her rather loosely. "For services rendered! I saw your letter mailed, all right and tight. You can't say I didn't."

"Dear Athalia, why should I say that? You did just as I asked—except that I did *not* ask you to note down the address and give it to Johann, which obviously you did." A very effective tear trickled down Delilah's freckled cheek. "I suppose you will accuse me of playing a May-game because I told you a little fib—but I couldn't say the letter was to my father, because it would've been too lowering to admit he might want nothing to do with me! Oh, was anyone *ever* so miserable as I? With each day I am plunged further into grief."

Athalia had a distinct sensation of being turned topsy-turvy, for which she didn't care. She gave it as her gruff opinion that Delilah's treatment by the nobs was no more than she would have expected; and that if Delilah had expected better, she was queer in the attic. Furthermore, if Delilah wished to be a young lady, which was to Athalia incomprehensible, because she wouldn't give a cuss for all the young ladies she'd ever encountered, which admittedly wasn't a considerable number, not that it signified—then it wasn't fitting that she should be kicking up a dust because the price was dear.

By these utterances, Delilah was not noticeably cheered. Positive torrents of tears now streamed down her face. "How unfeeling you are! As if I cared a button for being a lady! Why, I am bound to make a jackpudding of myself! Oh, it is no wonder I am in a pelter, with people always pinching at me, and saying I am not at all the thing!" Bravely, she straightened her spine. "It is my bed and I must sleep in it; don't think that I mean to turn craven because I don't. I have resigned myself to a thoroughly miserable fate. I had hoped that if I spoke with you, at least *you* might not hold me in low esteem. But it has not served! I will not trouble you further. Come, Jem."

It had become clear to Athalia, during this moving speech, that the heiress was in a rare taking. It was not like Delilah to be going on in such a maudlin way, and Athalia had come to a reluctant conviction that Delilah was telling the truth. Athalia wondered if there was any way in which that truth might benefit her. "Wait, *leicheen*," she said. "No hard feelings, eh?"

"Oh!" Delilah was radiant. "You have forgiven me!" Seeking something on which to dry her damp face, she approached a basket. It held not laundry, as Delilah had thought—which just went to show one should not allow oneself to be carried away by one's own histrionics; Athalia, being of the persuasion that dirty clothes only improved with the wearing, never did laundry—but a baby. Perhaps eighteen months of age, fair of hair and blue of eye, the baby stared serenely back at her. Delilah glanced curiously at Athalia. "Yours?" she asked.

Indignantly, Athalia let it be known that she was not the sort of woman who'd have a squalling, pulling brat forever at her heels. She was compelled by fairness to add that this brat, being mute, at least did not squall. And then she added, hastily, that since the brat was one of Johann's by-blows, it was none of Delilah's concern.

Delilah did not argue. "Johann," she said pensively. "The duke thinks he has frightened him off, but I know better. Johann can no more change his habits than a leopard its spots."

"What's a leopard?" Athalia inquired curiously.

"Well, I'm not exactly sure, but I know that it cannot. You know what I mean!" Somberly, Delilah stared into the campfire. "Johann will try again to extort money from my guardian, and my guardian will in turn take it out on me. Were I to tell you—but I shan't. It would only make you unhappy, too. And there's nothing I can do."

Great as had been Athalia's desire for revenge, she was not totally devoid of humanity. She found she did not relish the idea of Delilah's suffering. "Poor *leicheen*."

"Oh, Athalia!" Delilah flung herself upon Athalia's neck and hung there, in tears. "I have been so *very* unhappy."

"There, there!" said Athalia, rather helplessly. Jem averted his gaze, not out of embarrassment at this sentimental scene, but in an effort to maintain a straight face. Athalia's nose twitched. "What *is* that stench?"

Delilah drew away. "Horseradish and sour milk. I am not to be allowed to keep even my freckles! You see how they mistreat me?"

What Athalia saw was that Miss Mannering would be grateful to escape a situation where she was so sadly unappreciated. To simply run away would be useless; were the duke so wishful of laying his hands on the girl's fortune, he would move heaven and earth to find her. Once he did find her, he would not deal kindly with those who'd assisted her flight. Athalia had no desire to be hobbled, taken up for trial.

She had an inbred horror of that ignominious fate known as dangling in the sheriff's picture frame.

But all—"all" being the Mannering fortune—was not yet lost. Athalia did not despair of cutting her garment to fit her cloth. There must be some way to juggle Delilah out of the clutches of the duke and into her own, and at the same time to earn the heiress's undying gratitude. Perhaps if Johann diverted the duke? She must think on it. In the meantime, Delilah was safest with the duke, effectively, on ice.

Delilah had remained silent during these cogitations, the progress of which she very shrewdly gauged. "Athalia," she said earnestly, grasping the woman's hands, "have you any idea what Johann plans next? Not that I could stop him, but I might prepare myself!"

"Nay," lied Athalia. "Johann ever kept his own counsel. Never fret, *leicheen*: I'll help you if I can."

Nigh overcome with gratitude, Miss Mannering pressed a hand to her heart. "I shall never be able to repay you! You will know how to get me word."

"Aye." Athalia watched as the faithful Jem led Miss Mannering away. She decided she would not inform Johann of this little talk, lest he take it into his head to queer her lay. Johann thought no one capable of instigating brilliant schemes other than himself—which proved, in view of the outcome of those schemes, if one had not already known it, that he was touched in the upper works.

Athalia bent over the baby to ascertain that it continued in good health; with such a very quiet babe, one could never be sure. Athalia found the baby's silence rather unnerving, to tell truth. It was in excellent spirits, as it proved by pulling her hair. Then, as Athalia raised a hand to extricate herself from the baby's grasp, she saw that she no longer wore the golden wedding ring. Cursing, because she had meant for some time to hang it on one of the chains she wore, thus preventing its loss, Athalia scrabbled in the grass.

She did so to no avail: that golden ring was resting snugly in the bodice of Delilah's gown. Miss Mannering was a young lady of great resource, as she was explaining to Jem. "I had hoped to find them gone—which was very foolish of me, because it will take more than a sound drubbing to frighten off a snake in the grass like Johann. Still, it is always wise to reconnoiter the enemy camp. And one must expect to be put to various expedients and shifts in order to trounce the foe!"

Jem heard out this advice with a thrill of horror; Miss Mannering's confidences strongly hinted that he would be involved in further huggermugger activities. He stated a conviction that they were like to find themselves, if not all to pieces, involved in a terrible rowdydow.

"Balderdash!" uttered Delilah, deep in disillusionment. "Do *you* disapprove of me, too? Now that *truly* weighs upon my heart! I would not have thought you wished to be well wrapped in lamb's wool."

His courage thus impugned, Jem replied that Miss Mannering needn't fly into a pelter. He wasn't one, he stated stiffly, to turn tail.

"Don't pucker up! I didn't think you were! And it is quite right of you to harbor doubts because it is a very foolish general who doesn't admit the possibility of defeat—not that I *do* anticipate it, but one must be prepared." Delilah frowned. "This really is a pickle! There is nothing for it but to grasp the bull by the horns."

It was not Jem's place to point out that such activity often resulted in its instigator being very horribly gored. Diffidently, he begged to know what Miss Mannering wished him to do.

Delilah chewed her lower lip. That Athalia meant to serve her a bitter draught, she knew—but there was many a slip 'twixt the cup and the lip, as Athalia would learn. Since Athalia had not decided precisely how to slip her a dose of gall and wormwood, Delilah must first concentrate on Johann, who presented the most immediate danger. Never was any young lady, she decided, plagued by so many people determined to guide her innocent footsteps on the road to ruin.

It must not be deduced that Miss Mannering was dismayed by this realization. Miss Mannering was a young lady with a natural propensity for mischief, and a huge deviousness of mind; and she considered it a very kind fate that arranged for her to have to plot and scheme. As Delilah saw it, her only logical course of action was to engage in duplicity, and that suited her just fine.

But Jem awaited an answer, anxiously. "I don't mean to put all my eggs in one basket!" announced Delilah. "Johann will soon discover that I'm a damned knowing one! You recall that baby, Jem? Poor little thing! Listen: here is what we must do."

Obediently, Jem listened—and his heart sank down to his toes.

CHAPTER FIFTEEN

Lieutenant Neal Baskerville, as had become his habit of late, had once again taken more to drink than was advisable for a young gentleman of somber mien and upright habit who stood on the brink of matrimony. For this misconduct, he may be at least partially excused: Neal had developed a positive horror of the matrimonial adventure to which he was pledged; and additionally he was engaged, with the other officers of his regiment, for dinner with the regent at the Royal Pavilion, a treat for which Neal supposed he should be grateful, since it freed him of the necessity of passing yet another tedious evening with his fiancée.

For all that, gratitude was not among the emotions uppermost in Neal's mind. He failed to understand why invitations to the Pavilion were so eagerly sought, when Prinny's entertainments were so insufferably dull. No more than his cousin the duke did Lieutenant Baskersville appreciate porcelain pagodas or china fisherman, lamps shaped like elegant tulips, dragons darting everywhere—although, had Neal been aware of his cousin's sentiments on the subject, he would doubtless have found in himself a positive enthusiasm for the Oriental style of interior decoration so favored by his regent.

Prinny was in a very expansive frame of mind. Neal, sweltering in his dress regimentals—and he had never felt the same about his magnificently laced jacket, his gold-fringed red breeches, and his decorative yellow boots since compared to an ornamental monkey by elderly Choice-Pickerell—in the overheated rooms, was treated by his regent to a discussion of the renovations to the Pavilion soon to be under way. Prinny was full of enthusiasm for the plans put forward by the architect Wyatt, who had created the fantastic Fonthill; he anticipated that the Pavilion would assume an equally extraordinary Gothic style. The cost? A paltry £200,000, mere peanuts to a prince.

Neal's temples had begun to throb, a combined effect of the liquor he'd consumed and the efforts of the regent's German band. He was relieved to be informed by a servant that a footman had come to him from the Royal Crescent, and at the same time curious about what emergency had prompted such a breach of etiquette. The emergency must be of huge magnitude to warrant an intrusion here. Neal could only envision one disaster of such import. Fervently he hoped that Binnie had not been driven to murder the duke.

His questions were answered soon enough, by way of a note handed him by an ashen Jem. Neal scanned the missive, looked blank, then read it again. Still he could make no sense of it. "What the deuce," he inquired of Jem, "does this mean?"

Jem, trembling lest his sins catch up with him, and he be stricken down by divine retribution on the spot, looked agonized. "The young lady, sir!" he gasped. "It is a matter of great importance! She begs your assistance, sir!"

Neal's colonel had come up behind him in time to hear this explanation, of which he thought little; in Colonel Fortescue's opinion, the gentlemen of Neal's family were a great deal too much in the petticoat line. He voiced an opinion that for an officer in the prince's own regiment to be indulging in assignations right under the prince's very nose was altogether displeasing. Neal protested that the colonel misunderstood; the colonel stated firmly that men prone to misundertstandings did not achieve his exalted rank, and therefore that he had done no such thing. At this point their rather acrimonious exchange, which was inspiring poor Jem with a wish to sink through the floor before the nature of Delilah's summons was

128

published to the whole of Brighton, was interrupted by a gentleman of such exalted rank that he was second in consequence only to the mad king. Made aware by the colonel of the shocking antics indulged in by the lieutenant, the regent further demonstrated his genial frame of mind. He knew what it was like to be a young officer, said the regent, with a knowing glance. By all means the lieutenant must be given leave to deal with his emergency. And if the lieutenant would take a word of advice from his prince, he would keep all knowledge of this little emergency from the lovely Miss Choice-Pickerell.

Somewhat sobered by this exchange, during which he had been referred to by his regent as a "young reprobate," Neal took his leave. From Jem he gained no further explanation—Jem had no wish to bring down upon his own head the lieutenant's wrath—except that Miss Mannering awaited him on the seashore. Never had Neal known a damsel so fond of moonlight strolls, Neal thought, amused and exasperated. He uttered a strong determination to get to the bottom of this accursed affair. To this statement, Jem remained prudently silent. In his opinion, the lieutenant would discover, once he learned the truth of the matter, that he would much rather have remained in ignorance. It stood to reason. Jem would have much rather been ignorant himself.

Therefore, it was in silence that they walked to the beach. The first sight to greet Neal's eyes was Miss Mannering, bent over a large basket. Surely she had not dragged him away from the Royal Pavilion to indulge in an alfresco party? Actually, the thought of picnicking with Delilah in the moonlight was an alluring one. However, it simply wasn't done. So he informed Miss Mannering, as soon as he was within earshot. He did not intend, the lieutenant stated sternly, to help Delilah make a byword of herself.

Delilah straightened up to study him, a very easy task in the bright moonlight. "You're cast-away again," she said disapprovingly. "You must be, or you wouldn't be talking like a nodcock! I do think it very hard because I was relying on you for assistance."

"You are not," inquired Neal, regarding the basket, "picnicking?"

"At a time like this?" Delilah retorted indignantly. "Of

129

course I am not! Pray don't be a gudgeon. Oh, *why* must you be foxed when I need you most? I am at my wit's end!"

"I am *not* foxed," Neal responded, with equal offense. "Merely a trifle bosky. And I don't understand why that should put *you* in a tweak, Miss Mannering!"

"How could you? You have given me no opportunity to explain!" Delilah snapped, then looked rueful. "Pray forgive me for ripping up at you—I would not have done so were I not in such a whirl. You see, I cannot figure how to get into the house, and it is getting very late, and the case is *desperate!*"

From these remarks, Neal achieved no notable enlightenment. Why could Miss Mannering not gain access to the house on the Royal Crescent? Heaven knew she exited it easily enough! In search of further clarification, he glanced at Jem. "It's the baby, sir," the footman offered helpfully.

"Baby?" Neal echoed.

"Oh, yes!" With a doting expression, Delilah gazed upon the basket. "An excellent little creature, so quiet and well behaved. See for yourself. But I cannot think he will benefit from continual exposure to the night air, though I have wrapped him up very snugly. That is why I wished your help. You will know how we may sneak him into the house." Neal said nothing, merely stared. "He will be no trouble at all!" Delilah added anxiously. "I promise you. The poor little thing is mute."

Convinced that he was victim of some monstrous hoax, Neal bent over the basket, only to learn that for once Delilah spoke the truth. Within, bundled up as to endure an arctic chill, was definitely a baby. It stared serenely back at him. "Good God!" said Neal.

"You thought I was bamming you," Delilah observed shrewdly. "Now that you realize I was not, you may tell me what to do."

Neal made an effort to do so. He didn't know how Delilah had come by this baby, he stated disapprovingly, but there was only one thing to be done with it. It must be taken to a foundling home.

Delilah was horrified by this suggestion, and she was very disappointed that the dashing Lieutenant Baskerville should turn out to be an addleplot. So she informed him. "To think that a regular Trojan," she added, as he gaped at her, "should turn out to be so stiff-rumped! Highty-tighty behavior, sir! I am very sorry now that I asked your help. But I didn't know that you would prove so cruel and unnatural. Never mind, then! I will figure some way out of this fix myself!"

To these accusations Neal responded with a plea that Miss Mannering would refrain from enacting him further Cheltenham tragedies, since her histrionics had already inspired him with the devil of a head. Perhaps he did not fully grasp the situation. Why did Miss Mannering wish to introduce a baby into the duke's household? And since she did wish so, however queerly, why not simply carry the basket in through the front door?

Clever coconspirators, decided Delilah, were at a premium; certainly she'd never been blessed with one. She could not blame Jem for being on pins and needles, starting at a sound, or Neal for dragging his heels; but she wished that one of them would display a little initiative. She opened her mouth to render a full explanation, then paused, remembering Binnie's advice on the unwisdom of discussing Johann. Of course Jem had deserved to be acquainted with the whole, due to his involvement in the matter; Delilah thought Binnie would agree, were she told of Jem's endeavors, which Delilah did not intend she should be. The horse had already bolted; why worry about an unlocked barn door?

Neal, however, was an altogether different piece of goods. It was not that Delilah distrusted the young lieutenant; she had great faith in him, and was sure it was through no fault of his own that he'd fallen into cork-brained ways. As soon as there was time enough, she meant to demonstrate to him that one could, with the application of a little ingenuity and some good common sense, extricate oneself from even the most damnable difficulties. Unquestionably, Neal was in difficulties. Why else should he exhibit so relentless a determination to drink himself under the table at every opportunity? While the lieutenant was not of a sober nature, Delilah did not consider him yet sunk in dissipation. A clever girl, she could even put a name to the source of his difficulties. In a word, or three: Cressida Choice-Pickerell.

Though Delilah trusted the lieutenant, she did not trust him not to try and share with his fiancée a very good joke. Folly, that; Miss Choice-Pickerell demonstrably had no sense

131

of humor; a failing the enormity of which Neal clearly failed to comprehend. Therefore, lest Johann learn that the baby had taken up residence at the duke of Knowles's house on the Royal Crescent, which would ruin all Delilah's plans, the lieutenant must be kept in ignorance.

Miss Mannering drew a deep breath and blushed bright pink. "I will tell you all about it, although there isn't much to tell! We found this poor little creature, Jem and I, whilst engaged on a little stroll. Just fancy, Neal, he had been abandoned! Left in his little basket out in the cold! We couldn't leave him to such a wretched fate, and so I decided the only solution was to take him home." She paused; the lieutenant did not look entirely convinced. "It's no good telling me to carry the basket in the front door; the duke would only order it carried back out again! *You* know what he is! And I could not bear that. No one knows better than I how it feels to be abandoned, alone in the world, without family or friends!"

Quite naturally, confronted with a tearful damsel, Neal drew her into his arms and let her weep upon his chest. Tactfully, Jem gazed out to sea. "It would only be for a short while," sniffled Delilah. "Until I can find the baby a good home. He will be no trouble at all—I don't know much about babies. but surely nothing so small can create much fuss! We could keep him in the nursery, which Jem says is unused. No one ever goes there, and to make doubly certain we will lock the door. And I will put Caliban up there, which will make everyone relieved, because there's no denying Caliban is not a favorite with the household, and I will frequently visit him. As will Jem! So no one will smell a rat and let the cat out of the bag."

Despite the cool night air, Neal's head had not cleared, as evidenced by the fact that he attributed his continued intoxication to the large quantities of liquor he'd consumed, and not to the tearful young lady who fit so snugly in his arms. Due to that intoxication, whatever its true source, he did not pause to contemplate the very sketchy nature of Delilah's explanation, or the drawbacks to her schemes. That Delilah was on the hangout for his cousin the duke, Neal did recall. How the introduction of a baby into Sandor's house would help her to accomplish her goal Neal did not know, but he was quite willing to offer assistance. "What a clever puss you are!" he uttered, with the utmost sincerity.

Delilah drew back to stare, wide-eyed, up at him. "How nice that you should think so! But I must warn you that Lord Knowles will not agree. Oh, Lieutenant Baskerville, you are my very last hope! I throw myself on your mercy! But it would not be fair not to point out that if His Grace finds out about this, he will be *very* angry."

The lieutenant responded to this noble little speech as might have been expected: he first expressed utter disinterest in the duke's likes and dislikes; he secondly reminded Miss Mannering that she should call him Neal. What innate worth of character she possessed! he thought, as he gazed into her freckled face. To risk Sandor's wrath and the opportunity to feather her nest for the sake of an abandoned infant! But of course Delilah would pity the unfortunate creature, having herself been—as she had so sadly pointed out—similarly mistreated. Neal decided that Miss Mannering's misadventures had gained for her a wisdom and compassion denied more gently reared damsels. Miss Choice-Pickerell, for example, would have passed by an abandoned baby with her ladylike nose firmly in the air. Well, a fig for Miss Choice-Pickerell! Neal would render the assistance required of him. He knew exactly how to gain entrance to the duke's house on the Royal Crescent without attracting the attention of any-one. Being a mature adult, he no longer had recourse to it; but he was not of such mature years as to have forgotten the escape route of his salad days.

Thus the lieutenant pondered, gazing all the time into Delilah's brown eyes. Lovely eyes they were, he realized; large and luminous. Sandor, if only he could be brought to realize it, was a very lucky man. Neal succumbed to impulse, reached out and ruffled Delilah's carroty curls. She smiled at him. And then Neal wondered if perhaps his senses were a trifle disordered. Sour milk and horseradish were not among the scents common to the seashore.

Meanwhile, Jem, as he turned from the seascape to the basket, decided that there were no flies on Miss Mannering. He also decided, as he studied the complacent babe, that the little fellow was deaf as well as mute, since he had exhibited no awareness of the rather long-winded discussion that had

133

raged about his head. Perhaps deafness was a blessing, since the tyke seemed fated to confinement with a howling hound— Caliban did not take kindly to incarceration, as the household had learned. Jem hoped the hound had not chewed through the makeshift muzzle Delilah had tearfully applied before they set out on this night's expedition, had not made their absence known. Jem had not thought their progress would be hastened by the company of the hound.

Much as he might dread the consequence of what he suspected might be considered kidnapping by the law, Jem did not regret his part in it. On the contrary, he was proud of the deft way he'd pulled it off. Not that it had been difficult, since they had returned to the tinkers' campsite to find Athalia, Johann, and the horse all absent, and only the sleeping baby left behind in the caravan; but Jem had been prepared to do battle with the tinker if necessary, and though relieved that it had *not* been necessary, wasn't reluctant to give himself full marks for bravery. In fact, he was feeling distinctly proprietorial toward this babe, who greeted each new adventure with so serene an air. Due to this paternal attitude, Jem—who, due to his young siblings, knew a great deal about babies—had refrained from informing Miss Mannering that, in the case of infants, a great deal of fuss could come in very small packages. He bent over the basket and made a cooing sound.

To this friendly overture, the baby responded with only a blink of its blue eyes. Miss Mannering and Lieutenant Baskerville displayed more animation: they roused from their mutual trance. "What is it?" cried Delilah, rushing to Jem's side. "Why are you making that noise? Oh, I knew we should not have kept him out in the damp so long!"

Jem hastened to assure Miss Mannering that the babe had taken no harm. As proof, he lifted the child into his arms. "Snug as a bug in a rug, miss!" he said cheerfully.

Lieutenant Baskerville, who had followed Delilah to the basket—Neal, just then, would have followed Delilah anywhere, a sentiment which, had he considered it, he had never in the whole of their association cherished for Miss Choice-Pickerell—gazed upon the baby with interest, infants not generally coming in the way of young gentlemen of fashion. This infant, though deaf and mute, had perhaps benefited

134

from its acquaintance with Johann and Athalia and the devious Miss Mannering; or perhaps some digestive complaint inspired its action, and not instinctive recognition of an easy conquest. Whatever the motivation, the baby stared at Neal, and its round little face broke into an unmistakable smile.

"It *likes* you!" said Delilah, awed.

Neal was no less overwhelmed. Little had he known how much had been denied him by his previous lack of even a nodding acquaintance with a babe. What fascination it exercised, what perfection of tiny, exquisite limbs. Neal poked a gently inquiring finger into the baby's midriff. Amazing, the tenacity of the little hand that so firmly clutched his finger! Enthralling, that barely heard belch! But the poor little fellow must have a name.

A heated discussion ensued. Delilah suggested Osbert, Ebenezer, Faramond; Neal countered with Kenrick, Mortimer, Bartholomew; Jem interjected Charles, David, William. Too common! protested Neal. So exceptional a child deserved a brilliant name. Perhaps, Tobias? Here the baby belched again. A sign of accord, surely. Toby it would be.

CHAPTER SIXTEEN

On the following morning, Miss Sibyl Baskerville returned from a long and solitary walk upon the cliffs to be greeted by her cousin the duke with an irate demand for a clarification of the absurd on-dit with which he had been gifted by Edwina just moments past. Binnie adopted a blank expression. "What on-dit is that?" she asked innocently.

"This ridiculous rumor that you are to marry Mark," retorted

Sandor. "I can only conclude that Edwina has windmills in her head."

"Windmills?" Binnie pulled off her very unbecoming bonnet. "How can you say that, Sandor? Weren't you saying just recently that you *wished* me to marry Mark? I declare I do not understand you."

Obviously she did not. The duke could not blame her for it; he did not understand himself. Politely, he recalled to her their truce. "The word without the bark on it, if you please. *Are* you to be married?"

He sounded so skeptical, so incredulous, that Binnie decided he truly thought her at her last prayers. Destined to lead apes in hell, was she? It was with no small satisfaction that she disabused him of this notion. "Yes," she said baldly.

The duke was subject to the queerest sensation, as if he had been planted a facer as deftly as he'd tipped a doubler to the tinker Johann. This odd reaction did not leave him feeling especially charitable toward Miss Prunes and Prisms. "Binnie, *why?*" he inquired.

This not-unreasonable question left Binnie at a loss. Though she suspected her cousin the duke of innumerable villainies, it would hardly be diplomatic to inform him of her suspicions. She took refuge in her habitual irony. "But, Sandor, it is my duty to oblige you, is it not? You are the head of the family. If you didn't wish me to marry Mark, you should have told me so! I thought by accepting his handsome offer, I was no more than doing your bidding."

Sandor looked very much as if he wished to throttle his cousin, which in point of fact he did. "Tongue-valiant!" he uttered, wrathfully. "Confess, Binnie: you're cutting a sham."

Miss Baskerville regarded the duke, somewhat smugly. So he didn't approve her betrothal? So much the worse for him! "Not at all, Sandor; I have seldom been more serious. I have told Mark that I will become his wife, although the betrothal is not to be announced just yet." Very curiously, she awaited his next comment.

"Not Edwina!" snarled the duke. "*You're* the one with windmills in your head! To marry Mark—the devil, Binnie!"

Since these remarks were ambiguous, and since Miss Baskerville was well aware that the duke was in the habit of referring to her as Miss Prunes and Prisms, she interpreted his overt disapproval as stemming from concern for his friend. Sandor thought Mark could look higher for a female with which to settle in matrimony, that Mark should have chosen a wife both younger and more agreeable. Secretly, Binnie shared these sentiments. Still, that Sandor shared her lowly estimation of herself cut her, very irrationally, to the quick. Allow Sandor to know that his harsh words had very painfully struck home, Binnie would never do. "I had hoped you would wish us happy," she said quietly.

What Sandor wished was to know what had suddenly inspired Miss Prunes and Prisms to contract a singularly inappropriate betrothal—though why he considered that betrothal inappropriate was another thing the duke could not have explained. However, Binnie had already made clear the futility of asking questions of her. With a shocking oath Sandor spun round on his heel, strode down the hallway. Behind him the front door slammed.

Binnie savored the triumph attendant upon having had the last word, and found it very flat. What possessed her, that by her betrothal she should be rendered even more melancholy? Other ladies, having arranged for themselves so eligible a connection, would be all rapture. Binnie deduced that she was of a less romantic turn. Her marriage to Mark she regarded as a business arrangement through which she would receive assistance in dealing with her various problems. And Mark? she wondered suddenly. What would he in turn receive? Binnie lacked the faintest notion of what Mr. Dennison would require from his wife—or even why he wished for marriage with a dowdy female like herself. No matter! Binnie would keep her part of the bargain, whatever it entailed.

In this way reflecting, Binnie wandered through the house, giving the morning room in which Edwina was ensconced a very wide berth. Edwina was in alt, envisioning for herself any number of alternate residences; and Binnie did not care to hear further raptures on the topic of Mark. That this attitude was churlish, she knew. So very good was Mark that he had agreed to her request that they keep quiet their betrothal for a time without even inquiring why she wished to do so—which was very fortunate, since Binnie would have been hard pressed to come up with any reason at all.

Why *did* she wish to wait? mused Binnie. Having decided

to take the fatal plunge into waters matrimonial, why dither about getting one's toes wet? Perhaps, she concluded wisely, she wished to see certain other matters neatly tidied up. Or perhaps, as Sandor had so unchivalrously suggested, she really did have windmills in her head.

Binnie's ruminations, and her unguided footsteps, had brought her to the door that led to the nether regions of the house. She looked at it, unseeing—and then the door swung abruptly open, and the youngest of the duke's footmen walked through it. Or, to be more precise, he crept, laden down with a miscellany of items that included a cup of milk, a bowl of bread pudding, several other diverse receptacles the contents of which could not be ascertained, and a very large assortment of dish towels. Her curiosity pricked, Binnie reached out and gently tapped his shoulder. Jem was an excellent footman: he started violently and spun around; he stared and shook as if Miss Baskerville were a ghostly specter; and during all these contortions he spilled not a drop, nor dropped a single thing.

" 'Tis the hound, ma'am!" he gasped, in response to Miss Baskerville's ironic inquiry as to what he was about. "Miss Mannering's pet. Locked in the old nursery! Excuse me, my lady, I must go tend to it!" Permission granted, he fled.

The footman's conduct, decided Miss Baskerville, as she watched him mount—with more speed than decorum—the stair, was altogether perplexing. Delilah's decision to imprison her pet in the nursery was also a puzzle. Doubtless that young lady would have an explanation. Binnie thought she would like to be acquainted with it. She, too, mounted the staircase.

It was not so much that Binnie required enlightenment on Jem's queer behavior and Caliban's imprisonment; she was in the dumps, and there was no surer way to relieve a depression of the spirits than to laugh away an hour with Delilah. Anticipating an amusing encounter with Miss Mannering, Binnie approached the nursery door.

Voices came to her; she frowned. Neal should at this hour have been engaged in military duties elsewhere. How had he arrived in the house without attracting notice? And what was he doing in, of all places, the nursery? Talking about his fiancée, it would seem, from the comments that came faintly through the door. That was the strangest thing of all, decided

Binnie, who could not imagine why anyone would voluntarily discuss Miss Choice-Pickerell.

Actually, Neal was not doing so of his own volition, but in response to some very pointed questions asked him by Miss Mannering. Why Delilah should be so interested in his fiancée, Neal did not know, but he had done his best to satisfy her curiosity. "A beautiful refined profile," he said, in way of conclusion, "and a ladylike manner. Very high-minded."

"Why is it that high-minded people are often so very dull?" inquired Miss Mannering. "Not that I mean to imply that Miss Choice-Pickerell is a dead bore! Of course she must not be, since you want to marry her."

Neal had opened his mouth to inform Miss Mannering that her estimation of his fiancée's character was, unfortunately, correct, when he was distracted by the unmistakable squeak of door hinges. The lieutenant froze, lips parted. His fellow conspirators also paused motionless, anticipating disaster.

Consequently, Binnie was greeted with a paralyzed tableau. Delilah and Neal sat on the floor, one holding a bowl of bread pudding, the other a stuffed animal of undefinable breed; Jem, to whom had been assigned the more practical details of this undertaking, was attaching damp dish towels to an improvised clothesline. A cot had been set up in one corner. Caliban sprawled on it, sound asleep.

Dish towels? A cot? Binnie pinched herself. Surely that was not a *baby* on whom Delilah had so firm a grip? "Gracious God!" she breathed.

With her words, everyone relaxed. "I am so glad it's only you!" said Delilah. "Pray lock the door! For if Miss Childe—or, even worse, the duke—had come upon us, we would truly have been in a hobble." Neal was less charitable; he demanded to know what his sister meant by giving them such a nasty turn.

Binnie did as requested, she locked the door, and then she turned around again. It *was* a baby. She stared at him. As if aware of her fascination, and the use that could be made thereof, Toby wriggled immediately out of Delilah's grasp, and waddled across the room with amazing speed on his chubby little legs. Having safely reached his destination, he grasped Binnie's skirt, then leaned back to look up at her.

And then he lost his balance and sat down hard on his plump little behind.

Binnie was a lady with a very kind nature, despite her various megrims; she bent and swooped the baby up into her arms. Toby made a little gurgling sound, wrapped a fist in her hair, and treated her to a gap-toothed grin. Binnie could not help but smile back at him.

"Then *that's* all right!" said Delilah, rather enigmatically. "You'll be able to help us, Binnie! Because if Lord Knowles finds out, he'll turn poor Toby out into the streets, and that would be a terrible thing."

Certainly it would, Binnie promptly agreed; none but the most callous of monsters could so mistreat such a delightful child. That Sandor *was* the most callous of monsters, she could not deny. For all that, she was very interested in knowing just who Toby was, and what he was doing in Sandor's house. Briefly, Delilah explained. Since it was the same explanation she had rendered Neal, and a tissue of lies from beginning to end, in the telling she blushed bright pink.

Miss Baskerville, having become very closely acquainted with the devious Miss Mannering, had a very good idea what Delilah's blushes signified. Furthermore, even though on some subjects Binnie's thought processes were demonstrably muddled, she in general possessed very good sense. Toby was remarkably stout for a babe mistreated and abandoned and starved. In short, although Binnie heard out Delilah's explanation without interruption, she didn't believe a single word. "But how," she inquired, when Delilah had concluded, "do you mean to keep his presence secret?"

That, too, Delilah explained. Barring such errors as unlocked doors—Jem received a stern glance—she anticipated no difficulty. Toby was a great deal more energetic than she'd anticipated, she admitted; he ran around the nursery like a veritable whirlwind on his fat little legs and got into everything—and while it didn't matter if he crawled into the cupboards below the bookcases that lined the walls, the fireplace was a definite problem. "But he makes very little noise, Binnie! I mean, he may break things, but that we can blame on Caliban! You see, Toby is mute."

Binnie regarded Toby, whom she had returned to Delilah, and who was making a very large mess with the bread pudding.

Toby gurgled once again and waved his spoon, his serene blue eyes on Binnie's face. "Poor little thing!" said Binnie. Apparently content with this response, Toby resumed his meal, a great deal more of which adorned his person than went into his mouth.

"So you realize," continued Delilah, wiping bread pudding from her face, "that he cannot be left untended a single moment! It is very difficult with only Jem and me, and Jem forced to attend to duties elsewhere—and Neal of course cannot be forever hanging around the house!—but with *your* help, Binnie, we shall pull the thing off easily!"

"But Delilah!" Much as Binnie hated to spoil sport, she felt impelled to interject a note of reason. "You cannot hope to keep the child's presence secret indefinitely!"

"Oh, no!" With a doting expression, Delilah watched Toby totter over to Neal and collapse against his chest. Neal hugged the boy. Toby responded to this excess of affection by gaily pounding Neal's shoulder with his spoon, to the further detriment of Neal's uniform. "Only until we can make other arrangements."

Binnie offered no response, though she saw countless fallacies in this very hubble-bubble reasoning. Sandor missed little that went on, especially when it went on in his very house; he was not likely to long remain in ignorance of the fact that his household had suddenly been encumbered by a baby. Nor would the servants remain long unaware that something very untoward was under way in the old nursery, or that various supplies turned up missing. Binnie glanced around the nursery, where she had not set foot in years. Then she looked again at Toby, who had abandoned the spoon to clutch the disreputable stuffed animal. "Why, it's Button!" she exclaimed, glad to have at least one puzzle explained: Button was, or had been, a rabbit, fashioned for a much younger Neal by no less surprising a personage than his cousin the duke. Odd how very sad it made her, that memory of long-ago and much more congenial days.

"So it is!" said Neal, in a voice devoid of sentiment. "Good old Button! Toby found him in one of the closets." Here Jem—busy still with tasks more suited to a nurserymaid—felt obliged to insert a fond remark that Toby was slippery as a greased pig.

141

Miss Mannering had become aware, as her fellow conspirators apparently had not, that no assurances of assistance had been vouchsafed by Binnie. Unless matters were too soon to come to a crisis, assurances vouchsafed must be. "You have not said you will help, Binnie!" she wailed. "Does this mean you *won't*? Surely you cannot be so cruel!"

Much as she would have liked to be, because this situation was utterly appalling and Delilah guilty through the most noble of motives of the most reprehensible conduct, Binnie did not think herself sufficiently heartless as to inform Sandor of Toby's occupation of the nursery. Binnie had no doubt that the duke, as Delilah had predicted, would order Toby tossed out into the street. It then occurred to Binnie that noble motives were not something ordinarily associated with Miss Mannering. "I've said nothing of the sort!" she protested, as Neal berated her for the callousness of her conduct, and several tears slid down Delilah's freckled cheeks. "Nor am I likely to. Oh, do let me *think!*"

"Yes, do!" cried Delilah, and grasped Binnie hands. "Think of poor little Toby, who is mute! Without a proper home, or anyone to care what happens to him! Condemned to cruelty!" To ensure that Binnie's cogitations followed those lines, she surreptitiously prodded the babe. Nothing loath, Toby abandoned Button and flopped down with an utter lack of ceremony in Binnie's lap, for Binnie had joined the others on the floor.

Binnie stared at the child. Had she, when Delilah grasped her hands, felt on Miss Mannering's finger a wedding ring? Covertly, Binnie glanced at the girl's hand. A wedding ring it was. What could it mean?

In this manner Binnie pondered, and the answer was not difficult to find. Previously Binnie had thought Delilah enamored of someone; now she realized that Delilah had been sufficiently enamored to engage in wedlock. But how did Delilah mean to form an eligible connection, an intention stated several times, if she already had a spouse? Perhaps the girl did not realize the laws concerning bigamy. And to whom was Delilah wed?

Nor did that answer prove elusive. Delilah was amusing herself and Toby by instructing him in Shelta, tinkers' talk. A *mush-faker* was an umbrella-mender, explained Miss

Mannering; a *ghesterman*, a magistrate, a *dinnessy*, a cat. A *nyock* was a penny, a *midgic*, sixpence; and a *tripo-rauniel*, a pot of beer.

Johann! Binnie thought unhappily. Scant wonder the tinker had dared brave Sandor in his den; he had more than ample grounds for blackmail. The idea of introducing to society a young lady who was secretly married to a tinker made Binnie's blood run cold. Then it turned to positive ice. The implications of Delilah's championship of Toby had burst upon Binnie. She groaned.

The others were looking at her, curiously. Binnie could hardly announce her suspicions regarding Toby's parentage. "I'll help you," she said, firmly if faintly—it would be cruel beyond bearing if a mother were parted from her babe. "This seems as good a moment as any to tell you that I am going to marry Mark."

Dead silence greeted this announcement, which was delivered with as little gusto as if its speaker was en route not to the altar but to the guillotine. Neal was first to speak. "Why?" he inquired.

Binnie had not the energy to embark upon a discussion of pros and cons. "It seemed like a good notion at the time," she said, rather gloomily.

This lack of enthusiasm did not strike Neal as odd, perhaps because he viewed his own approaching nuptials in a similar light. "We must decide what's to be done with Toby," he remarked. "Perhaps Cressida will be willing to adopt him."

Gently, because she was devoted to her brother, Binnie pointed out that Miss Choice-Pickerell was unlikely to look with favor upon such a suggestion. "Mark is more understanding. Perhaps I may take Toby into my home."

Miss Mannering, paying little heed to this bird-witted discussion, was regarding its subject. Toby was slobbering in a friendly manner on Binnie's skirts, and kicking his chubby heels in the air. The Baskervilles, Delilah decided, had an astonishing knack for going from bad to worse. Heartily, she deplored the tendency of the objects of her benevolence to make the straightening out of this tangle ever more difficult. Naturally, Miss Mannering did not despair. To straighten out even the most dreadful of tangles was not beyond her abilities.

Or was it? She matched Toby stare for stare. The babe bore not the least resemblance to his alleged sire, Johann. But if Toby was *not* Johann's child, then whose was he? Why had he been in Johann's custody?

Definitely, Delilah had acted without sufficient forethought. Had she in her zeal to get the goods on Johann, also failed to take Athalia into enough account? Would Athalia add two and two together, associate Toby's disappearance with Delilah's visit to the campsite, and achieve an accurate total? In that case, if Johann realized Delilah had spirited Toby away, he would have a very sharp sword to hold over her head instead of, as she had intended, the opposite. With the fervor of the thousand troopers, Delilah cursed.

CHAPTER SEVENTEEN

Because she was in mourning, Miss Mannering's social debut was a small, intimate affair. No more than a hundred invitations had been issued to the cozy evening reception held in the duke of Knowles's bow-fronted house on the Royal Crescent. Thus obliged to curtail her guest list, Edwina had extended invitations only to the *crème de la crème*.

Not a single member of the Upper Ten Thousand who sojourned in Brighton this season, and who consequently graced Edwina's guest list, had rendered polite apologies. Edwina was not especially surprised by this gratifying development. The *ton* were very curious about newcomers to their ranks, and ever eager to scrutinize young heiresses, the means by which many old, titled families managed to live in the style to which they had become accustomed before inflated prices and imprudent sons had diminished their income. Miss Mannering was a considerable heiress indeed.

She was also a considerable success, having created a sensation on her entrance, clad in a lovely gown trimmed with knots of ribbon. Luckily, Delilah appeared to advantage in black, the requisite color for a young lady recently bereaved. There was no dancing, due to that bereavement, which was rather a pity: Edwina would very much have liked to see the duke of Knowles engage Delilah for a waltz. Or several! she amended. Let the polite world be made aware of which direction the wind blew.

Of course Sandor could not conduct himself in a manner so shocking, not to a damsel under his own care. Too, Delilah was prohibited by mourning from marrying for almost a year. That, too, was a pity; perhaps the unwritten rule might be bent a bit in this case. After all, Sandor was a duke and had no need to bend his knee to the conventions that bound less exalted folk. Edwina decided she should drop a gentle hint, lest some gazetted fortune hunter in the interim made Delilah his prey.

What a pleasure it was to see Miss Mannering deporting herself like a well-brought-up young woman, for a change. Not a single vulgar expression—and Edwina had been listening sharply, ready if necessary to cover any slip—had this evening been heard to pass her lips. She was very natural, amiable but not forward, a young lady of distinct breeding.

Currently she was holding court, surrounded by a number of admirers, in the drawing room. This was a lovely chamber, furnished with pier tables, commode and elegant fire screen; and a gilt suite consisting of large and small sofas, a confidante and armchairs, all of a simple design that incorporated scrolled endpieces and straight legs, adorned with flutings, paterae, palm leaves, and honeysuckle. The plaster walls boasted rectangular panels of stucco design alternated with Zucchi paintings of Piranesi-style ruins. The design of the carpet—a circle within a square, and in the center a star surrounded by paterae and swags—echoed the Kauffman medallions in the ceiling. Edwina beamed upon Miss Mannering, then turned her attention to another young lady who stood at her side.

Edwina, as has previously been stated, rather admired

Miss Choice-Pickerell. Since the Choice-Pickerells were the only persons on the guest list who were not included in the ranks of the Upper Ten Thousand, and consequently might be expected to feel somewhat ill-at-ease, Edwina was making a special effort to compensate for any natural sensations of inferiority. "Lovely, isn't she?" she now inquired of Cressida. "Our little Delilah has made quite a hit, it seems!"

Much as she disliked the necessity of doing so, Miss Choice-Pickerell agreed. Cressida did not find Miss Mannering at all attractive; it could only be the heiress's fortune that exercised such allure; it certainly wasn't the distinctly common-place combination of freckles and flaming red hair. Cressida may be forgiven these conclusions, which were as unfair as they were uncharitable; Delilah may have been no beauty, but she possessed an abundance of charm. However, Cressida knew herself perfectly qualified to receive the compliments of persons of the first consideration, and that she was being ignored in favor of a dab of a girl with no manners and less countenance piqued her vanity.

Not only by persons of rank was Miss Choice-Pickerell being overlooked. Rather irritably, she inquired after Neal.

"Why, I don't know where he's gotten to." Edwina looked around the room. "Perhaps he's in the supper rooms, my dear, or engaged with a hand of cards." Though dancing was out of the question, Edwina had provided every other possible diversion for her guests. Cressida did not appear pleased, she thought, that Neal found other diversions more pleasant than herself. "Neal," Edwina added tactfully, "is not one to neglect his duties."

Since Miss Choice-Pickerell made no response, Edwina considered her ruffled feathers smoothed. Again she contemplated the guests—or those of the guests within her range of vision—and congratulated herself on the arrangement of a very gay affair. She did so in all justice; her idea of presenting Delilah to polite society in this manner had met with little enthusiasm from her family. Sibyl, in particular, had been against it, though the reason for her opposition was beyond Edwina's comprehension. For that matter, Sibyl was altogether inexplicable these days. Edwina could think of no reason for her sudden skittishness. Perhaps finding herself betrothed after so many years of unloved spinsterhood had unhinged Sibyl's brain.

But Miss Choice-Pickerell was growing sulky, poor thing; it was hardly kind of Neal to subject his fiancée to such arrant neglect. Edwina craned her neck. She saw not the missing Neal but his sister, engaged in a desultory conversation with Mark Dennison. For once, and after lengthy prodding, Sibyl was dressed becomingly, in a dress of embroidered silk gauze worn over a sarcenet slip. Even her hair was arranged attractively, due to the efforts of Miss Mannering, in a mass of loose intricate curls atop her head. Alas, Sibyl's expression was at odds with her finery. She looked almost grim.

"Come, my dear!" said Edwina to Miss Choice-Pickerell. "Let me make you known to a gentleman who is also soon to become a member of the family. It is not yet public, but I do not scruple to tell *you* that Sibyl and Mr. Dennison are to achieve the utmost felicity."

Sibyl and Mr. Dennison, thought Cressida, did not look like two people on the brink of bliss. She offered no objection, but allowed Edwina to usher her through the crowded room. "Mr. Dennison and I," she murmured, "have already met."

"Excellent!" Edwina spoke rather absently. There was Sandor, regarding his guests with distinct hauteur, as could only be expected from a gentleman of exalted rank and debased temperament—but where was Neal? Edwina would have a few stern words to say to that young man when he chose to reappear. To that end, she inquired of Sibyl her brother's whereabouts.

Binnie looked, Cressida thought, positively guilty. "Neal? I don't know! But I will find him!" gasped Miss Baskerville, and fled the drawing room.

"God bless my soul! What ails the girl?" muttered Edwina. Then Delilah beckoned, and she left Cressida with Mr. Dennison, after an arch comment that they would find much to talk about, since they would soon be almost related, as it were, by marriage. These remarks were uttered in a very complacent manner. Edwina was beginning to think herself no mean matchmaker—like her regent, envisioning herself responsible for all matter of stirring developments at which she hadn't been present.

Mr. Dennison and Miss Choice-Pickerell looked after her, a rather comical figure in a gown of gossamer satin with festooned trimming, bordered with satin rouleaux, the bodice and sleeves slashed with scarlet, and a cap ornamented with roses on her yellow hair. It was hardly an ensemble suited to a lady of mature years. But Mr. Dennison and Miss Choice-Pickerell were far too well-bred to make mock of their hostess. Instead Miss Choice-Pickerell embarked upon an erudite discussion of the correspondence between the prince and princess of Wales regarding their daughter, as published in the *Morning Chronicle;* and Mr. Dennison countered with a description of the festivities with which the prince customarily celebrated his birthday, which included oxen roasted whole, free-flowing liquor, fireworks, and races for every imaginable kind of quadruped, and much ringing of bells.

These civilities concluded, Mr. Dennison and Miss Choice-Pickerell regarded the young lady who was uppermost in both their thoughts. By the fact that Miss Mannering was conducting herself in an irreproachable manner, neither was reconciled to her. "I should not say so," Miss Choice-Pickerell said, "but I am very much afraid that Miss Mannering is not quite the thing. At least this evening she is not displaying her usual oddities of manner and *sauvageries.* One concludes she has been well rehearsed. And one can but hope one is mistaken in thinking her guilty of duplicity."

Mr. Dennison saw nothing untoward in these comments, which is an excellent indication of the opprobrium with which Mr. Dennison regarded Delilah: Miss Choice-Pickerell had with her outspoken spitefulness greatly overstepped the bounds of propriety. However, she had gauged her audience to a nicety. With Cressida's sentiments, Mark agreed.

So he informed her. Miss Choice-Pickerell, thought Mr. Dennison, was an unexceptional young woman with a great deal of countenance and a very proper delicacy of feeling; and on the subject of Miss Mannering—indeed, on every subject that he had been privileged to discuss with her—felt exactly as she should. He intimated—presumptuous as it might be on the short basis of their acquaintance—that he held her in the highest esteem. Cressida thought it only fitting that she should look gratified, and therefore she did.

"A tinkers' camp!" uttered Mark, still staring in a pained

manner upon Miss Mannering. "I have always deprecated Sandor's decision to bring the girl to Brighton. You see the result! The whole family has been sadly taken in."

A tinkers' camp? What was this? Cressida was too clever to betray her ignorance. Soberly she agreed with Mr. Dennison. The introduction of such a girl into a fashionable household, she remarked, could not fail to result in domestic difficulties.

"Very true!" Mark was struck by Miss Choice-Pickerell's sound good sense. Also, he was delighted to have found someone whose abhorrence of the heiress marched with his own. "Sandor might have expected by it to leave himself open to blackmail."

Blackmail! Cressida almost gasped. By mention of tinkers her curiosity had been pricked; now she itched for knowledge. Deftly, she set herself to draw Mark out. In mere moments, she had learned all he knew of Delilah's history. Pondering what use to make of this newfound knowledge, she fanned herself vigorously.

"There is Lieutenant Baskerville!" remarked Mr. Dennison as Neal, looking somewhat flushed, strolled into the room. Before Cressida's astonished gaze, the lieutenant made his way not to her side but to Miss Mannering, then bent to whisper a few words. Delilah nodded, murmured, then gestured unmistakably toward Miss Choice-Pickerell. Neal looked up, caught his fiancée's fulminating gaze, and walked toward her. He could only be said to have done so halfheartedly.

Mr. Dennison had missed none of this byplay, and he thought Neal's behavior very cavalier. Binnie's was no better, he decided; she had not accompanied her brother back into the drawing room. If Binnie had treated the object of her long-ago infatuation in the same distinctly offhand manner as she was currently treating Mark, he could see perfectly why her infatuation had come to naught. Politely, he relinquished Miss Choice-Pickerell into the keeping of her fiancé. Smarting under a sense of ill-usage, he strode into the supper room. Rapidly devouring several cups of excellent punch, he wondered what had ever led him to think he wished to marry a lady so unappreciative of himself as Miss Baskerville.

Cressida regarded her husband-to-be with little more favor, but much more triumph. Neal looked like the cat that had swallowed the canary. Little did he realize that he was about to choke on that forbidden fruit! With this fact, Cressida speedily made him acquainted. "Mr. Dennison and I have just had a *very* interesting conversation," said she.

"Did you?" Neal responded with some dubiety, wondering what Mr. Dennison could have found of interest in Cressida's infernal prose. "What about?"

"Well you may inquire!" Cressida snapped shut her fan. "I fear, Neal, that you are impractical and impetuous, much too concerned with the trivialities of life."

Was he again to be scolded for frivolity? Suppressing a rude response, Neal cast a glance of abject longing at Miss Mannering. Delilah would not rake a fellow over the coals for having a little harmless fun. But Neal had not had much time for frivolity of late, what with his upcoming nuptials, and the rigors of keeping Toby's presence secret, and his newly acquired habit of drinking himself under the table at every opportunity. He made bold to inquire what the devil Cressida was prosing on about.

Cressida may have been a high-minded young lady, but she was not above such very human emotions as jealousy. She had seen the look bestowed on Delilah by Neal, had understood it, and consequently was enraged. "I am quite out of charity with you, Neal! Your behavior is unspeakably odious. It gives me a thorough disgust!"

That Miss Choice-Pickerell should hold him in disgust was the most encouraging news Neal had learned in many days. He eyed her. "You've decided we won't suit!" he suggested helpfully. "You leave me nothing to say. I'm sorry for it— brokenhearted!—but I must agree. We wouldn't!"

Miss Choice-Pickerell, who had intended to threaten to break off her betrothal as a harsh lesson to her fiancé, realized that the lieutenant wished her to do precisely that, and immediately changed her mind. "Oh, no!" she said irately. "You shall not so easily throw *me* over, and for the sake of a creature who is no better than she should be." The lieutenant stared at her blankly, and inquired if she was paperskulled. "Not at all!" snapped Cressida. "Don't attempt to further deceive me. Already I am distressed beyond measure that you have kept me in perfect ignorance as to what is going on!"

The ominous nature of that latter remark did not immediately strike Neal; he was pondering Cressida's prior intimations. A creature no better than she should be? Delilah was the sole candidate for that description. But Delilah was an arrant adventuress. Surely Cressida did not think he nourished a tendresse for that thorough minx? Startled, he studied Miss Mannering.

She was a hoyden, a baggage, an abominably rag-mannered brat; she would never bore a man, or moralize over him, or seek to reform his frippery ways. In fact, decided Neal, carried away with these rhapsodies, Delilah would enter with enthusiasm into one's wildest larks, would preside over one's household in a delightfully ramshackle manner. Good God, he *was* in love with her! Much good the revelation did him. Neal was only too aware of the net Delilah had set for Sandor.

He additionally became aware that Cressida was observing him balefully. "Eh? I'm sorry, Cressida, but if you don't cry off, I must myself. Shabby as it may look! Surely you see that we wouldn't rub on together at all well. Too bad, but there it is! Much better to find out now than later, don't you agree?" There was the possibility, remote but ever-present, that he might divert Delilah's attention from Sandor to himself. Perhaps she was unaware that upon his marriage he would come into an inheritance that, while not so large as Sandor's fortune, was not inconsiderable. Why Miss Mannering should want another fortune, Neal could not imagine, unless she was extremely mercenary. What if she was? Delilah might possess all the known vices, and Neal would want her all the same.

But it was not to be so easy. Miss Choice-Pickerell had no intention of allowing herself to be tossed aside like a worn-out shoe. Clearly the lieutenant was in one of his hey-go-mad humors. She would tolerate his fits and starts no longer. So she intimated subtly. "I have told you that Mr. Dennison and I passed some little time in conversation, and very agreeable it was. To speak without roundaboutation, Neal, I Know All."

This remark, which suggested to Neal that Cressida was aware of Toby's presence in the house—perhaps Binnie had told Mark? She'd been acting very harebrained of late—affected him most extremely. He gaped.

Cressida was pleased that her fiancé had proven so quick on the uptake. In case he harbored an erroneous notion that

151

she would hesitate to use the information so luckily come by, she added, delicately: "The poor girl's reputation would be sullied beyond all belief were that to be blazoned about. Goodness, a tinkers' camp! You would not wish that to happen, I think, Neal? No? I confess it pleases me immensely that we begin to understand one another so well!"

Neal understood. Dared he try and thwart Cressida, she would see Delilah ruined. That the newly discovered object of his adoration should become the subject of censure, scandal, gossip, and moreover through an act of his, was unthinkable.

Frantically, the lieutenant sought a means out of this dilemma, and found none. He knew of no one with sufficient influence to stay Cressida's hand, save Sandor, and after years spent perpetually vowing vengeance against the duke for meddling in his life, Neal would liefer have applied to the great fiend himself for assistance. Betrothed to Miss Choice-Pickerell Neal was, and so he was destined to remain, and Delilah would never know the great sacrifice made on her behalf.

Cressida rapped his arm, sharply, with her fan. "I'm waiting," she said sternly. "Give me your word on this."

Ah, the folly of indulging, even briefly, romantically roseate air-dreams! Neal had been much less unhappy before realizing the object of his adoration, and realizing also that he was doomed to worship from afar. As if from an immense distance— and very much in the manner of the hound Caliban contemplating an especially juicy bone—he gazed upon Miss Mannering. She glanced up, espied his expression, strongly reminiscent of a man but newly sentenced to hang, and looked puzzled.

Cause tears to spring into those innocent eyes, those freckled cheeks to blush scarlet with shame? Never! "It will be as you wish, Cressida," Neal said, miserably.

CHAPTER EIGHTEEN

Sandor was not unaware that various of his dependents were exhibiting behavior that was bizarre. Miss Mannering had been mysteriously absent from the reception held in her honor for a noticeable period of time; and upon her reappearance the youngest of the duke's footmen was nowhere to be found. Then Neal had vanished. He reappeared at length, but now Sibyl was gone. Something, Sandor decided, was afoot. Sandor did not relish the idea that subterfuge was underway in his house—subterfuge, that is, in which he had no part. He decided to get to the bottom of it. To this end, he collared the one member of the seeming conspiracy who would not dare refuse him an answer.

" 'Tis the hound, my lord!" gasped poor Jem, pale as candle wax. "He gets lonesome locked away. Nothing to signify, I assure Your Grace!"

The duke stood in no need whatsoever of assurances from his youngest footman, who looked to be on the verge of a convulsion fit. He did, however, require verification of Jem's statements, the veracity of which he was very strongly inclined to doubt. Accordingly, he suggested that Jem lead the way to the nursery. Lord Knowles had an urge to witness for himself the lonesome hound. Wishing that some cataclysm of nature might intervene—to be swallowed whole by the earth would be infinitely preferable to the undoubted reaction of the duke to the discovery of a babe in his nursery, a reaction that in its mildest form would require that the duke's youngest footman was skinned alive—Jem obeyed.

They arrived at the nursery door. The duke reached out an elegant hand to the knob, and discovered that the door was locked. He then extended that hand toward Jem. Lest those fingers move next to Jem's defenseless neck—which, judging from the duke's expression, was a definite possibility—Jem tapped on the door. A feminine voice inquired who wished admittance. Jem cast an anguished glance at his employer. The duke looked both impatient and annoyed. "Miss Sibyl," said Jem, feeling as though he was introducing the wolf into the sheep pen, "it's only me."

There was a moment's silence, and then the sound of footsteps on the other side of the door, and a key turning in the lock. The door opened slightly and Binnie peered out. Her astonished gaze fell on her cousin. She tried to push the door shut.

"I couldn't help it, Miss Sibyl!" cried Jem. "He made me bring him!"

"Don't tease yourself!" came Binnie's voice, through the door. "I realize you had no choice. Sandor, go away!"

Naturally, Sandor had no intention of obliging Miss Baskerville. Obliging other people, especially such aggravating people as Miss Prunes and Prisms, had no place in Sandor's scheme of things. Too, he was on the trail of a mystery, and was very curious as to what was hidden behind this particular closed door. He dismissed Jem. Then he informed Miss Prunes and Prisms that if she did not immediately grant him entrance, he would break the door down.

Binnie—none better!—knew the duke's temper, and that he wouldn't hesitate to carry out his threat. She picked up the sleeping Toby and clasped him against her breast. The poor little fellow was exhausted after a day spent getting into every variety of mischief available to him, in the process demonstrating an amazing tenacity; and chewing on any number of diverse things, most notable among which had been Caliban's tail, an activity that the knowledgeable Jem had explained as attendant upon the acquirement of additional teeth. "Very well, if you must, come in!"

Undeterred by the gracelessness of this invitation, Sandor pushed upon the door. The first sight to greet him was Sibyl, who clutched what appeared to be a large bundle of linen to her breast. The second was Caliban, who roused from slumber to spring with great enthusiasm upon the latest intruder into his domain. Some several moments—during which Binnie prayed in a very unchristian manner that the hound might savage the duke—passed in a very frantic fashion. As matters evolved, and they evolved to Binnie's disappointment, Caliban's intention was not to roust an enemy, but to welcome a friend.

"Yes, yes, but that will do!" the duke said irritably, holding Caliban at a distance with one hand, and with the other attempting to remove from his dark double-breasted dress coat and his florentine silk breeches a large quantity of dog hair. "Binnie, if you love me, call off this beast!"

Of course Binnie did not love her cousin, but she called Caliban to order all the same. The fat was already in the fire, and there was little point in seeking to delay the dreaded moment of confrontation with the duke. She had hoped Sandor would not tumble to Toby's presence until after some definite plan for Toby's future had been made, a question that remained very much up in the air. Delilah, to whom the resolution of that question should have been of paramount importance, seemed to have more immediate concerns than Toby's upkeep. Remembering Delilah's violently vulgar reaction to the schemes put forth, which Binnie attributed to the natural reluctance of a mother whose child was soon to be wrested from her arms, Binnie glared at her cousin the duke. "You will not," she said indignantly, "toss poor Toby out into the streets!"

Sandor, who had been thinking that Miss Prunes and Prisms was looking unusually lovely, even though her gown of embroidered silk gauze had since his last viewing acquired some damp stains, and even though her intricate coiffure showed evidence of coming loose from its pins, begged that she make an effort to engage in rational conversation. "Who the devil," he added, "is Toby?"

"*This* is Toby!" cried Binnie, and shook her bundle in an agitated manner that would have caused a less serene child to shriek. Toby merely blinked sleepily. "You may think what you will, Sandor, but I will not permit Toby to be mistreated! He is mute! And even if he weren't, I would not stand for him being abused!"

The duke's reaction to these remarks defies analysis. He

155

sat down abruptly on the cot. Caliban leaped up and laid his large head on the duke's knee. The duke glanced blankly at the hound, and then at his cousin. "A *baby?*"

"Of course a baby!" Binnie retorted scathingly." "Gracious God, Sandor, what else would it be?"

For this rather illogical question, the duke had no response. Babies were not on the duke's list of favorite objects, and less so now than ever. He stared at it somberly. Having decided that he was not about to be dropped on his head, Toby resumed his slumbers. Binnie rocked him in her arms, crooning tunelessly.

As he stared, Sandor pondered the situation. Being unacquainted with the reasons underlying Miss Mannering's introduction of Toby into his household, or even of the clankers Miss Mannering had told the gullible Baskervilles; indeed, being unaware even that it was Miss Mannering whom he was to thank for this bewildering development, the conclusions reached by the duke were extremely unflattering to Miss Prunes and Prisms. But how to broach the matter tactfully? Obviously, broached it must be. Discreetly, the duke ventured a query as to Toby's paternity.

"Heavens, how should *I* know?" What a fascinating little fellow Toby was, even when asleep. Binnie gazed fondly upon his chubby little face. "I could venture a guess, but what purpose would it serve? The question of primary importance now is, since you have found me out, what you intend to do."

For perhaps the first time in a long and misspent life, the duke of Knowles was rendered speechless with shock. He stared at his cousin, dumbfounded. Stunned by Sibyl's tacit admission that she had fallen into licentious ways, he had tried to tell himself that even the most virtuous of ladies could occasionally make a slip. But then to be informed that Binnie neither knew nor cared to know the identity of the baby's sire—it confounded the imagination! Not a brief madness, but positive paroxysms of debauchery! "Sibyl!" he uttered, with what he considered laudable restraint. "Your behavior leaves very much to be desired!"

Binnie, who had no notion that her cousin the duke thought her no better than one of the wicked, set on the downward path to perdition, preoccupied with sin, deemed his remark very typical. "What would you have had me do? Leave the poor little fellow to starve in the streets? How like you, to spout such fustian. No matter how foolhardy you think me, Sandor, I cannot bring myself to regret a moment of it!"

Sandor was trying very hard to be fair, an endeavor in which he had no prior experience, and one he found increasingly difficult. That Binnie should have conceded the ultimate favor was bad enough, but Sandor reminded himself of the infinite number of ladies who had bestowed similar boons on him, and not all of whom had numbered among the frail and fair. Furthermore Binnie, though no longer a green girl, was obviously not up to snuff. That some heartless blackguard might have taken advantage of her unworldliness, Sandor might have forgiven—but with each word, Binnie revealed herself as further sunk in turpitude. Still, he tried to impose a check on his rapidly growing rage. "Is Mark aware of this?"

Strenuous as were Sandor's efforts at concealment, Binnie was aware of his anger. Perhaps he regarded her championship of Toby as the latest move in their eternal game of one-upmanship. "Why should I tell Mark?" she inquired, puzzled. "It's nothing to do with him!"

Nothing? When the lady the poor deluded Mark planned to marry was given to philandering, to foibles and indiscretions of a staggering magnitude?

Binnie had become aware of the duke's expression, which was nothing short of thunderous. "Why," she inquired, not unreasonably, "are you staring at me?"

Was she grown so iniquitous that she did not realize her conduct was shameful? Extricating himself with some difficulty from Caliban, Sandor rose. "I make you my compliments," he said in a grim tone. "You have duped me very thoroughly."

So she had, though not for long; Binnie had not expected Sandor to accept the situation so readily. Perhaps his impatience lessened with the passage of time. "Didn't I just?" she inquired cheerfully, as she placed the sleeping Toby on the cot. "It is very good of you, Sandor, to take it so well. I thought you would go into high fidgets once you found out."

The duke regarded Miss Prunes and Prisms, bent over the cot, making very mawkish noises as she tucked the baby in next to Caliban. Sibyl, he decided, was deranged. How else explain what appeared to be countless sordid intrigues? That he himself was as likely a candidate for Bedlam Asylum as was his shameless cousin did not occur to the duke, who due to the discovery that he had nursed an adder in his bosom—an adder, moreover, that had displayed a deflating absence of consideration for himself—was feeling increasingly resentful.

Puzzled by Sandor's continued silence, Binnie turned to look at him. There was a glint in his cold eyes that she intensely disliked. "You *are* angry! I am sorry for it—but, Sandor, what else could I do?"

"You could have trusted me." Still attempting to restrain his temper, the reins of which were rapidly sliding out of control, Sandor strode toward her. "Deuce take it, Binnie! How could you think I would turn your brat out into the streets?"

Binnie was uncomprehending. "But, Sandor—"

Surely she did not think to further deceive him? Sandor grasped her shoulders and shook her. "Take a damper!" he said roughly. "I expect I should be grateful that you did not decide to put a period to your life. A pretty mess *that* would have been! As if this is not bad enough. Binnie, I find it difficult to believe you could do such a thing!"

Binnie was no simpleton, when all is said; and Sandor had said quite enough to make Binnie realize he thought her guilty of engaging in an *affaire de coeur*. "Gracious God, Sandor! Have you taken leave of your wits?"

Perhaps he had. Certainly it did not occur to Sandor, engaged in revising his opinion of Miss Prunes and Prisms, that not a breath of scandal had attached itself to her name, a laudable accomplishment for a lady of myriad indiscretions, not one of which had inspired the malicious gossip of the *ton,* who were in the habit of thinking the worst of everyone. He had always known Sibyl was lovely; how could he not, seeing her each day? But now he realized that in addition to mere loveliness, she was a very desirable woman. Doubtless she had encountered little difficulty in treading the primrose path.

Which brought him to the source of his discontent. Miss Prunes and Prisms had with some justification cast aspersions upon His Grace's state of mind: Sandor was mulling over not his cousin's breach of every precept of propriety, but her failure to cast the eye of love upon himself. The duke was ot accustomed to being ignored by ladies in the process of alling from grace. No one, he fancied, was more familiar with the primrose path than himself. Not vanity prompted his reflection, although His Grace possessed his share of hat—and every other—failing. His Grace had set feminine hearts aflutter from a very early age.

He thought he understood. Binnie had sought to bring herself to his attention. Perhaps she thought him indifferent—a chuckleheaded notion, but females were prone to such—and had sought balm for her wounded pride. Silly girl! He must make clear his appreciation of her efforts, which if a bit more strenuous than necessary, had not been in vain. Whatever emotion Sandor felt toward his cousin, and the nature of that emotion remained elusive even to His Grace, it was not indifference. Generously, he made known these sentiments.

Not one *affaire de coeur,* realized Binnie, as the duke laid bare his soul, but several. She was left breathless and bewildered by the calumnies that rolled so easily off her cousin's tongue. She was also, and understandably, left furious.

"You utter fool!" she cried, and smartly slapped his face. "You think that *I*—the injustice of it! How *dare* you make these odious accusations, when it is *you* who are a Monster of Depravity?"

Sandor gazed in an annoyed fashion upon his cousin. Naturally she would cut up stiff on being confronted with the reasons underlying her naughty actions; his understanding would be a blow to her pride. However, to slap him was to carry sensibility too far. "Doing it a little too brown, Binnie!" he snapped. "Come down out of the boughs."

Had the duke not grasped her wrists, Binnie would have slapped him again. Since he did hold her virtually immobile, she contented herself with glowering malevolently at him. "Depravity!" she continued, as if no interruption had occurred. "And deceit! A truce you offered me, and yet you have not made the least effort to break up Neal's engagement to Cressida!"

This abrupt change of subject left Sandor a bit confused. He begged to know what Neal had to do with the present situation.

"Everything!" cried Binnie. "Why do you think I agreed to marry Mark? To try and prevent you from further putting my brother's money to your own use! Don't bother to deny it. Or that you are dangling after a rich heiress for the same vile motive! Well, I shan't allow you to ruin Delilah's life as you have ruined mine."

To this rather incoherent outburst, the duke could have made any number of retorts. He could also have done any of several things, among them strangling his aggravating cousin. Of the retorts; he chose to inquire how he had ruined Binnie's life; and of the actions, to take her face between the palms of his hands.

"That's a damned silly question." Binnie's voice was thick due to the proximity of tears. "You said I had an unbecoming *levity!*"

This incomprehensible accusation made perfect sense to Sandor. "That was many years ago," he said reasonably. "Beside, it's true. One does not make mock of men who are making you declarations of their sentiments, my girl! Is *that* what's inspired you to make a storm in a teacup?"

In the conducting of unintelligible conversations, Miss Baskerville had no peer. "You married Linnet," she said belligerently.

And in the unraveling of irrational remarks, Sandor excelled. "Yes, but you didn't want to marry me, and I thought I should marry *someone*. If you minded, you should have said so at the time!"

Binnie twisted her head in a futile effort at escape. "Mind? Why should I mind? You suffer an overweening vanity!" This setdown was not so devastating as intended, its delivery being lachrymose. "I suppose because you didn't want me, you thought no one else would."

The majority of Binnie's statements the duke was helpless to counter; this particular accusation, he could easily disprove. Hence, the duke kissed Miss Prunes and Prisms, very thoroughly. When this most pleasant of activities was at length concluded, Binnie stared up at him. "Oh, Sandor!" she breathed.

But then Toby stirred, making the strange little noises with which he indicated a wish to be fed. Caliban, very protective of his charge, leapt down from the cot, butted Binnie's knees with his large head, and for good measure snapped at Sandor's heels.

As diversion, it was very effective. Binnie pulled away

from the duke and rushed to Toby. The duke, thusly reminded of Miss Baskerville's descent into amorality, and reminded also of the various unflattering observations made by Miss Baskerville upon his character, the impact of which had just begun to sting, deemed it politic to hint to his cousin that no matter what degree of ardor he might harbor for her, he was not to be trifled with. Not a man to mince words, Sandor put forth a warning that he was not to be made a fool by any light-skirts.

Binnie's breast swelled with outrage. Naturally Sandor dared embrace her; considering her already sullied by countless diverse embraces, why should he refrain? Having embraced her, an embrace to which she had not offered any appreciable protest, an omission for which Binnie could think of no reason save that she had been stunned by his insolence, Sandor must assume that she would next succumb altogether to his legendary and highly overrated charm. *That* misapprehension he would cherish no longer! Binnie bid her cousin go and be damned.

CHAPTER NINETEEN

The polite world might accord Miss Delilah Mannering a tolerable success, and the reception held in her honor a very gay affair; but Miss Mannering had grave doubts on both scores. Undeniably she had received a great deal of attention, if not from the only person whose attention she sought, but Delilah was wise enough in the ways of the world to realize that the attentive gentlemen who had paid her such gallant court were in uniform need of financial assistance. Delilah had not been impressed by the Upper Ten Thousand, or the members thereof included among Edwina's guests. She had not found the reception to her taste, and thought it dull to be forever minding one's manners, and tedious to be on public view. The *haut ton,* decided Delilah, had a strange notion of gaiety. Fortunately, the *ton* were unaware that the duke had stormed out of his house in the midst of the festivities. Currently, Delilah was trying to determine just why the duke had done so. Her endeavors were meeting with no little difficulty.

She was in the nursery, watching with Miss Baskerville as Toby and Caliban engaged in a game of tug with Toby's blanket. "And?" Delilah inquired patiently. "The duke forced poor Jem to bring him up here, and demanded to be let in."

Binnie knew she should not sully Delilah's delicate ears with so shameful a tale, but if she did not share that tale with someone she would burst with indignation. "Sandor," she said bluntly, "has undoubtedly gone mad! He asked who Toby's father was, and I said I didn't know; then he asked if Mark was aware of Toby's presence here, and I said I saw no reason why he should be told. And then—oh, the brute!" In great agitation, she walked up and down the room. "Delilah, he as much as accused me of—of perseverance in loose morality!"

This blunt announcement was beyond the comprehension of the needle-witted Miss Mannering. She understood what Binnie had said, of course, but the suggestion that so decorous and diffident a lady should be mistaken for a fair barque of frailty was so absurd that Delilah decided she could not have heard aright. "He didn't!"

"No?" Binnie's amber eyes burned with remembered rage. "I assure you he did! He also said he was grateful I didn't try to put a period to my existence—from the shame of it, I suppose!—because it would have made a dreadful *mess!* And even that was not the worst!"

Utterly fascinated by these disclosures, Delilah pleaded to be told the rest. Binnie, who had spent a sleepless night working herself into a dreadful frenzy, was not reluctant to oblige. "He let it be known that he was prepared to overlook my indiscretions, and that he wouldn't toss Toby out into the street." She wrung her handkerchief as if it were her cousin's neck. "Me, an object of his charity! And so I made him privy to my opinion of *his* character! Gracious God, it's not *my* honor that's besmirched! *I'm* not the one who makes a habit of deceit and duplicity! *I* don't take all manner of encroaching fancies!"

More and more interesting! decided Miss Mannering. "Encroaching fancies" had an encouraging ring. She did not expect Binnie to view the manner in a similarly rational light, however. "Devil take the man! *Then* what happened?"

"I slapped him." Binnie looked very guilty, and so she felt, having convicted herself of grave misconduct. "What else was I to do? He had intimated that I was a—a bird of paradise! I had no choice but to administer a stinging rebuke." Delilah's silence, she interpreted as censure. "And he kissed me, the beast!"

But Miss Baskerville had misread the character of her protégée: Delilah was not censuring such arrant misbehavior, but struggling to repress an untimely fit of levity. "Naturally he kissed you!" she gasped. "I was sure that at some time during this encounter, he must have! What did you do?"

At least, reflected Binnie, she need no longer worry that Delilah would succumb to the duke's practiced allure. Obviously Delilah realized the duke was a Monster of Depravity. But there remained the worry that the Monster of Depravity might succumb to Delilah and unwittingly lend his assistance to that young lady's aspirations toward bigamy—though why Binnie should care if Sandor ruined himself she didn't know, unless it was for the sake of the family. "What do you *think* I did?" she retorted irately. "After he had accused me of throwing out lures, had intimated that I might be privileged to be his favorite of the moment! Treated me, in fact, as if I were no more than bachelor's fare!"

"What's this?" inquired Neal, from the doorway. Binnie, in her agitation, had failed to turn the key in the lock. "Who is no more than bachelor's fare? I must tell you, Binnie, that it is hardly proper for you to be discussing bits o' muslin with Miss Mannering!" He entered and locked the door behind him, then sternly regarded his sister and her protégée. Binnie looked to be in a rare taking, and Delilah was distinctly red-faced. He concluded that she was embarrassed at having been caught out in a highly exceptionable conversation. "Never mind, puss! It's not *you* that's blotted your copybook!"

This kindness almost proved Delilah's undoing. "No!" she gasped. "It's Binnie who's tossed her bonnet over the windmill. I mean, she hasn't, but he thinks she has—oh, fiddlestick!" She dissolved into giggles.

Neal stared at his sister, whose unhappy frame of mind had led her to take even less trouble than usual with her appearance, and who consequently appeared a very far cry from her brother's notion of a soiled dove. Her nose was red, her expression forbidding, and her hair was coming unpinned. Binnie, set upon the path to perdition? Neal fell into whoops.

That Delilah and Neal should laugh themselves into stitches at the notion that she might pursue an infamous career pleased Binnie as little as had the notion itself. "Well!" she said indignantly, hands on her slim hips. "I don't see why you should think it all so amusing! I daresay I would make a very good, er, bit o' muslin, if I wished it! Not that I *do* wish it, but it is hardly kind of you to act as if I *couldn't!*"

This irate observation did little to instill sobriety. Delilah offered an assurance that Miss Baskerville could indeed, if she chose, be a prime article of virtue; Neal, between guffaws, inquired if Binnie was suffering a fever of the brain. Miffed, Binnie turned her back on them. Toby, tired of a useless effort to reclaim the blanket on which Caliban had gone to sleep, ran to her. Thus reminded of a further reason for offense, Binnie picked him up.

"It is especially unkind of you, Delilah, to make game of me! When the whole misunderstanding came about because I withheld the truth for your sake."

Aware that she had wounded her benefactress's feelings, Delilah strove for self-control. "How's that, ma'am?" she asked, wiping her damp cheeks.

"Here!" Neal produced a handkerchief. "Let me!" Under Binnie's startled gaze, he dabbed tenderly at Delilah's freckled face.

As a result of her brother's considerate action, Binnie found herself in a very sad fix. She realized that Neal was far from impervious to Miss Mannering. It wouldn't do, alas; even less than Sandor was Binnie eager to see Neal engaged in bigamy. Furthermore, he was betrothed to Miss Choice-Pickerell— and for the first time, Binnie considered that betrothal a blessing in disguise. While engaged to one young lady, Neal could hardly pay his addresses to another. Or could he? Neal appeared to be doing exactly that. There was but one way to nip this dreadfully blighted blossom in the bud: the truth had to come out. "I refer," Binnie said severely, "to Toby's parentage."

Delilah glanced away from Neal's handsome face to Binnie's somber one: could Binnie know something she did not? "What about Toby's parentage?"

"Oh, my dear! Have done with this!" Binnie hugged Toby and looked at Delilah reproachfully. "Surely you cannot be so heartless as to deny your own son?"

"*My* son?" echoed Delilah, taken aback. Equally astounded, Neal inquired first if his sister had been making inroads on the brandy bottle, and then proceeded to read her a dreadful scold. "Wait!" cried Delilah, gratified that on her behalf Neal should ring a regular peal over his sister, and curious as to why Neal's sister should have leapt to so very illogical a conclusion. "It accomplishes nothing to give poor Binnie a trimming, Neal!"

"Certainly it does not!" Unhappy at the necessity, Binnie persevered. "Especially when I do not deserve it! Instead of roundly denouncing me, Neal, you would do better to ask Delilah why she wears a wedding ring!"

Neal had not passed a pleasant morning. During the daily drill he had endured an unpleasant encounter with his colonel, who seemed to think the lieutenant should be capable of rendering an explanation of the recent erraticisms displayed by the fair Phaedra. Colonel Fortescue's wife had progressed from making a fool of him all over the town, it evolved, to teetering on the brink of a decline. Naturally, Neal had been able to render no explanation, having never exchanged more than polite civilities with the colonel's wife. Nor was he in his cousin the duke's confidence. These circumstances he had tried tactfully to make clear. It had not served; Colonel Fortescue had subjected him to a severe tongue-lashing. Had not the colonel's irascibility stemmed from an obviously genuine concern for his wife's welfare, Neal might have retorted in a manner guaranteed to ensure that he was straightaway cashiered out of his regiment. Instead, he had bitten back the angry words and had tried to view the matter objectively. And now Binnie made addlepated accusations about a young lady who, though undoubtedly an adventuress, was aside from that minor failing above reproach. It was beyond human bearing!

"That wedding ring," he snapped, "belonged to Delilah's mother. So she would have told you, had you bothered to ask."

Binnie paid scant heed to Neal's displeasure; she gazed upon Delilah with horrified sympathy. "You're *not* married? You poor child!"

It had become apparent to Miss Mannering that her benefactress was laboring under a severe misapprehension—perhaps any number of them. "If I was married," she said reasonably, "I could hardly hope to form an eligible connection, could I? But I daresay that did not occur to you. Oh, I see! You *did* think of it, and thought that I was hoaxing you! I expect I might have, had it been necessary, but you see that it was not."

Miss Baskerville had developed a raging headache, alleviated neither by the daggers Neal was looking at her, or Toby's tugs at her hair. Wincing, she set him down. Toby immediately waddled over to Neal and gazed worshipfully up into his face. "I don't understand, Delilah! What about Johann?"

"Johann," Delilah answered bravely, "was a mistake. I freely admit it! But I thought Toby was his child—Athalia told me as much! And I was very anxious to steal a march on Johann because he was trying to blackmail the duke. Binnie, you are turned white as parchment! Pray try not to faint! It may look bad—it *does* look bad!—but we are not yet undone."

Guilty of misjudging Miss Mannering every bit as badly as she'd been misjudged, Binnie sank down on the bunk. Feebly, she requested a full explanation.

Delilah didn't like the look of Miss Baskerville at all. In fact, Binnie appeared on the verge of hysteria, or vapors, or both. "Truly I didn't do it for a lark! But I thought you wouldn't let me keep Toby here if you knew I'd *filched* him! Rather, *Jem* filched him, but he mustn't be blamed, because I told him to." This attempt at reassurance fell short of its intended mark. Binnie moaned. "Are you going to swoon?" Delilah inquired anxiously. "Shall I go and fetch Edwina's vinaigrette?"

Since the fetching of Edwina's vinaigrette would doubtless bring Edwina trailing in its wake—of the various stirring events under way in the duke of Knowles's bow-fronted house on the Royal Crescent, Edwina thus far had been kept in blissfull ignorance—Binnie refused this offer of assistance. "Please, Delilah, from the beginning!" she begged.

Delilah drew a deep breath. The moment of revelation had come. Bravely, she faced up to it. Baldly, Binnie was gifted with the circumstances leading to Toby's presence in the nursery. "I thought I could blackmail Johann in turn," Delilah concluded. "And if Toby was really his son, it might have worked very well! But I have decided Toby *isn't* Johann's son—though he does put me very strongly in mind of *someone*—Toby, that is, not Johann. Johann reminds me of no one at all, which is fortunate, because it would be sad to think there are two such perfect blocks in the world! However, if Toby *isn't* Johann's son, then whose is he? And what was Johann doing with him? I have thought about that very much, as you can imagine—and I have decided that maybe *Johann* filched him. If so, we did Toby a great favor by removing him from Johann's wagon, because it's certain that Johann's intentions weren't honorable. And in *that* case, it may still work out to our benefit!"

This speech was concluded with an air of triumph, which Neal perfectly approved. "Gad, what powers of reasoning!" said he, amid various other awed comments on Miss Mannering's ingenuity. "Binnie, don't you agree?" There was no answer. Neal tore his fascinated gaze away from Delilah to glance irritably at the cot. Binnie lay sprawled across it, in a dead faint.

She was not long allowed to enjoy this blessed state of unconsciousness, was awakened in but moments by a dreadful stench. Prohibited from fetching Edwina's vinaigrette, the resourceful Delilah had burned Toby's feather pillow in the grate. "There!" said Miss Mannering, as Binnie cautiously opened one eye. "You are yourself again! You must not worry: I am aware I have gotten us all into a dreadful scrape, but you may trust me to get us out again! On the square! Because I may be an incurable humbugger, may make rare mulls of things, but I *always* manage to fix them up all right and tight in the end!"

Binnie had been inspired by Delilah's assurances to screw both eyes shut and pray for a resumption of her swoon. Hidden away in the duke's nursery was a child the identity of whom was unknown, a child stolen from what appeared to be its rightful guardians. Perhaps that very moment anxious parents were in search of Toby, hot on the heels of his kidnappers. What would happen when that search brought them, as eventually it must, to this very house? Delilah and Jem at the best would be transported, at the worst would hang. And what of herself and Néal? As accomplices, they could hardly expect a more beneficient fate. Odd how often good fortune favored those who deserved it least. With all his wards thus disposed of, the duke would be a fabulously wealthy man. "Trust Sandor!"

Delilah considered this odd remark as only natural from a lady so recently recovered from a swoon. In case Binnie had not totally recovered, she waved some burned feathers under her nose. "Yes, but do you think we *should?* Trust the duke?"

"Gracious God!" Sneezing, Binnie sat up. "Above all, we must not acquaint Sandor with this. He's already decided that I'm a marvel of indiscretion; let him go on thinking it! I'm sure *I* don't mind."

It was clear to Delilah that Binnie minded very much, not the duke's misjudgment of her character, but that he had held her so cheap, and not that he had dared embrace her, but that he had done so out of expedience. Delilah was glad that she was no lady, and therefore not subject to the confusion attendant upon high principles. She wondered if she might delicately hint to Binnie that gentlemen did not generally go around kissing ladies to whom they were indifferent, or scolding ladies for whose misconduct they had no concern.

As Delilah pondered, Neal spoke. He had paid scant attention to the conversation between his sister and Miss Mannering, being totally bemused by the various expressions that flicked across Delilah's enchantingly freckled face, but one aspect of the conversation had caught his interest. "Binnie!" he said, in a very deadly tone. "*Who* accused you of being a lightskirts?"

Unhappily reminded of that debacle, Binnie dropped her face into her hands. Delilah might vow to make things right as a trivet, but Binnie didn't see how that was possible.

'erhaps she *should* put a period to her existence. That empting notion she abandoned; it would suit the odious duke ll too well. "Sandor! Who else would dare?"

Sandor! Everything always came back to Sandor! "By God!" ttered Neal. "He'll pay for this! Lucky for Sandor that he's ot here or I'd—I'd carve out his damned gizzard!"

Thrilled by so forceful an attitude, Delilah clapped her ands. Before Miss Mannering could further encourage Neal's loodlust, Binnie intervened.

"Stuff!" she responded, unappreciatively. "You'll do no such hing! I forbid it, Neal! Leave Sandor to me! Where *is* he, by he bye? He generally doesn't emerge from his bedchamber efore noon."

"He can hardly emerge from what he didn't go into!" Neal oked at the stuffed rabbit, one appendage of which Toby was hewing. Toby looked quite blissful, Neal the opposite. "It eems he hasn't come home since he left here last night. And know for a fact that he hasn't called upon the fair Phaedra, ecause she's locked in her bedroom, teetering on a decline. The colonel told me so. So where Sandor may be is anybody's guess. Maybe somebody has murdered him!"

This explanation should have gratified a lady with a burning desire for revenge, one who had spent many sleepless hours assuring herself she wished never again to find herself in the duke's untrustworthy presence; but Binnie was so sadly pulled-about that she could not be expected to react rationally.

"I bid him go and be damned!" she wailed. "But I didn't think he really *would!* Go away, that is! Not that I should care if I never laid eyes on him again—but he may be lying somewhere, hurt! We must do something!"

Neal was quite eager to do something, he professed: he would break the head of the man who had reduced his sister to such a sorry state. Binnie protested; she might wish to see the man responsible for her unhappiness boiled in hot oil, but she didn't wish him dead. To this fine feminine illogic, Neal retorted scathingly. Binnie burst into renewed sobs. Lest matters deteriorate into total chaos, Miss Mannering lent a hand.

Before any retribution could be dealt the duke, Delilah pointed out, the duke must be found. With that necessity in

mind, she suggested that she and the lieutenant might tak
the air. A stroll through the streets of Brighton might tur
up some clue as to the duke's whereabouts. Were they to fin
the duke himself, she consoled Binnie, she would endeavor t
see that Neal dealt him no mortal blow. Once the matter o
the missing duke was resolved, they would turn their ener
gies on the problem of Toby. Victory was achieved, after all
one step at a time.

The lieutenant professed himself agreeable; taking Caliba
with them, he and Delilah departed according to plan. Binni
was left to preside over the nursery. Gloomily, she stared a
Toby. A sympathetic youngster, he immediately ran acros
the room, leaned against her knees, thrust the stuffed rabbi
in her face.

This generous offer of solace, Binnie gently refused. Wer
her fears groundless? Was it possible that the insolent, dis
dainful duke of Knowles could have met with dire mishap'
True, to this point the duke had led a charmed life—bu
Binnie had a strong presentiment that his luck had abruptly
run out. Naturally it was not concern for Sandor's well-being
that prompted Binnie's disquiet; were retribution to be exacted
from her cousin, she wanted to be the one to give the devil hi
due.

The nature of that retribution, she anticipated pleasurably.
Tar and feathers? The rack? The duke's mocking head would
admirably adorn a pike. At this ghoulish point in her
reflections, Binnie was interrupted by Toby, who was attempting very energetically to climb into her lap.

The child's chubby face *was* tantalizingly familiar, Binnie
decided as she lifted him. There was a distinct resemblance—
but to whom?

CHAPTER TWENTY

Although his mocking head did not adorn a pike, nor his handsome body a rack or a vat of boiling oil, the duke of Knowles had encountered a fate almost as dire as any wished down on him by Miss Baskerville. Slowly, His Grace was becoming aware of this unpalatable development.

First to penetrate His Grace's consciousness was an abominably aching head; second was that the world had gone utterly black; third, that he could not so much as an inch move any of his limbs. A lesser man might have been thrown into a state of panic by these discoveries. The duke was not. The duke was unaccustomed to going down to defeat; he had so little notion of bearing his losses bravely that he found it impossible to comprehend that loss might be his fate. Some reasonable explanation for his dark immobility must undoubtedly exist. He searched for it.

After his confrontation with his shameless cousin, Sandor had left his house in a rage. He had gone to Raggett's, then to the Cider Cellar, then to an establishment of such low estate that it lacked even a name. His recollection was a trifle hazy; he believed he'd consumed a large amount of diverse intoxicating beverages. Perhaps this accounted for his throbbing temples, the sensation that at any moment he might cast up his accounts. But if the duke's malaise was the wages of sin—said sin being an overindulgence in the grape—his was definitely the most monumental hangover ever inflicted on mortal man. His skull felt as if it had suffered repeated blows from a heavy object. . . .

Ah! A glimmer of enlightenment! Sandor recalled that perhaps due to the quality of the refreshment served in the establishment of low estate, he had taken a notion for a moonlight ride along the seashore. It was a pastime in which he occasionally indulged, when he was drunk as a lord and the tide was coming in, sending his horse galloping across the sand, through the splashing waves. Sometimes the beast would shy when a foamy breaker rolled under his feet and retreated as abruptly, as if in sport. Once the duke, caught unawares, had taken a drenching.

Not so on this occasion; his clothing was not damp. Indeed the duke had no memory of fetching his steed. Valiantly despite the pain attendant upon rumination, he strove to piece together his progress. He had left the establishment of low estate—Oho! A fragmented memory of difficulty encountered in the control of his extremities, of a dark side street, a figure with arm upraised.

Drugged, then, and set upon. For what purpose? Not simple robbery, or he would have been left where he'd fallen—and what criminal existed so desperate as to attack the duke of Knowles, who was of a temperament to see such presumption punished on the Nubbing Cheat? But if no simple ruffian, then who was responsible for the duke's current plight? Thinking clearer now, if with no less difficulty, the duke explored his predicament. His immobility, he discovered, was due to ropes that tightly bound him; his sightlessness attendant upon a blindfold. Additionally, he was rendered speechless by a foul-tasting strip of cloth.

The duke's temper was not improved by the discovery that he was trussed up like a chicken ready for the cooking pot. Anger lent lucidity. Somehow, decided the duke, he had made an enemy. Further cogitation led him to admit—the duke was cold and selfish and stern; humorless and compassionless and dissolute; but he was perfectly capable on occasion, albeit rare, of recognizing his own shortcomings—that there might be several people with good cause to wish him ill. This realization caused the duke not an instant's chagrin, nor did it inspire him with unease. Since he lacked any more amusing way to pass the time, his lordship compiled a mental list of his potential enemies.

No short time later, the duke abandoned this pursuit, having narrowed a staggering number of potential ill-wishers down to the few who were capable of utilizing a practical outlet for their malice. Colonel Fortescue, the fair Phaedra? Had the colonel learned the extent of his wife's indiscretion, he might well have been driven to seek redress. But the colonel was a man of honor, and therefore would have been far more likely to challenge his rival to a duel than to have him set upon by ruffians. That suspect, then, Sandor erased from his list.

Phaedra was a far more likely candidate; despite her threats, the duke had not been especially attentive of late. Perhaps she had chosen this queer way to exact revenge. It made little sense; Phaedra could hardly make her husband jealous with a gentleman who was locked in some filthy hovel—that his prison was no model of good housekeeping Sandor had determined; his sense of smell was unimpaired, and the stench of his surroundings, a pungent aroma comprised of unwashed bodies and soured food and even less wholesome items, made his fastidious nostrils twitch. Unable to imagine what advantage it would serve Phaedra to reduce him to such straits—and Phaedra had already shown herself in possession of a very calculating foresight—the duke also dismissed her.

Which brought him to the members of his immediate family. Sandor did not even briefly consider that Edwina should wish him harm. He accorded a great deal more thought, however, to the Baskervilles.

That Neal heartily resented his guardianship, Sandor was aware: Neal would have resented anyone in a position to wield authority over him. Sandor had not been deterred by Neal's dislike of the situation from keeping a firm hand on the reins, nor was he especially disturbed that Neal failed to comprehend the benefits to himself of such discipline. Neal had bid fair, at the time Sandor took up his guardianship, to become a rare young blood, damnably hot-at-hand, and ripe for any spree, having from his cradle been indulged in everything by his doting parents and his equally doting sister. Had Neal been allowed to pursue the path he wished to tread, he would have speedily been in the hands of moneylenders and Captain Sharps, another of the countless young bucks who set out to sow their innocent wild oats and ultimately reaped ruin. Sandor had not allowed that to happen, had ensured that Neal, if still damnably hot-at-hand, had developed from a pampered brat into an unexceptionable young man. Additionally, he had done so without breaking the boy's spirits. That Neal should resent his guardianship did not surprise the duke, nor did it cause him distress. He had imagined Neal would come round, in time.

Could he have been mistaken? Could he have pushed Neal too far? Sandor thought not. He had not been unreasonable, had provided Neal with the lieutenancy in the Hussars that he craved, had permitted his singularly inappropriate betrothal to Miss Choice-Pickerell. Neal's resentment had no reason to so suddenly overboil.

The duke was left with only one remaining suspect. Her, he didn't want to think about at all. Yet he must; if he was to free himself from this predicament, he must first determine how it had come about, must prepare for the next action of the enemy. What would that next action be? Was death to be the only means by which he was released from this stinking place? The duke contemplated that notion with singular disfavor. Surely, if murder was intended, it would have been best accomplished in that dark street? Perhaps the plan had somehow gone awry, some providential interruption had made it necessary that instead of being bludgeoned to death on the spot he had been conveyed to his odiferous prison.

It must not be thought that the duke trembled in terror at the prospect of imminent demise; he did no such thing. His Grace had no intention of dying to suit anyone, and certainly not the misguided Miss Baskerville. But why should Binnie wish him dead? If she was so desirous of protecting her guilty secret, she should have never brought it to his house. Surely Binnie didn't think to keep her by-blow—what had she called the brat? Toby?—forever hidden from the world.

A bit belatedly, the duke wondered how she had managed to do so for this long. And why had she allowed the child to be born out of wedlock? If not the man responsible for her predicament, there had been other gentlemen who wished to marry Binnie. A very large number of gentlemen, now that Sandor counted them. He should not have been surprised; Binnie was first-rate, fine as fivepence, despite her retiring habit and her adder's tongue; but surprised he was, perhaps because Binnie's amused rejection of his own proposal had led him to conclude she wished to marry no one.

At all events, abruptly, she had become betrothed to Mark, the man among all her suitors most unsuited to her. Mark was a perfect gentlemen—and therefore hardly of a nature to long retain the interest of a lady accustomed to keeping assignations with gay and profligate men. Perhaps Binnie thought Mark would be easily led.

That was not the explanation she'd rendered, of course; but one could hardly expect even a straw damsel to admit the depths of her duplicity. Those depths astounded Sandor, who even now found it difficult to credit that Binnie, while conducting herself in public with the utmost decorum, had in private indulged in veritable paroxysms of intemperance and debauchery. And what the devil had led her to turn his house into a hotbed of scandal? Furthermore, what had induced her, when he had subtly indicated his awareness of her intimate acquaintance with the fleshpots, to slap his face? Sandor thought he had displayed an admirable tolerance of her shortcomings. So little had Binnie agreed that she had called him a monster of depravity.

Working futilely to loosen his tight bonds, Sandor remembered what else Binnie had said. This required no effort; Binnie's words were branded as if with fire in his memory. Could she seriously believe he harbored avaricious intentions toward Neal's inheritance? Surely she could not think he was on the dangle for Miss Mannering! The claim that he had ruined his cousin's life was the most outrageous accusation of the lot. Were Binnie's life ruined, it was through no action of the duke's. Odd that she should remember a vindictive remark made so many years ago. It had been no more than the truth: Binnie *did* possess an unbecoming levity.

He did not mind it, especially; he was well accustomed to Binnie's ironic manner, her knack for seeing humor in a situation that looked serious to him; he had learned to appreciate partly Binnie's love of the absurd. Because she joked about a matter did not mean she failed to appreciate its seriousness, merely that she was not a lady who wore her heart on her sleeve. Still waters, the duke decided in a burst of originality, could run very deep.

With that profound realization, his head threatened to burst. Had he misunderstood her levity, those many years ago? Had he not lost his temper, accused her of making mock of him—

Speculation was fruitless. Whatever Binnie might once have been, she was now a lady fallen far from grace, and one furthermore who had the unmitigated impudence to introduce a love child into the duke's nursery. For what possible purpose—unlike lightning, revelation struck again. Sandor was in the habit of seeing his cousin daily. In no way could Binnie have hidden from his keen eye the fact that she had grown happily advanced in pregnancy.

Sandor wasted no time in pondering whose child, if not Binnie's, Toby might be; if not Binnie's child, Toby aroused no interest. Frantically, Sandor tried to recall the exact words he'd said to his cousin.

He'd accused her of unbecoming behavior, certainly; but had he made apparent what he believed that behavior consisted of? On due reflection, Sandor decided he had. It was a reflection far more lowering than the realization that someone wished him dead. What a coxcomb he must have appeared, so convinced of his own devastating charm that he concluded that Binnie had proceeded from a want of his affection to embark upon an infamous career. To accuse Binnie, of all people, of being a sylphid! Scant wonder she had slapped his face. Had she ever worn the willow for him, she would no more.

This, of all the conclusions arrived at by the duke, caused him the greatest discontent. That chagrin was inspired not by the fact that he, a man of the world who was well versed in the ploys of romantic courtship, a man whose far from pristine reputation as concerned the opposite sex was very well deserved, had made a cake of himself; but by the decision that his atrocious arrogance could have only roused Binnie's repugnance.

At this point in his reflections, the duke paused to wonder why he should care so deeply that he might have caused Miss Prunes and Prisms to hold him in disgust. His conclusions, after all, had not been illogical. What else was he to think than what he had, given the circumstances? Galling to think that Binnie had obviously considered the duke's youngest footman more trustworthy than the duke himself. Even more galling to realize she'd been right. Jem would never have been so addlepated as to suspect—even worse, to accuse—Binnie of being a light-skirts.

Had the duke been able, he would have cursed loudly. Taxed so unjustly, Binnie would have naturally misinterpreted the events that preceded the accusation. She would have thought him, frankly, to be desirous of mounting a mistress, would have thought he intended she should play that rôle. And in all justice, although Sandor's ardor had not been feigned, he had intended nothing of the sort. Had not Miss Prunes and Prisms bid him go and be damned, he would have made her a candid confession of his sentiments.

Very well, what *were* those sentiments? His Grace was not a man given to introspection, and he was rather astounded at the torturous workings of his mind. Moreover, he was astounded that he could have been so obtuse. Binnie would have found the situation amusing, had she not been so furious with him; nothing could be more droll than the duke of Knowles, berating a lady for shameful conduct, when the cream of the jest was that he wanted the frail one for himself—not as a *petite amie*, but as his wife. Sandor marveled at his capacity for self-delusion. It had become appallingly clear to him that he had never forgiven nor forgotten Binnie's rejection, had been embarked for an unconscionable time upon a systematic extraction of revenge. That this boorishness had been unconscious excused it not one whit.

Would she, could she, forgive him? The suspicion that she would not alarmed him not a little. In point of fact, the duke was driven nigh distracted by the thought that Binnie might never so much as speak to him again. Such a reaction would not be unreasonable.

Briefly, he allowed himself to savor the few favorable aspects of that fateful interview. Binnie had been jealous of Linnet, which was surely a hopeful sign; she had returned his embrace with enthusiasm, which was equally encouraging. Hold herself aloof, would she? He wouldn't stand for it!

As becomes apparent, the duke of Knowles did not long wallow in remorse. He had behaved badly; he would make amends. Even without cooperation, atone he would; even if to do so he must kidnap his cousin, lock her away, keep her on starvation rations of bread and water until she proved amenable to reason, as proffered by himself. Countless years had been wasted; time now to act. If he had to drag her protesting to the altar, the duke meant to marry his Miss Prunes and Prisms.

Alas, Sandor then recalled his own predicament. Pleasant as it was to contemplate dragging off his viper-tongued lady to a long overdue rendezvous with the parson and the marriage bed, Sandor was hardly in a position to conduct himself like some prehistoric caveman. Frustrated beyond measure by being held down by circumstance, and at a moment when prompt and decisive action was imperative lest his quarry act in a manner that placed her forever beyond his reach, such as marrying Mark in a fit of pique, the duke struggled violently against his ropes.

He was prevented from doing himself bodily injury by the sound of approaching footsteps. Motionless he paused, ready to achieve escape by whatever means. On that end he concentrated, pushing aside even the tantalizing prospect of throttling his cousin until she was forced to confess her sentiments toward him.

A door opened. The footsteps came closer. There was a rustle of clothing, a pungent sweaty scent. Then came the prick of a knife-blade against His Grace's neck.

CHAPTER TWENTY-ONE

Miss Mannering and Lieutenant Baskerville, with Caliban in tow, had made a leisurely progress through Brighton. They had inspected shops displaying toys and rare china, knickknacks and tea; the library on the Marine Parade where

ne might read the London newspapers, or through a telescope
aze out to sea. Miss Mannering waited under the colonnade
f the establishment across the street while Lieutenant
Baskerville went into Raggett's to ascertain if the duke of
Knowles had recently been there; she acted similarly when
he likewise broached the Cider Cellar off the Steine. Then
hey paused at the corner of the Marine Parade and refreshed
hemselves with gingerbread and apples purchased from
Phoebe Hessell, who cheerfully exhibited for the lieutenant
her bayonet wound.

"Curses!" said Delilah, in a rather garbled tone, due to a
mouthful of gingerbread, as they proceeded down the street.
"A man like the duke of Knowles cannot disappear into thin
air! I'll lay a monkey there's mischief afoot."

Neal made no response. If mischief was afoot, it had doubt-
ess been set in train by the duke himself, and he hoped
Sandor might perish in his own intrigues. He did not expect
Miss Mannering, with her sights set firmly on Sandor, to
share this point of view. Did she truly care for him, or did she
seek merely to feather her nest? By the suspicion that Delilah
might have formed a lasting passion for Lord Knowles, Neal
was put in a passion himself. Lest he take out that passion on
Delilah, he gritted his teeth shut.

To the Downs they went, after pausing to observe a cricket
match under way on the Steine. There was no sign of the duke
of Knowles among the beaux and belles *en promenade*. Nor
was he among the people on the seashore, gathering shells,
gazing out to sea through spyglasses, being steamed and
shampooed and plummeted in the Oriental baths. Their
progress was not rapid, Caliban being in a sportive mood.

"This accomplishes nothing!" Delilah said, at last. "Neal,
you know your cousin's habits. Where can he have gone?"

"Hopefully, to perdition!" snapped Neal, then bit his tongue.
"I'm sorry, puss! I know you are concerned for him. It does
you great credit."

"Pooh!" Delilah fed the last of her gingerbread, not entirely
by design, to the faithful Caliban. "It is my fault that the
duke stormed out of the house, and *that* does me no credit at
all. Because if I had not taken Toby there, the duke would not
have found him; and if the duke had never set eyes on Toby,
he would have had no reason to accuse Binnie of being a

179

light-skirts." Her freckled face was contemplative. "Which was not what I had planned, though I daresay it will serve very well. *I* would have gone about the thing with considerably less fuss."

Neal, unaware of the sentiments harbored by his sister for the duke and vice versa, hadn't the least notion of what Delilah meant, unless she referred to her own campaign to ensnare the duke. She intended, then, to go on with her plans? "You still mean," he inquired delicately, "to form an eligible connection?"

"Of course I do!" Delilah wiped sticky hands on her skirt. "I assure you I am quite incorrigible. And very determined once my mind is made up! What is it they say? Faint heart never won fair maiden? Or fair gentleman, in this case."

"The devil! " ejaculated Neal. "You can't mean you're *fond* of the brute!"

Miss Mannering paused to look up at the lieutenant, a little frown upon her freckled brow. "Fond? You might say so! Indeed, I did precisely what I said I wouldn't, and tumbled into love with him after the briefest acquaintance, which just shows how foolish it is to anticipate!"

Bad enough to think of Delilah coldheartedly set out to land a plump fish; far, far worse to realize she meant to savor her catch. "Give it up!" Neal said abruptly. "He'll lead you a merry dance. You *can't* think he'll make you happy, puss! He doesn't care a button for anything but himself. Look at Binnie! He once wanted to marry her, and now he accuses her of being a light-skirts!" He watched with fascination as Delilah's cheeks turned pink. She appeared to be laboring under some strong emotion. "I'm sorry if this makes you unhappy, but I can't stand by and watch you set your cap at a brute like Sandor. Even if you did manage to marry him, you would find yourself plunged into grief!"

Nobly, Miss Mannering attempted to restrain the merriment attendant upon so cork-brained a notion as that she was enamored of the ill-tempered duke. She had a high regard for him, certainly; a clear-sighted young lady, Delilah recognized virtues in the duke that were apparently well hidden from his family. However, she had never briefly contemplated settling with Sandor in matrimony. Now that she did so, she perfectly agreed with Neal that to do so would be a prodigious misstep. But this was hardly an appropriate moment to acquaint Neal with the extent of his error, lest she make a sad botch of the whole affair.

"Oh!" Her voice, due to the preceding reflections, was strangled. "I fear it is midsummer moon with me!"

Confronted with a mulish young lady, prohibited from attempting to lure her away from a man who could only cause her grave unhappiness, Neal tried a different tack. Subtly, he recalled to Delilah the reception held in her honor, at which she had enjoyed such success. Any one of those admiring gentlemen, he intimated, would be a better catch for an enterprising young lady than the duke. To this, Delilah responded that those gentlemen had been gazetted fortune hunters all. Miss Mannering had no intention of placing her fortune in such a person's hands.

Thus reminded of Delilah's avaricious nature, Neal put forth the suggestion that, could she but restrain her greed, she could surely discover some gentleman who suited her needs. Since Delilah looked extremely startled by this remark, and since Neal interpreted that amazement as resultant upon his understanding of her motives, he added that she mustn't think *he* minded that she was dangling after wealth. It was not unnatural, the lieutenant professed, that a young lady already possessing one fortune should yearn for yet another—if she *did* possess a fortune, and wasn't laying claim to something that wasn't truly hers—or he supposed it was not unnatural, though he admitted that to him it didn't make a great deal of sense.

Miss Mannering reflected, with considerable amusement, that she had gotten herself involved with a uniformly cockle-brained family. Never had she met a group of people so set on misjudging one another. In Neal's case, at least, there was some excuse: Edwina had warned her that her behavior was open to very unfavorable interpretations, and Edwina had been correct. But she was ignoring Neal. With keen interest, she waited to see what absurdity he would utter next.

Lieutenant Baskerville did not disappoint Miss Mannering: after acquainting her with his suspicion that she was an adventuress, he informed her that she erred in choosing Sandor as her dupe. The duke's mind was of a mean and little structure, Neal explained, and he possessed an insuperable vanity, but all shortcomings aside, there were no flies on the duke.

Delilah could bear no more, lest she burst into laughter, which would doubtless cause Neal to take offense. "Come out of the mops!" she gasped. "I promise I shan't come to grief. But where is Caliban?"

Obviously the subject was closed. What a dreadful fix this was, decided Neal, for all concerned. He must marry a lady for whom he had not the least affection, lest she ruin the lady for whom he harbored the greatest affection possible; while the latter lady was set on contracting an alliance with a cold and heartless brute. Naturally she was set on finding Sandor; of course she was determined that, for Sandor's insult to Binnie, Neal should not wreak vengeance. Accordingly, Neal was not to be permitted to carve out his cousin's gizzard. Feeling very frustrated, Neal looked around for the missing hound.

They had, during their conversation, reached a poorer part of town, one with which Neal was not familiar. Nor did he care to be. The silent squalor of his surroundings struck him as ominous.

"There!" cried Delilah, tugging on his arm. "That alley-way!"

Sure enough, Neal caught a glimpse of a hideously multi-colored tail. He also heard a frantic barking. Neal did not deem it expedient to be running into alleyways in this particular section of town, and so he said, but he spoke only to air. Delilah was already in hot pursuit of her pet.

Resigned, Neal followed. As if things were not already bad enough, now Caliban must hold at bay some unwary pedestrian, who would doubtless seek legal redress for injuries sustained.

Once more, Neal was guilty of misjudgment: Caliban was, after a fashion, very well trained, that fashion being that he did not harry strangers, only prior acquaintances. Of this fact, Neal was made aware as soon as he stepped into the alleyway. Not only with Caliban was this gaudily dressed, villainous-looking female acquainted. Delilah was addressing her in terms of great, if irate, familiarity.

"It will do you no good to try and bamboozle me, Athalia!" Delilah said sternly. "Everything is at sixes and sevens, and you are at least partially to blame! You and that nodcock Johann! You might as well unbosom yourself, because until you do so I will not call Caliban to heel."

With a wary eye on Caliban snapping at her ankles, Athalia sought to put forth a defense. Delilah should not hold it against her, she protested, that she had been very wishful to escape an existence the high points of which were sleeping under hedges, telling fortunes, begging for one's bread in the streets. And furthermore, Athalia added, she was mortal afraid of Johann.

"Moonshine!" retorted Delilah. Neal said nothing, being fascinated by the deft manner in which Delilah handled her victim. "I should have realized before that you had your fingers in the pie, and have smelled a rat! Because it is very much like Johann to be cramming his fences! Make a clean breast of it, Athalia, and I *may* forgive you. If not—" She paused, meaningfully.

Athalia required no further explanation; Caliban was barking and snarling energetically. "You're a rum one, *leicheen*. Haven't I always said so? Stands to reason I wouldn't be after making *you* out a flat!"

Miss Mannering was not so easily misled. "Balderdash!" said she. "You and Johann pinched that baby from someone. I very strongly suspect that filching babies is a hanging offense."

Athalia, who suspected similarly, disavowed all knowledge of the baby's origin. Johann, she proclaimed, had grown very enterprising—in her opinion, daftly so—of late. Were she to tell them of his latest undertaking, Miss Mannering would be positively horrified. And speaking of pinching babies, Athalia suspected Miss Mannering was not entirely blameless in that line, in which case Miss Mannering should contemplate the possibility of having her own neck stretched. "Not that I'll run rusty," she added hastily, as the lieutenant took a furious step forward and Caliban's bark took on a menacing note. "It's no bread-and-butter of mine!"

"No?" By threats of hanging, Delilah was not swayed. "I should think, considering you are his accomplice, that Johann's enterprises should be very much your concern. Don't try again to throw me off the scent! You must know *something* about the baby. You had better tell me, Athalia, because if you do not, I shall turn you over to the nearest magistrate!"

In Athalia's opinion, Delilah would not dare, being herself not above reproach. Delilah was very interested in that baby, which led Athalia to conclude that Delilah had been responsible for its disappearance from Johann's wagon. What Delilah wanted with a baby Athalia could not imagine, but she wished Delilah joy of it. Miss Mannering was in need of good wishes, though she could not know it yet. Athalia figured Miss Mannering would discover the enormity of her meddling soon enough. Athalia additionally figured that she'd best be clear of Brighton when the truth came out.

With that decision in mind, she sought to delay the dé-nouement as long as possible. She disclaimed all knowledge of the identity of the child, vowed that Johann had only told her it was some great lady's illegitimate offspring, put out to a female with a large number of offspring of her own. "He reckoned the lady'd pay him well for the return of the brat," she concluded, and shrugged. "But you pinched it before Johann had a chance to put his plan into effect. He was in the devil of a temper. You'd best steer clear of Johann, *leicheen*."

"Rather," murmured Delilah, "I think I should have a serious talk with him, if I am ever to learn who Toby's parents are. Poor thing, to be put out to pasture like an old horse! But that's neither here nor there! Tell me the nature of Johann's latest enterprise."

At that, Athalia balked. Eager as she was to cooperate with Miss Mannering, she averred, she dared not get on the wrong side of Johann. Already he was gravely out of temper with her, due to the disappearance of the babe, for which she had been unjustly blamed. Lest Delilah doubt the severity of Johann's displeasure, Athalia displayed several bruises. "Damned near did for me!" she added, soulfully. "Never was I so mistook in a man! But I've made my bed and now I must sleep in it—of course, it'd be different if I had a *choice*."

"One always has a choice," Delilah responded severely. "If you don't wish to stay with Johann—and it is inconceivable to me why anyone should wish to stay with a perfect block like Johann!—you may simply leave. I contrived to do so, did I not? I would not have thought you so lacking in courage."

"Damn your eyes!" cried Athalia. This remark was adressed not to Miss Mannering but to Miss Mannering's hound, who

184

had leaped up, paws on Athalia's shoulders, to lick at her face. She shoved the dog away. Caliban was not so easily dissuaded from friendly exuberances. An energetic tussle ensued.

Though Neal was positively enthralled by these proceedings, and Delilah's skilled handling thereof, the proceedings saw them little advanced. Toby's parentage remained a mystery; Sandor still had to be found. Therefore Neal suggested that in exchange for Athalia's cooperation she might be rewarded with sufficient money to remove herself out of the range of Johann's wrath.

"You shouldn't," Delilah said repressively, "encourage her! But I see time is of the essence, and so it will have to do. Athalia, if you tell us what you know, this nice gentleman will give you some money, and I will give you back my mother's wedding ring."

Athalia was agreeable. "I'll talk!" she gasped. "Call off your hound!"

Delilah did so, then dangled the wedding ring in front of Athalia's nose. "It will be yours to keep this time, I swear. And now, if you please? I will make it easier for you! I have a very strong hunch that Johann is involved in the disappearance of the duke of Knowles."

"Damned if you *aren't* a rum one!" Athalia snatched the ring. "It's right you are, lass; Johann means to hold him for ransom. I told him it was a cursed paperskulled idea, but he's set on getting hold of some rhino."

"Paperskulled!" responded Delilah, in amazement. "I should think it is! The duke's family is more likely to pay Johann for *keeping* him! Anyway, the duke is of so vicious a temper that he is like to cut up *very* stiff! If Johann values his skin, he'll let the duke go."

Athalia chuckled, evilly. "That one won't be cutting up stiff for a while! Stretched out stiff as a corpse he is, on the wagon floor!"

"Aha!" said Delilah, triumphantly. "So *that's* where Johann has taken him!" Neal, observing Athalia's expression, guessed that she had not intended to let the cat so far out of the bag. He extended a handful of coins, without comment.

"Miss Delilah! Master Neal!" came a harried, breathless

voice. Jem ran panting up to them. "I've been looking every where! If not for the barking of the hound, I'd still be looking Miss Sibyl is very anxious to know what you've found out!'

Succinctly, Delilah informed Jem of their discoveries Caliban, weary of teasing Athalia, turned his attention or the newcomer and washed the footman's face. Athalia, no longer the center of attention, took immediate advantage of her opportunity and slipped down the alleyway. In a very short time she had shown the town of Brighton a singularly dirty pair of heels.

Meanwhile, Jem was rendered corpse-white by the intelli gence that his employer was being held to ransom, a devel opment for which he feared his employer would hold him to blame. "And so," Delilah concluded, "matters draw rapidly to a crisis! Here is what we must do. You will take Caliban back to the house, Jem, and inform Binnie of what's transpired Neal and I will go and rescue the duke."

"We will?" inquired Neal, stunned. "Don't you think the matter might be better dealt with by the proper authorities?"'

"Piffle!" Delilah retorted. "The odds are in our favor. You and I together are more than a match for a clodpole like Johann." Neal did not look convinced. "What would the duke say, do you think, if all Brighton learned he had been kid napped by a tinker? It could not help but come out. The duke would be a laughingstock."

This argument, though not in the manner Delilah had intended, weighed strongly with Neal. He did not mind if a man whose gizzard he wished strongly to slit should become the object of rumor and speculation; but he minded very much that the lady whom he revered above all others should be prey to scandalous on-dits. Johann, brought to the attention of the authorities, was not likely to remain silent on the subject of Delilah's sojourn in his camp; the authorities, made a present of such a titillating tidbit, were unlikely to keep it to themselves. Next they might expect to see blazoned in the newspapers Delilah's entire history.

He must do his best to prevent that, no matter how reluctant his best might be. Delilah was regarding him hopefully. Neal forced a smile and for good measure tweaked her nose. "Why do we tarry here? Sandor awaits!" he said, a halfhearted hero indeed.

CHAPTER TWENTY-TWO

Jem hurried back, as instructed, to the duke's bow-fronted house on the Royal Crescent, there to inform Miss Baskerville of the startling information brought to light by her protégée. He could not guess how Miss Baskerville would react, and thought perhaps he might have to deal with an hysterical female. As matters evolved, Jem was not reduced to such straits, at least not just then: Miss Baskerville believed not a word of his breathless account. She did not accuse Jem of spinning tarradiddles, merely of allowing himself to be gulled by an unconscionable humbugger. Then she left him to preside over the nursery while she put in a belated appearance in the morning room, where callers awaited. She did not sally forth, thought Jem, with any appreciable enthusiasm. Poor Jem was in a cleft stick. He could not leave Toby unattended, either to try further to persuade Miss Baskerville that a very real danger threatened the duke, or to set out himself as a backup force. Nor could he sit idly by while his idol walked boldly into the lion's den. He regarded Toby, engaged in decapitating stuffed rabbit, and cursed in a manner strongly reminiscent of Miss Mannering.

As did Binnie, though not aloud, when she walked into the morning room. Awaiting her there were the man whom she had agreed to marry and Miss Choice-Pickerell.

"God bless my soul!" said Edwina, who had been trying without great success to entertain the callers. "Wherever have you been? Miss Choice-Pickerell and Mr. Dennison have been waiting for you this age!"

187

"I'm sorry." Binnie sank down upon a striped silk sofa and smiled weakly at Mark. "I came immediately I had word."

In the opinion of Mr. Dennison, the onetime charmer of his heart and soul would have been better advised to take sufficient time to tidy herself first. Binnie wore a simple dress of white muslin, creased and stained; her hair was in a tangle; there were exhausted shadows beneath her eyes. He could not help but remark the difference between Binnie and Miss Choice-Pickerell—elegant in a pristine Spanish pelisse of shot sarcenet trimmed with Egyptian crape and antique cuffs trimmed with Chinese binding, lemon-colored kid gloves and slippers—to Binnie's discredit. "My dear," he murmured, "you are looking shockingly worn-down. How came you to allow yourself to be reduced to such a state?"

Quite naturally, this patent lack of appreciation roused no animation in Miss Baskerville. Still, she owed Mark some explanation for her seeming neglect of himself, and she had fallen into the habit of confiding in him. She cast a cautious glance at Miss Choice-Pickerell, deep in conversation with Edwina. "It is a long story. Suffice it to say that Sandor has accused me of being a marvel of indiscretion, of perseverance in loose morality."

This information affected Mark most extremely: he started, then stared, then laughed outright. "Loose morality? You? Come now, Binnie—you can't have taken him seriously."

Oddly, this skeptical reaction caused Binnie to feel wholly out of charity with her most persistent suitor, who apparently considered her totally unfit to be a ladybird, and much more charitable toward the outspoken duke, who despite his myriad sins at least had sufficient good taste to find her desirable. "I bid him," she said gloomily, "go and be damned. Not that I suppose it will answer the purpose. Things have come to a pretty pass! To think that I once fancied myself *smitten* with the brute!"

By this absentminded statement, Mark was rendered considerably less amused. *Sandor* had been the object of Binnie's long-ago infatuation? He supposed he should have guessed as much. Because he had not, he felt very much a fool. "You might have told me," he said irritably.

"Told you what? Oh!" Binnie tried very hard to concentrate her mind. Could Jem's wild tale be true? Was Sandor being held to ransom? If so, what was she to do? "To own the truth, I thought you'd guessed."

Mark wondered if this omission was sufficient grounds on which to honorably break off his betrothal, and decided it was not. "There is something *you* should know, Binnie," he said quietly. "I made discreet inquiries—you were wrong about Sandor. He has not been trifling with your brother's inheritance, but on your brother's behalf investing in the 'Change. And to very good effect, I might add! By the time Neal comes of age, he will be in a position to command every luxury."

"You mean—" Binnie gasped.

"I mean," Mark retorted sternly, "that Sandor is *not* a Monster of Depravity. I don't know why I ever allowed you to convince me that he *was*. You owe your cousin an apology, Binnie."

So she did, any number of them. Binnie felt as though she was being buffeted by a series of ill winds. Shamed, she recalled her hateful accusations, in which it now appeared there had not been a single word of truth. Scant wonder Sandor had stormed out of the house! Apologize she must and would, and the sooner the better—but what if Sandor refused to listen? What if the evil Johann disposed of Sandor before Binnie had the chance to render her apology? She could only pray Neal and Delilah reached the duke in time. But Neal still labored under the delusions from which she had just been freed. "Gracious God!" she wailed. "Neal will *murder* him!"

"Angels defend us!" uttered Edwina, thus interrupted in mid-speech. *"Murder?"*

By this further evidence of the Baskerville lack of stability, Miss Choice-Pickerell was depressed. She inquired who it was that Neal would murder. More to the point, she inquired her fiancé's whereabouts.

"It was only a matter of speaking," said Binnie, in a desperate attempt to remove her foot from her mouth. "I did not mean that Neal would actually commit murder, merely that he is incensed. Oh, it would take too long to explain! As to where he is, I'm not sure exactly—with Delilah somewhere."

"I see!" said Miss Choice-Pickerell, rather awfully.

Hastily, before Miss Choice-Pickerell could make public the precise nature of what she saw, which clearly was sufficiently annoying to provoke a saint, Edwina put forth a conversational gambit. Since this concerned the notorious Harriette Wilson—whose partiality to the military, especially the Tenth, took such diverse forms as riding habits daringly modeled on the Hussar uniform, and riding lessons provided by the officers; and who was frequently invited to dine in the mess rooms, and had been recently ordered off the parade grounds for flirting so indelicately that she'd occupied the attention of the entire regiment—by it Cressida's agitation was not soothed.

Binnie, relieved to escape further explanations, paid scant heed to Miss Choice-Pickerell. Her thoughts were frantic. Should she send Jem after Neal, to prevent him doing Sandor bodily injury? But in that case, what was to be done with Toby? She could not leave the child alone in the nursery, and she was too overwrought to attend to him herself. And *who* did Toby resemble? On that very perplexing question, she could not concentrate. Sandor wholly occupied her thoughts.

"You cannot have meant that," said Mark, not for the first time. "Your brother surely doesn't mean Sandor harm. I fear, Binnie, that you tend to exaggerate."

Miss Baskerville was in no frame of mind to tolerate a discussion of her less admirable traits. "So I do not!" she snapped. "As I recall, Neal expressed a wish to carve out Sandor's gizzard. Nor do I blame him; I wished to see Sandor boiled in oil myself! And you needn't give me a rake-down, Mark. Am I privileged to see Sandor again alive, I intend to atône most handsomely."

Mark was so little enjoying converse with the lady to whom he was betrothed that he searched even more frantically for some reason why the betrothal should be broken off. "I don't know where you learned your fantastic notions. Sandor dead—inconceivable!"

"To you, perhaps, but you do not know the whole." Nor did Binnie intend to acquaint him with it. She studied him. A man of dignified appearance, reserved in his deportment—knowledge of her difficulties would deprive him of consciousness. It would also inspire him, once recovered from his consternation, to moralize over her. Mortifying to realize she'd agreed to marry Mark only to resolve her problems—problems, she now suspected, against which he wouldn't have

190

aised a hand. And then she realized that those previous
roblems had been no more than the result of a fevered
magination. In attempting to deal with chimeras, she had
rought herself to point nonplus. She had pledged herself to
man she didn't love in order to escape a man she thought
he loathed—only she did not loathe Sandor and now, en-
aged in conversation with Mark, could think of nothing
han that the duke might be at death's door.

In the doorway of the morning room appeared a footman,
earing before him a missive on a silver tray. Binnie, in
nxious expectation of more news, leapt to her feet. She
erused the note, which was both filthy and nigh unintelligible.
Delilah was exonerated of falsehood; this was a ransom
lemand. Binnie blanched.

"Merciful powers!" cried Edwina, fluttering her hands.
"What's amiss? Sibyl, *not* Delilah? She can't be in trouble
again!"

Of this opening, Cressida made good use. "You have my
deepest sympathy, Miss Childe! I am not one to put myself
orward, but I do not scruple to say that the girl's conduct has
een abominable. I never can look at her without shuddering
o think that she may at any moment make a byword of
herself."

This observation may not have been without foundation,
ut Binnie could not let it pass unchallenged. Cressida grated
ike chalk against slate on her shattered nerves. "I would not
like to accuse you of impertinence, Miss Choice-Pickerell, but
I shall have to do so if you continue in this vein. As I have
said before, Miss Mannering's conduct is none of your concern."

Cressida also labored under strain, and she deemed it time
that her future sister-in-law be put firmly in her place. "And
I would not wish to accuse *you* of highty-tighty behavior,
Miss Baskerville! I hope that I am not *priggish*, but anyone
with a grain of proper feeling must deplore Miss Mannering's
fits and starts."

Clutching her dirty *billet-doux,* Binnie paced the carpet.
Somehow she must lend her assistance to securing Sandor's
release. At least, if held to ransom, the duke must be alive.
She could only hope he didn't goad Johann to murder him
before help arrived.

Mark decided that Miss Baskerville was acting very

strangely. Perhaps she was unaware that her own conduct must appear graceless. Since he was betrothed, albeit reluctantly, to the lady who was cutting so ill-behaved a figure, he might as well make use of his authority.

Miss Baskerville, informed that by subjecting so high-minded a lady as Miss Choice-Pickerell to a scolding she had performed a disservice that was iniquitous, paused in her pacing to stare. "Miss Choice-Pickerell's comments are not without foundation," Mark added. "She is acquainted with the whole."

Since Binnie had been thinking of Sandor stretched out stiff as a corpse, a description presented her verbatim by Jem, a contingency once ardently desired and now ardently abhorred; and alternately of Toby's puzzling parentage, she was briefly at a loss. "The whole of what?" said she.

"The whole history of Miss Mannering," Cressida responded triumphantly. "I know that the duke brought her here from a tinkers' camp. Outrageous! Abominable!"

Amazing, how this new disaster concentrated Binnie's mind. She looked first at Edwina, whose extreme pallor and frantic recourse to her vinaigrette made it obvious that Cressida's knowledge had come as a grave blow. Then she looked at Mark.

He did not care for the expression on Binnie's face, which suggested he was a viper that she wished to crush underfoot. "Miss Choice-Pickerell had every right to know," he said sternly. "I beg that you will not make a scene."

Beg, would he? Well he might! "Is Neal aware of your enlightenment?" Binnie inquired of Miss Choice-Pickerell.

Rather relieved by this reasonable query, which she interpreted as an indication that Miss Baskerville would as requested refrain from flying into a pelter, Cressida saw no reason to withhold response. "Naturally I acquainted him with my knowledge," she said primly. "There should be no secrets between husband and wife."

Came a brief silence, during which Binnie's expression grew even more murderous, and her golden eyes flashed. Edwina knew that expression, which on its rare appearances was usually directed at the duke. She knew, too, the futility of interference. Therefore, she closed her eyes and prayed.

But Mark was not similarly well acquainted with the moods

192

f his future wife, and consequently made a grave misstep: he ead her a gentle scold. For the disservice done Miss Choice-Pickerell, who had as always acted with a fine regard for propriety, he required that Binnie render apology.

Binnie turned her amber eyes on him. Sternly, Mark met er gaze. Her lips parted. He continued to frown, thusly ndicating that he would not relent until gifted with the requisite apology.

"Propriety," uttered Miss Baskerville wrathfully, "be damned! Likewise, apologies! It is you who should apologize to Delilah, for being a prattle-box! As well as to myself, for telling me to mend my tongue regarding a scheming, heart-less wench! Oh, certainly Miss Choice-Pickerell is a pattern card of respectability! She is insipid, humdrum, prosy, and mealymouthed; her conversation is flat as a street pavement! She possesses all the virtues, in fact." Here Cressida gasped, Edwina groaned, and Mark uttered angry protest.

But Binnie was not to be denied having her say. She glared at Miss Choice-Pickerell so fearsomely that the lady quailed. 'She is also common to the core, of which you would be aware, were you not such a slow-top, Mark. Shall I tell you what use she has made of your confidences concerning Delilah? It's plain as the nose on your face! Your so-proper Cressida was afraid that Delilah would steal a march on her—which in point of fact Delilah has!—and used your confidence to throw a rub in Delilah's way. In short, I'll wager anything you wish that Cressida has threatened Neal with Delilah's exposure. Which is utter nonsense because Delilah has done nothing wrong—but Neal, being head over heels in love with her, would have no choice but to knuckle down."

Mark, engaged in comforting Miss Choice-Pickerell, who had with these vile accusations turned chalk-white, had been for some time trying to get a word in edgewise. At this point he did so, several of them, and all uniformly unappreciative.

Binnie was beyond remorse. In fact, Binnie was feeling rather pleased with herself for having finally taken a step that, however rag-mannered, was constructive. "Inexcusable, am I?" she interrupted. "That settles it: I am quite decided *not* to marry you. I beg you will release me from a betrothal that was patent folly on both our parts."

"So it was!" snapped Mark, so seriously angry with Binnie

193

for abusing Cressida that he failed to feel relief. "I release you with the greatest pleasure on earth, ma'am!"

Binnie cast a contemplative glance at Cressida, but could not determine if Miss Choice-Pickerell had understood the point of this object lesson—to wit, the ease with which betrothals could be brought to an end. In case Cressida had not, Binnie determined to underscore the moral of the thing. She stalked across the room, paused dramatically at the door. "I will leave you to console Miss Choice-Pickerell, since your thoughts accord so well. Time will prove which of us is correct, will it not? If Miss Choice-Pickerell is the proper-thinking lady that you believe her, she cannot but declare off from a marriage to a man who loves someone else." On that killing sally, she sped through the door.

She sped also up the stairs, pausing only to enter the duke's bedchamber and rifle through his dresser drawers before she entered the nursery. Having taken one positive action, with what she fancied would be very happy results, she was eager to accomplish more. To that end, she demanded to know of Jem the exact whereabouts of Johann's caravan.

Jem could not but tell her, though he wondered if he should: Binnie was looking very wild-eyed. Also, she was clutching a pistol. As he was winding up his explanation, Edwina burst into the room. She stared blankly at Binnie, who held a pistol in one hand and with the other had scooped up Toby, who contentedly straddled her hip. A *baby?* Surely Binnie could not have— Did she mean to— So *this* was why Binnie detested Sandor, and Neal meant to murder him! Edwina swooned.

Binnie had no time to waste on hysterical females; and it was certain that Edwina would indulge in awesome hysterics as soon as she revived. Callously, Binnie instructed Jem to deal with the unconscious woman. And then, with the pistol in her hand and Toby on her hip and Caliban panting at her heels, Binnie set out to accomplish a rescue.

CHAPTER TWENTY-THREE

That Miss Baskerville had indeed been prompted to desperate action, though not the action he had anticipated and
not for the reasons he foresaw, might have relieved Sandor,
had he known, which alas he did not. The duke was in the
foulest temper possible for him which, in light of the fact that
His Grace's usual temper was far from sanguine, was nothing
short of demoniac. He was uncomfortable and hungry, infu-
riated by his captivity, and thoroughly inimicable toward the
instigator of these misfortunes.

"The Nubbing Cheat!" he said, with relish. "It's all you can
hope for if you persist in this insanity. You'll dance the
sheriff's waltz. Perhaps you don't realize how long it takes a
man to die by hanging? Sometimes the body jerks and twitches
for as much as an hour."

As becomes evident, the duke was not conducting himself
like a model prisoner. Johann's direst threats aroused only
his scorn; Johann's graphic descriptions of what fate awaited
were the ransom to be unpaid gained only a caustic rejoinder
concerning Johann's mental faculties, which the duke apparently held in very low esteem. "The devil, man!" he said
now. "Give it up! You have bungled the thing completely.
Release me and I'll see you come to no harm."

But Johann was possessed of an admirable tenacity. He did
not intend to let so plump a pigeon out of his snare. "I knew
you was a knaggy gager as soon as I laid eyes on you!" he
continued. "A right peevy cove! But it's no use trying to
hoodwink *me*, guv'nor. If I let you go you'd see me in Rumbo
quick as a greased pig."

The duke attempted to shift positions, and failed. Johann had removed the filthy gag from his mouth, but the duke's extremities remained tightly bound. Sandor wondered if he would ever regain feeling in his limbs. Too, he wondered if it mattered, since the tinker obviously planned some unpleasant fate for him.

"Have it your way, then!" he responded, with fine indifference. "I needn't tell *you* about the horrors of prison life. Perhaps you won't mind jail fever or starvation rations or being nibbled by rats. Assaulting a peer, holding him for ransom—you cannot hope to escape being taken for a capital offense."

Johann's patience, with this nasty suggestion that he might straightaway be nicked by hornies, wore thin. He was at a loss as to how to deal with a prisoner so uncooperative. Lest the duke realize his uncertainty and use it to advantage, Johann brandished his knife. He put forth the suggestion that the duke should close his trap lest his throat be slit open without further ado.

"Very well!" responded Sandor. "You can't say you weren't warned."

The tinker may not have possessed any marked degree of native wit, but he had come to realize, somewhat tardily, that he was in a bit of a pickle. He should not, he decided, have allowed the duke to learn the identity of his kidnapper. Johann did not wish to commit murder, but now he saw no other means by which to avoid the duke's vengeance. Even Johann was not sufficiently caper-witted to think that the duke, released from captivity, would fail to move heaven and earth to achieve revenge. Perhaps Athalia might put forth some solution to this problem. In line with that, where *was* Athalia? She should have returned to the wagon some time ago. Had she been taken up by constables? Run rusty, hopped the twig? Johann suffered a distinct twinge of alarm.

"Mayhap, guv'nor," he ventured, "we might strike a bargain. I'm not wishful of doing you any harm, only to get my dabbers onto some rhino. You understand! Once the ransom's paid, I'll set you free and we'll forget all about this. No harm done, eh?"

The duke understood, perfectly, that the fox was on the run. Briefly, he contemplated the inevitable uproar in his

196

household when Johann's note—composed with much labor and knuckle-chewing, assisted by various unhelpful suggestions from the duke himself—arrived. Would Binnie, faced with the prospect of his imminent demise, regret her unkind words, admit the nature of her sentiments for him? Or would she, as was much more probable, greet with delight so effective a means by which to remove a thorn from her flesh? Sternly disallowing himself further reflection on that flesh, of so lovely a complexion and so pleasingly packaged, Sandor hoped he might live to find out.

"No bargains!" said he. "Release me and I'll press no charges against you, but I won't be bled one farthing."

Johann considered this a very selfish attitude, especially from a man as rich as Croesus. He thought the gentleman so plump in the pocket could be a bit more generous toward a man whose pockets were perennially to let. All he wished, he stated, was the means by which to be beforehand with the world. It was very uncharitable of the duke, he added, as he strode indignantly toward the door, to be trying to sconce the reckoning. He could only conclude that the duke was a nipfarthing.

"Oh, he is!" came a cheerful voice, as Delilah appeared in the doorway. "But we cannot blame him too much for cheeseparing, because he is all to pieces! That's what I've come to tell you, Johann: the duke of Knowles hasn't a feather to fly with. He is extravagant and undisciplined, a spendthrift and something of a rogue—in short, he's whistled his entire fortune down the wind. There will be no ransom paid; you will have to let him go. What are you doing, you ninnyhammer? Release me immediately!"

That Johann had no intention of so doing, he made quickly clear, not only to Miss Mannering but to Lieutenant Baskerville, who had rushed into the wagon to find Delilah being held at knife-point. His Grace, meanwhile, settled back to watch the proceedings with a distinctly sardonic air. Even more sardonically, he murmured his appreciation of so splendidly executed a rescue.

"Oh, do hush!" snapped Delilah, who was struggling manfully, if to little avail, with Johann, and wishing fervently for a frying pan. "Johann, you are a nodcock! A gapeseed! A clodpole! *Now* what hubble-bubble notion have you taken in your brain?"

197

As Johann disposed of these two additional fish who ha[d] floundered into his net—a disposal accomplished not withou[t] difficulty, Miss Mannering being prompted to energetic protes[t] every inch of the way, and the lieutenant being rendered very reckless by the sight of a tinker laying violent hands or Miss Mannering—he explained. Miss Mannering's assertions that the duke lacked a fortune, he regarded as a prope[r] take-in. However, were it true, Miss Mannering's own fortune remained intact. Johann had evolved the nacky notion o[f] holding Miss Mannering to ransom, along with her guardian.

The duke inquired of whom Johann meant to extract that ransom, since the person enabled to pay it—himself—was likewise in captivity; Neal offered to draw the tinker's claret, could he but get his hands free; Delilah cursed like an entire regiment of troopers, which rendered everyone else silent with shock, including Johann. With a hint of admiration, he informed her that young ladies shouldn't say such things. Then he added that he wasn't to be diddled by a slyboots.

"Fiddle-faddle!" responded Delilah, impatiently. "You are a cabbagehead! Only a cabbagehead would go about kidnapping babies and dukes! Don't deny you meant to hold poor Toby to ransom also—Athalia has already told us you wished to extort money from his mother for her return. That was very poorly done of you, Johann! Even if she had put him out to pasture like an old horse—which does not at all suit *my* notion of conduct fitting to highborn ladies, but clearly I do not fully comprehend the ways of the polite world!—she cannot help but be concerned for him."

Miss Mannering's audience was affected strongly by these remarks. While Lieutenant Baskerville admired her bold courage, Johann was chopfallen to learn Miss Mannering had held converse with Athalia; and Sandor was positively flabbergasted by the references to Toby. "Good God!" he said.

"It is enough," muttered Delilah, "to send one off in an apoplexy! And *that* would serve you right, Johann, because you can hardly ransom a corpse!"

That much, Johann understood. He begged that Miss Mannering would not fidget herself. All would work out for the best, she need just wait and see.

"Of course it will—it generally *does*—but if it doesn't you will be to blame!" Delilah scowled so dreadfully that her

yebrows met above her freckled nose. "And I shall make as
reat a piece of work of it as I wish. Oh, go away, you
udding-heart! You make me cross as crabs."

To this request, Johann proved obedient—not in an effort
o placate the tempersome Miss Mannering, but because he
eeded time in which to contemplate these new developments.
ohann's processes of thought, which at the best of times
round slow as the mills of God, were not hastened by verbal
buse. Athalia had tipped the wink to Delilah? Doubtless she
vas halfway to London by now. Strongly, Johann was tempted
o follow suit.

Yet he could not abandon all hope of gaining a fortune so
asily. It was a dreadful coil. Perhaps Delilah had been cor-
ect in suggesting that he wasn't a downy one, unkind as it
vas of her to speak so beggarly.

And perhaps, which was more likely, she'd been pitching
im gammon once again. Never had Johann known so young
a lady with so large a deviousness of mind. In that case, the
ntimation that the duke's fortune had been frittered away
night also be a hoax. Viciously, Johann kicked at a wagon
wheel. It was enough to make a man's head spin.

Neal's head was spinning also, as a result of the wagon's
tench. Silently he watched Delilah inch across the floor
ntil she reached a position halfway between Sandor and
im. Sandor did not seem appreciably disturbed by the grave
langer that loomed over them. Unless Neal's vision failed,
Sandor was actually smiling. Did he not comprehend that
hey might all momentarily have their throats slit? Neal did
ot mind that Sandor's neck should be cut; and for himself it
would be a fate preferable to marriage with Miss Choice-
Pickerell. On behalf of Delilah, however, he mourned so
premature an end.

"So that's why," he said bitterly, "you've kept me without
money for common necessaries. You haven't sixpence to scratch
with yourself! Not that I'm surprised—I suspected as much!
It is just the sort of thing that is typical of you. Binnie was
right to call you a Monster of Depravity!"

"Did she?" Even with his dark dress coat and black florentine
silk breeches in deplorable disarray, Lord Knowles retained
his dignity. "Ah, yes, I believe she mentioned something
of the sort. Amazing, the opinion formed of me by the

pair of you. I begin to wonder if I have given you basis.

Neal squirmed violently, trying to rid himself of the tight ropes in which he'd been trussed, rather like a butterfl cocooned. "By God, if I hadn't promised Binnie—and if I coul get my hands free!—I vow I *would* murder you!"

"What's this?" The duke quirked a brow. "Your siste *doesn't* wish me murdered? You surprise me."

"I shouldn't!" snapped Neal. "She only told me not to be cause she wanted to do it herself! And when she finds out tha you've spent all my money, I daresay she'll be *happy* if I carv out your gizzard! And even if she *doesn't* wish it, I mean to d it anyway!" Having run out of threats, he glared.

Delilah had listened contemplatively to this tirade. Sinc Johann had surely heard enough to convince him that she' spoken the truth about the duke's financial affairs, sh interrupted the hostilities. "Johann will hang, I expect! Goo riddance, *I* say!" she uttered briskly; and then, in a lowe voice, "Neal, this is the height of ingratitude. It was all hum."

"*What* was?" The lieutenant looked blank. Of all people, h would not have expected Delilah to take him to task.

"Lower your voice!" she hissed, with a meaningful glanc at the door. "Do you want Johann to hear? Well, Your Grace you do not look too terribly misused, though very much th worse for wear! We have been looking all over Brighton fo you. Binnie is *very* concerned for your welfare."

Neal understood why Delilah was being so kind to th duke—obviously she still meant to marry him—but if Delilal still coveted the duke's fortune, then a fortune the duke mus still retain. "Wait! Do you mean Sandor *hasn't*—"

"Of course not!" Delilah shot another glance at the door "Or I don't think he has. *Have* you, sir?"

"Of course not!" Sandor's sense of humor was acquiring rapidly broadening horizons. "Why should I?"

"That is an excellent question," approved Delilah, "anc one for which I had no answer, which is why I decided you had not." She contemplated Neal, who looked very uncomfort able. "But that is fair and far off!"

"So it is," agreed the duke. "Having expended such efforts to find me, now what do you plan? Though I hesitate to poin this out, the omens are not encouraging."

"Nonsense!" retorted Miss Mannering. "I would not have thought you one to easily cry quits. We need only to be patient; something will occur to me. And even if it doesn't, we need not despair. I daresay Binnie will send help when Jem tells her what we learned."

The duke's sense of humor may have been growing by leaps and bounds, but with this intelligence it received an abrupt check. Binnie, in receipt of information from Delilah—and well he remembered the dramatic style of messages fashioned by Miss Mannering—as well as Johann's ransom note? Miss Prunes and Prisms would be wholly overset. Without the slightest hesitation, he aired his displeasure.

Though Miss Mannering was not abashed by this tongue-lashing, indeed endured it with an expression of extreme interest, Neal was considerably less self-possessed. The information that Sandor was not fleecing him had not inspired him with any greater fondness for his cousin. "If that's the way you talk to Binnie," said Delilah, as Neal drew breath to utter a tongue-lashing of his own, "it's not at all surprising that she should think you don't like her above half. I would've thought *you* better versed in the way of women, Duke!"

Diverted, Sandor confessed that in regard to Miss Baskerville, he had behaved with less than his usual sangfroid. However, as he pointed out, Miss Baskerville was not in the ordinary way. And why, he begged to be informed, had Delilah sent word to Binnie instead of to the authorities?

"It was a mistake," Delilah admitted handsomely. "I have been making a great number of mistakes of late! I would weep with pure vexation, were I of a melting mood! Fortunately I am not, because weeping does not accomplish much. And anyway I am not to be entirely blamed, because so many people have had irons in the fire. I may be an unconscionable little liar, and always getting into scrapes, but never before have I stirred up such a hornets' nest. Oh, the authorities! I did not think you would wish a public washing of your dirty linen, sir!"

"The devil!" said the duke. "I would much more prefer a scandal to being held to ransom, my girl!"

"Oh," responded Delilah, subdued.

For Neal, his cousin's ingratitude was the last straw. That Sandor should behave so callously toward the young lady who for some inconceivable reason wished to marry him was the outside of enough. So he stated. As a result of that blunt statement, he received a blank look. "Marry *me?*" echoed Sandor.

Delilah sighed heavily. "I suppose I had better lay my cards on the table, though the time is not propitious! That is the trouble with playing for high stakes; one cannot but trust to the luck of the draw. And all too often one draws a deuce, when one is wishing for an ace!" Mournfully, she regarded Neal. "I have deceived you. At least, I have allowed you to be deceived, which comes out to the same thing."

Miss Mannering's unhappy little face, which had turned bright pink, her shamed and soulful manner, tugged at Neal's heartstrings. "Never mind, puss!" he said gruffly. "I've already guessed."

"Guessed what?" inquired the duke, intrigued.

"I think, sir, that Neal has guessed I am an adventuress." Delilah regarded her bound wrists. "Which is not an unreasonable conclusion. He has also guessed that I am on the lookout for a fortune, having no real claim on that of the Mannerings."

"An impostor! Why didn't I think of that?" For a gentleman hungry and tired and lacking sensation in his extremities, the duke was enjoying himself inordinately. "Probably because you're the spitting image of your father! Do continue!"

"You're *not* an adventuress?" Neal asked. "But you said—"

"I say," Delilah responded sadly, "a great deal of flummery! Anyway, Neal decided that I'd taken a marked fancy to your fortune, Sir; and also that you fancied my fortune to an alarming degree. It has had him in quite a pelter, because he's convinced we shouldn't *suit.*"

"So we shouldn't!" agreed the duke.

"But you said," Neal persisted in his struggle toward enlightenment. "that you wished to form an eligible connection."

"I did. And I do!" There was nothing for it, decided Delilah, but to confess the whole, even if that confession was a trifle premature. "It has been deuced difficult, too! In ordinary circumstances I should have simply swept the gentleman off his feet, but it is much more difficult to fix one's interest with a gentleman who is otherwise bespoken, because he is too honorable by half and therefore not even aware that one is laying siege!"

To this tender declaration, the lieutenant responded with utter bewilderment. Delilah was in love with a man promised to another? Well he understood her predicament, poor girl! The duke, rather more perspicacious, gazed upon Delilah's rosy cheeks and Neal's stricken expression, and succumbed to a paroxysm of mirth.

Neal ignored his cousin's outburst. "Poor puss!" he said gently, then expressed a curiosity concerning the identity of the gentleman so thickskulled as to fail to realize he held the admiration of the most divine young lady ever to set foot on an unworthy earth.

"Why, Neal!" Delilah raised her huge brown eyes to his somber face. "Do you *still* not realize?"

How could he? She had said nothing that gave him a clue to the lucky man's identity. He begged she be more specific.

How the deuce, wondered Delilah, should a young lady properly conduct herself in a situation like this? She would not wish the lieutenant to think her bold as a brass-faced monkey, or a pushing sort. "I cannot!" she lamented. "Modesty forbids me. The devil, Neal! It's clear as noonday."

The lieutenant was growing very frustrated by being denied the identity of his rival—not that he could ever honorably enter the lists. Irritably, he requested that Miss Mannering cease being missish. If she did not mean to name the possessor of her affections, he averred, she should never have introduced the subject.

"Missish!" echoed Delilah, incensed.

Sandor, lest he expire of a fatal paroxysm of mirth, could listen to no more. "Young cawker!" he uttered, between guffaws. "The lady is speaking of yourself."

CHAPTER TWENTY-FOUR

With breathless stealth, Binnie approached the caravan. Toby, who'd fallen asleep on her hip, had grown remarkably heavy for so young a child; Caliban, restrained by a hastily fashioned leash, required considerable energy to curtail his exuberance. Definitely, Binnie was in need of several more hands. She wondered if, in rushing off *ventre à terre* to the rescue, she had perhaps not rushed her own fences.

No matter, the thing was done. She could but put forth her best efforts and pray for success. Thusly ruminating, she crept closer.

Irritable voices came to her, engaged in argument. Actually, Binnie had become aware of those voices some time previous, but had been unable to gauge the source of disagreement. The voices sounded familiar; she paused. Frowning, she strained to hear.

Surely that could only be Neal, simultaneously making a confession of his sentiments and spouting a great deal of nonsense about unrequited love. Unrequited? Binnie listened even more carefully. Her brother, it appeared, momentarily anticipated his deathblow. He did not wish to shuffle off this mortal coil without making Miss Mannering aware that he was unalterably devoted to her. However, Miss Mannering was not to consider this declaration as particularly encouraging. Neal was promised to another. He begged that Miss Mannering would not wear the willow for him, or sink into a decline.

Miss Mannering's response to this loverlike speech was

exactly what might have been expected from that intrepid damsel. "Flimflam!" she cried. "Johann has had a very bad influence because now *you* are talking like a nodcock! First you profess to be my very ardent admirer, and next you suggest that I should be trained in a school of sorrow. It makes me cross as a cat! You must have windmills in your head."

Binnie felt as though she might suffer a similar affliction. She had rushed boldly to the rescue, only to break in on a singularly bird-witted lovers' quarrel? Could that be Sandor *laughing* in the background? She hitched Toby further up on her hip and peered cautiously around the corner of the caravan. In so doing, she came face to face with Johann.

Came for them both a moment of stunned immobility. Johann, who after prolonged reflection had concluded that he was *not* a downy one, couldn't think what to make of this disheveled female who was clutching a baby, a pistol, and a singularly ugly hound. Furthermore, he knew both the baby and the hound. The pistol, though unfamiliar, looked most businesslike.

Johann was not enamored of strange females brandishing pistols in his face. Quick action was the ticket. He lunged.

Binnie, faced with the alternatives of dropping Toby or loosening the hound, shrieked and let fall Caliban's leash. Caliban, delighted at this unexpected release, and anticipating a pleasant tussle with his old acquaintance the tinker, also leaped. He and Johann collided in midair. Johann lost his balance. His head thwacked against a wagon wheel; he sank senseless to the ground.

"Oh, *good* dog!" cried Binnie, who was very shaken by her close escape. Gratified, Caliban wagged his tail, lolled his tongue, and sat down smack on the tinker's chest. Johann would go nowhere for a while. Binnie cautiously approached the wagon door.

The sight therein—the caravan was indescribably filthy and her friends in dire straits—sent her quickly out again, to scrabble fastidiously in the unconscious Johann's belt for his knife. Toby, who still slept, and the pistol she set aside. Then she once more entered the wagon, after drawing a deep breath, and freed the captives. By unanimous consent, they speedily adjourned outside. In the case of the duke, this was not accomplished effortlessly. His Grace had no feeling whatsoever in his limbs.

Miss Mannering cast a speculative glance around the campsite. She saw the sleeping Toby and the pistol, a smug-looking Caliban perched triumphantly atop the spoils of battle. "Thunder and turf!" she uttered. "Is he *dead?*"

Neal bent over the tinker. "No, but he's going to wake up with the devil of a head." The duke, sitting on the caravan steps while Binnie attempted to restore by brisk massage some feeling to his limbs, aired a hope that the tinker's head might ache as if danced upon by *all* the imps of hell, for eternity. And even that, continued Sandor, would not be sufficient punishment. To this, Miss Mannering offered the opinion that any recourse taken against Johann could not be rebound on themselves, and unpleasantly; Miss Mannering was not adverse to scandal, but she suspected her companions were rather more nice to their notions. And then she turned her attention back to Neal.

"And I am *not* missish!" she stated sternly. "Nor am I bold as a brass-faced monkey, or *pushing!* But I never thought *you* would have used me in this manner, and it has rather raised my spleen. Perhaps the trouble you have been in has deranged your ideas? Because it makes no sense that you should say you have a decided partiality for me, and in the next breath be shabbing off!"

Damned difficult it was to be honorable when one wished more than anything to cast all principle to the winds and ride off into the sunset with the object of one's affections tossed over one's saddlebow. But he could not. "Try and understand!" begged Neal.

"What I understand is that we shall come to cuffs if you keep nattering on about the straight and narrow path!" Perhaps the lieutenant might prove more receptive to a less logical approach? Delilah sniffled. "Perhaps you *want* me to fall ill of a galloping consumption! It makes me very *melancholy.*"

Naturally, Neal could not bear that Delilah should be made unhappy on his account. "Oh, no, puss!" he cried, grasping her hands. "Never that!"

"I see how it is!" wailed Delilah, tears streaming down her

cheeks, which were a telltale pink. "I *have* been too bold! You are only being *kind* to me! You *wish* to marry Miss Choice-Pickerell! The shame of it! I daresay I shall never recover. But do not concern yourself. I shall bear with resignation my irreparable loss, shall reap what comfort I can from the knowledge that my beloved has won the lady of his choice, which will be the only consolation left me on earth."

The lieutenant was impelled to reassert his adoration of Miss Mannering; Miss Mannering retorted that a gentleman who adored one young lady wouldn't marry another, and therefore she concluded that the lieutenant cared nothing for her at all. She had exhibited an unbecoming violence of feeling which she hoped he would forgive; she hoped also that he would not consider her vulgarity of expression as a symptom of light-mindedness; he must realize that she would not behave in so unmaidenly a manner were not her feelings wounded and her heartstrings cracked. Neal protested; it was honor that bound him to Miss Choice-Pickerell, not affection. Delilah was adamant; did he but love her, which obviously he didn't, she wouldn't care a groat if he was thoroughly dishonorable. The preceding is a faithful example of the entire conversation conducted between Lieutenant Baskerville and Miss Mannering, which though of the utmost interest to the participants, was too tedious to be related here in its entirety.

"Gracious God!" uttered Binnie, at the point when Delilah asserted dramatically that her heartstrings were cracked. "What has put Delilah in such a tweak?"

Sandor, who had paid not the least attention to Miss Mannering's histrionics, being a great deal more interested in Miss Baskerville's ministrations to himself, and additionally having grown bored with the antics of what he considered a singularly bird-witted pair, responded absently. "What tweak? Binnie, I owe you an apology."

So generous an admission cast all other considerations—in particular the consideration that perhaps she should inform her brother that Miss Choice-Pickerell was due to break off their betrothal, though Binnie suspected that Neal would refuse to allow Cressida to cry off if he knew how shamelessly she'd been manipulated—from Binnie's mind. "Pray, don't! It is I who must apologize to you! Those horrid things I said—Mark has told me they weren't true."

The duke—who it must be remembered had been recently laboring under any number of difficulties—was not especially delighted by this introduction into the conversation of his friend. "And you told *me* that you decided to marry Mark only to prevent me from further inroads on Neal's inheritance." Having regained mobility in his hands, he grasped her shoulders. "Goose! What do you think he would have done?"

Binnie was feeling extremely shy, a circumstance for which she took herself to task. Sandor was irresistible to most women; birds of paradise vied for his favors—and why not? With his golden hair and sun-bronzed features, his blue eyes and athletic figure, Sandor was surely the most handsome of gentlemen!—and would have scant interest in a female who could not even properly order her thoughts in his presence. Lest she cause him to hold her at a distance—or worse, inspire him with pity—she must not let him guess that she loved him quite desperately. If only she had not laughed, those many years ago! But this was no moment to cry over spilled milk.

"What? Oh, Mark! He would probably have done nothing. At least nothing to the purpose. I'll tell you what he *has* done, Sandor: told that odious Choice-Pickerell female about Delilah and Johann! I wished to sink."

It was obvious to the duke, whose attraction for various diverse ladybirds his cousin had not underestimated, and who as a result was very familiar with the illogical workings of the female mind, that he must proceed cautiously. "What *did* you do?"

"Behaved abominably!" Briefly forgetting her embarrassment, Binnie cast him a mischievous glance. She acquainted him with the whole. The duke's mood was considerably improved by the intelligence that Miss Baskerville had decided *not* to marry Mark. His hands tightened on her shoulders and his blue eyes gleamed. Binnie stared at him, breathless. And then Johann stirred.

He pushed futilely at Caliban, snoozing on his chest, then clasped his aching head. Then he looked cautiously around. Nearby, gurgling in his sleep, lay Toby. "Dashed if it ain't his nibs!" uttered Johann.

Thus recalled to the present, Binnie snatched up the gun.
"Of course it is!" she said reprovingly. "You knew that when
you kidnapped him, you dreadful man! How could you be so
stupid as to try and ransom a duke? You deserve to hang!"

With that sentiment, Johann did not agree. Moreover, he
thought he saw a way to avoid so distasteful a contingency.
He regarded the duke, who was testing the mobility of his
legs, and proceeded with great relish to try and make that
high-and-mighty gentleman squirm. "Not the rum cove!" he
explained. "The brat!" He glanced at Miss Mannering, still
engaged in lachrymose argument with her lieutenant; and
expressed a strong wish that the lieutenant might pop the
question so that Delilah would get her cursed dog off his
chest.

Thus abjured, Delilah briefly abandoned her campaign.
"Now what are you up to?" she inquired sternly of Johann, as
with great expenditure of energy she hauled Caliban off him.
"Because it would be most unlike you not to be up to
something—and I must say it is very tiresome of you, Johann,
to forever be such a perfect block!"

Once again, Johann marveled that the heiress could harbor so little liking for a fine specimen like himself. He decided that Miss Mannering's fortune was above his touch.
However, he had not yet despaired of the duke. "Shall you
tell them, guv'nor?" he suggested slyly. "Or shall I? 'Course,
was you not to come across with some rhino, I might be persuaded not to spill the beans."

His Grace, much to Johann's disappointment, didn't appear
at all perturbed by this threat. In fact, he ignored Johann
altogether, and picked up the sleeping baby. Toby, his slumber
rudely interrupted, yawned hugely and opened his blue eyes.
Serenely, he regarded the duke. Then he smiled.

"So that's it," said Sandor thoughtfully. "I rather suspected
it might be. Now I suppose you will expect me to reward you
for bringing me the brat."

That particular notion had never crossed Johann's mind;
he had supposed the duke to have no special interest in his
by-blows, of whom he conjectured there were any number in
existence. Certainly Johann was agreeable to reward—so
agreeable that he professed himself willing to round up any

number of misbegotten brats. He was, Johann added modestl›
very good at pinching things. His Grace expressed a rath
wry appreciation of this offer, but explained that Johann h;
overestimated his prowess; this was the only of his by-blow
Or, he amended, the only by-blow of which he was aware, a›
his awareness of Toby's existence had only come about latel
the fair Phaedra having kept very quiet on the subje‹
with an intention of using the brat as a second stri›
to her bow. "But you very neatly spiked her guns!" tl
duke concluded. "Perhaps you *do* deserve to be rewarded.'

Delilah had, during these startling revelations, be‹
watching Binnie's face. She could not decide if her benefa
tress was benumbed with shock, or verging on an apoplex
Nor could she determine why the duke was so quick ›
take the word of a confirmed scoundrel like Johann. "Pooh
she said briskly, before Johann's ambition ruined th
segment of her master plan. "This is all a fudge!" Ar
then she stared at Toby, who she had taken from Sando›
lest Sandor, due to lack of experience in handling babie
drop Toby on his head. "Hell and the devil confound it
gasped Miss Mannering. "So *you're* who he reminded n
of!"

"Well, yes, I think I might be," said the duke, a trifl
apologetically. Since he was feeling a trifle bemused by th
sudden confrontation with his offspring, he did not immed
ately realize that the existence of that offspring might caus
a certain lady a very justifiable offense. Warily, he eye
Binnie.

With that same unreadable expression, she returned hi
regard. A suspenseful silence descended. "I never claimed,
the duke remarked, "to be a saint."

"Nor a monk," responded Miss Baskerville, ironically. "Doe
this mean we have to give Toby back, Sandor?"

"I don't see why." Sandor, deflated beyond measure tha
his cousin had not flown into alt upon being presented wit
evidence of the extent to which he had been in the petticoa
line, approached her cautiously. "Phaedra doesn't wan
him, and she'll dare not make a fuss lest her husband fin‹
out."

"But how did she keep it from him?" Binnie achieved, witl

at effort, a semblance of impartial interest. In point of
t, and for any number of reasons, Binnie longed to scratch
e fair Phaedra's eyes out.

As a result of Binnie's eminently reasonable outlook, which
 feared sprang from indifference toward his peccadilloes
d therefore himself, Sandor was tempted to shake her
til her teeth rattled in her head. "I neither know nor
re. Binnie, there are matters we must discuss."

"Indeed there are!" snapped Neal who, due to his discovery
at he was beloved of Miss Mannering, and his further
scovery that Miss Mannering felt herself grievously abused
 his avowed intention to behave honorably, was not in the
st cheerful of moods. "Such as how you dared accuse my
ter of being a prime article of virtue! *You*, a paragon of
ofligacy!"

"Neal, do hush!" Miss Mannering pinched him. "If Binnie
s forgiven him, so must you."

Of that forgiveness, the duke was not convinced. "*Have*
u?" he inquired of Binnie.

Binnie, stricken with a sudden burning desire to be pressed
th almost savage violence against his lordship's breast,
ghed. "I really *could* be a prime article of virtue," said
e.

Sandor, well acquainted with the illogical ways of women,
as far too wise to argue. "Of course you could!" he responded
omptly. "Demure immorality in satin and lace, quite at the
p of the trees! And so you shall be, if you wish. But I am a
lfish man, my darling, and I would much rather you mar-
ed me!"

Miss Baskerville stared at her cousin the duke, who was
ry much begrimed as a result of his misadventures, and
ho additionally was looking as awkwardly hopeful as the
eenest sprig, and strove for a sense of decorum. She failed.
Oh, Sandor, I cannot help it! You are so absurd!" She burst
to laughter.

That Binnie should again greet his ardent declarations
ith merriment did not amuse His Grace; but this time he
ould not by that amusement be deterred. Sibyl was going to
arry him, willing or no. Recalling his intention of throttling
s cousin into compliance if necessary, he grasped her

211

shoulders and shook her ungently. Binnie raised her hands
either push him away or draw him closer, he was not su
which. Nor did he find out. She still clutched his pist
Sandor was deafened by the discharge.

CHAPTER TWENTY-FIVE

The gunshot was heard throughout the surrounding cou
tryside. It caused no consternation to the locals, who we
through long experience inured to the goings-on of the ge
try; but it caused great consternation to Edwina Childe an
her entourage. "Angels defend us!" gasped Edwina. "She h
murdered him. And who can blame her, poor girl? But all th
same—" Words failed her. Silently, Jem proffered the vina
grette. With trembling fingers, Edwina grasped her smellin
salts. Deeply, she inhaled.

Jem was not happy to be part of this expedition, which
addition to Edwina included Miss Choice-Pickerell and M
Dennison, both of whom had burst into the nursery up
hearing Edwina's hysterical outburst, which had resounde
throughout the whole house; and who had thereupon bee
gifted with a jumbled account that consisted largely of broa
hints that the duke of Knowles had led his cousin Sibyl int
the deepest depravity, as a result of which both Sibyl and h
brother wished to murder him. Nor could Edwina fault the
bloodthirst—if any man ever deserved to be murdered, tha
man was the duke—but she could not help thinking of th
scandal. Nor could Miss Choice-Pickerell or Mr. Denniso
since with the potential murderers their own names wer

fortunately linked. At Mr. Dennison's strongly worded
ggestion, they had set out to try and avert the disaster.
But it seemed they were too late, which was not surprising,
nce Edwina was so overcome by the depravity of her cousins
at she frequently came over faint, and had to stop and
ncap her vinaigrette and rest. Now they were only a few
eters from the camp, could see Johann's wagon in the dis-
nce. Abandoning both his charges and his dignity, Jem ran.
The sight that greeted him upon his breathless arrival at
e camp stopped Jem dead in his tracks. Lieutenant Basker-
lle and Miss Mannering and Miss Mannering's hound were
ddled by a fallen figure, beside which crouched Miss
askerville. For some queer reason, Sibyl had hitched up her
irts and was tearing frantically at her petticoats. Of Johann
ere was no sign. (In brief explanation it must be stated that
hann had taken to his heels at sound of the gunshot, never
be seen again in Brighton or its environs. During the
mainder of his long career, which was far from exemplary,
never again tried his hand at kidnapping, though he was
nd of recounting the tale, with suitable embellishments, of
e day when in his power he'd held no less than a duke. Nor
d Johann's path again cross that of Athalia, who set herself
p in a very old profession with the proceeds of the sale of
elilah's mother's wedding ring.)
Everyone was talking at once, save Sibyl, who appeared
vercome by grief. "Don't make a piece of work of it!" abjured
eal, irritably. "You've only nicked his ear, worse luck!"
"Do hush!" remarked Miss Mannering. "I don't know why
ou should be in a fit of the blue devils, Neal! It is *my*
eartstrings that are cracked, and all because of you! Binnie,
on't cry. The duke is perfectly all right, I assure you. Were
e *not* perfectly all right, he would not be cursing you so
readfully!"
Decidedly, the duke was cursing, though his imprecations
ere directed not at the tearful Miss Baskerville, but at
aliban, who was taking advantage of the duke's supine
osition to thoroughly wash his face. "Fiend seize you!"
ellowed the duke. "Get away from me! No, not you, Binnie!
his accursed hound!"
"Of all the unjust things to say!" uttered Miss Mannering.
Caliban is only trying to *help* you, sir. There, you've hurt his

213

feelings. Never mind, Caliban; *I* appreciate you!" To th
assurance the hound responded by sitting back on h
haunches. While so doing, he espied the dumbfounded Je
With a welcoming bark, Caliban raced off to greet his frien

Thus rid of the main impediment to his recovery, Sand
achieved a sitting position. He removed from Binnie's ha
the strip of petticoat with which she had been dabbling f
tilely at his face, being too blinded by tears to properly se
and applied it to his wounded ear. Binnie sobbed. Sando
who had been about to read his cousin a thunderous lectu
on the use and abuse of firearms, abruptly changed his min
"There, there!" he said soothingly, and drew her comfortab
against his chest. "That pistol has a hair trigger. My darlin
it is no great calamity."

Binnie was not so easily consoled. Aghast that she ha
almost killed her cousin, and at the most untimely of m
ments, for he had offered her marriage and she had not on
laughed but nearly murdered him, she burst into renew
tears. Sandor patted her, rather helplessly. Toby, ever
compassionate youngster, was inspired by the duke's dilemn
to abandon the mysterious and complex game he'd been playin
with some pebbles to climb into the duke's lap. The duke eye
his son, rather quizzically.

Jem, meanwhile, endeavored to fend off Caliban's exube
ant greeting. "Why, it's Jem!" Delilah announced. "Have ye
come to our rescue? It's very good of you, even if you are t
late!" And then her voice faded as around the side of th
wagon came Edwina and Cressida and Mark. "Oh, blood
hell!" said she.

"God bless my soul! He *isn't* dead!" ejaculated Edwin
staring at her cousin. "Sandor! Binnie! How *could* you?"

"How could we what?" inquired the duke, rather absentl
The duke was finding it surprisingly pleasant to clasp in on
arm a tearful lady and in the other his own offspring. Mut
was the lad? Sandor thought he'd see what the doctors had t
say about that. No son of his was going to labor under
handicap. "My darling, do stop this sniveling! You're worryin
the brat."

Of course Binnie did not wish to do that. She raised he
head from Sandor's shoulder to gaze mistily upon Toby. Tob
smiled. She kissed him.

I never!" gasped Miss Choice-Pickerell, who had herself
[be]en temporarily deprived of speech by so perverted a scene.
[T]his is a pretty thing! And to think, Miss Baskerville, that
[you] accused *me* of being scheming and heartless! Words fail
[me]!"

For this failure, no one expressed regret. "*Did* you?" in-
[qu]ired the duke of Miss Baskerville.

"I did." Binnie awarded an unappreciative glance to Miss
[Ch]oice-Pickerell. "I also said she was insipid and humdrum,
[pro]sy and mealymouthed, and that her conversation was flat
[as] a street pavement. Moreover, I don't regret a word of it!"

"That's my girl!" said the duke. "Incidentally, Miss Choice-
[Pi]ckerell, I have decided that I don't care for this betrothal of
[yo]urs. Neal won't do for you. I withdraw my consent."

"Well!" gasped Miss Choice-Pickerell.

For a young man abruptly released from an unpleasant
[fat]e, Neal exhibited scant relief. "That won't wash," he said
[bit]terly. "But thank you, Sandor, all the same! Cressida's
[al]ready made it clear that if I don't marry her she'll spread
[sto]ries that you found Delilah living in a tinkers' camp. And
[sh]e *would!*"

"Neal!" Delilah's freckled face was alight. "You *do* love
[m]e!"

"Confound it, puss!" retorted the lieutenant. "What do you
[th]ink I've been trying to tell you? I think I've loved you ever
[si]nce that first minute."

"When I was calling Johann a nodcock?" inquired Miss
[M]annering, with burning curiosity. "It just goes to show that
[on]e can suffer Cupid's sting in the most unexpected situations!
[B]ecause that is precisely when I fell in love with you. But I
[w]ish you'd told me sooner, Neal, because I daresay I should've
[co]ntrived somehow that Miss Choice-Pickerell shouldn't hold
[yo]u to blackmail!"

"Well!" cried Miss Choice-Pickerell again. "As if I would
[be]have in so vulgar a manner! I am shocked by your
[al]legations, Neal! Your conduct verges on outright lunacy!"

Brutally, the duke broke into these protestations of inno-
[ce]nce. "Miss Choice-Pickerell," he said, in a very dangerous
[vo]ice, "would not dare slander *my* family."

"Dash it!" Neal was by this simple sentence remarkably
[en]thused. "Does that mean I *don't* have to marry her?"

"Yes." Sandor had grown noticeably bored with this change, being anxious to continue with his own pursu which had at a most untimely moment been interrupted b gunshot. "I never meant you *should* marry her. In truth always wondered why you wanted to get leg-shackled t pattern card of respectability!"

Neal wondered likewise, having during this exchange gro so in charity with Sandor that he quite forgot that once overriding ambition had been to remove himself from une Sandor's thumb. Blissfully he regarded Miss Mannering, w was enacting rosy-cheeked ecstasy.

Before she could be given her *congé*, the presentation which appeared imminent, Miss Choice-Pickerell erupted in outraged speech. Rigid with indignation, she expressed firm determination to be freed from a betrothal that had be a ghastly mistake. For some time, she asserted, she had f that her prospective alliance with the lieutenant would unsuitable; she had been, she claimed, grievously misled his character. He was frivolous and frippery and odiou hot-at-hand; he did not on any subject feel as he should; s was sadly disappointed in him. A young lady with her stro sense of propriety, declared Miss Choice-Pickerell, could r be expected to ally herself with a family who were so lacki in awareness of the amenities as to conduct themselves in manner that was positively debased.

"Debased?" echoed Edwina, from the wagon steps. "Mer on us!" With newly acquired expertise, Jem wielded t vinaigrette. So vigorously did he do so that Edwina sneeze

"Debased!" asserted Mark, grimly. Miss Choice-Pickerel nobly delivered denunciation speech had recalled to Mark h own considerable chagrin. He had been led a merry dance the garden path by a lady who was clearly no better than o of the wicked. Had not Sandor so accused her himself? Obv ously Sandor should know! But before he raked Miss Baske ville over the coals for her infamy, he required a confirmati of fact. "Sandor, is that child *yours?*"

The duke regarded Toby, currently engaged in pulling tl gilt buttons off his dark dress coat, with paternal pride. "O yes!" he said cheerfully. Miss Mannering, at this poin interjected an opinion that Toby was as like to the duke two peas in a pod. Thereby roused from his fascinate contemplation of Miss Mannering's freckled face, Lieutenant Baskerville asked her to marry him. Without the slightest hesitation, Miss Mannering agreed.

"That tears it!" uttered Mark. "You *are* a Monster of Depravity! *Both* of you are! While I was paying your cousin very proper court, *you* were paying her attentions that were *much* too pointed! And while I am not surprised at your philandering, I am shocked to my soul that you should have engaged your own cousin in a squalid little debauch. It surpasses everything!"

With these accusations, Binnie aroused from her stupor—which was attendant upon her speculations as to whether the duke had seriously meant his proposal of marriage, and conjectures about how she might persuade him to repeat the offer, so that she could valiantly refrain from laughing at him. "Gracious God!" she said. "You think that Sandor and I have, er, persevered in loose morality? That Toby is—" His expression was answer enough. "Merciful heavens!" cried Binnie, and subsided onto Sandor's shoulder once again.

Miss Mannering, observing the proceedings with interest, put forth an opinion that Mr. Dennison had shot the cat—or perhaps he was merely bacon-brained? The duke was the highest of sticklers, after all, and the highest of sticklers was not likely to act the rogue toward his own cousin, who additionally hadn't the slightest appearance of a lady preoccupied with sin. Not that appearances could be trusted, but in this case Miss Mannering was prepared to wager her reputation that her benefactress was of unblemished character. For Mr. Dennison to hint otherwise, she added sternly, was cursed unchivalrous. Mr. Dennison, highly incensed at receiving a lecture from this source, responded ungallantly that Miss Mannering had no reputation to wager. At this, Lieutenant Baskerville stated an intention to murder Mr. Dennison. And in the midst of all this brouhaha, which so fascinated Jem that he quite forgot the vinaigrette, Edwina fainted dead away.

It was the duke who put an end to the contretemps, in his inimitably bad-tempered way. "Quiet!" he roared. Instantly, he was obeyed. Briefly, he looked down at Miss Baskerville, whose face was hidden against his chest. "Are you laughing or crying?" he inquired.

"Oh!" Binnie, flushed and disheveled and absolutely mag
nificent, sat up. "Laughing, of course! You recall my un
becoming levity!"

"I do." Sandor regarded his cousin with an expression tha
caused her giggles abruptly to cease, due not to dread of hi
anger but to a curious shortness of breath. Then he looked a
Mr. Dennison and Miss Choice-Pickerell with a singula
lack of appreciation, and informed them that Toby was no
as so uncharitably alleged, the result of a liaison betwee
himself and his cousin, but of a liaison between himsel
and someone else. The identity of that other lady he di
not choose to reveal. Nor did he intend to endure furthe
slurs upon his moral character which, though hardly in a
pristine state, was no worse than that of any other gentle
man, and rather better than some. And then he made ver
clear to Miss Choice-Pickerell and Mr. Dennison the dir
repercussions to themselves if a word of their uncharitabl
allegations were to be breathed to anyone. Having inspire
them both with a very healthy terror, he demanded that the
immediately depart.

To say that Mr. Dennison turned craven at the intimatio
that, were he to displease the duke, Lieutenant Baskervill
would be allowed to carve out his gizzard, as the duke ha
asserted with the greatest gravity, would be to malign Mr
Dennison. However, Mark was only too eager to remove
himself from a situation that was distasteful in the extreme
Solicitously, he escorted Cressida homeward, during which
journey they exchanged a great many barbed comments on
the perverse nature of the Baskervilles, and professed a mutual relief at having escaped entanglement with so profligate
a family.

"And now," said the duke, as he rose, deposited Toby in
Edwina's lap, and pulled Binnie to her feet. "Where were we?
When you so ungraciously shot me?"

"God bless my soul!" muttered Edwina. Having wrenched
her vinaigrette away from Jem, who was currently engaged
in an unwilling game of catch-as-catch-can with Caliban, and
having inhaled deeply and repeatedly of it, she was much
more herself. Why Binnie should have shot Sandor, if Sandor
hadn't ruined her, which it now seemed Sandor had not,
Edwina couldn't conceive. Curious, she regarded Toby. Toby,

nsing another potential conquest, gurgled and beamed. hat mattered a by-blow? Edwina decided abruptly. Any umber of people had them! Gentlemen were expected to sow eir wild oats—look at the royal family!

"I didn't *mean* to shoot you!" protested Binnie, stricken at Sandor might think the mishap deliberate. "I may have d you go and be damned, but I didn't mean to see to it yself! I mean, I didn't mean it at all! Sandor, how *dare* you ugh at me?"

Sandor grasped his cousin's arms and drew her to him. "My arling," he said, with great gravity, "if you wished it, I ould go to the devil for you."

"Sandor!" Binnie stared entranced into his ill-tempered nd diabolically handsome face. "But I *don't* wish it!" And en she said no more. Sandor, so wise in the illogical ways of omen as to understand precisely what manner of action ould please his cousin best, had crushed her with almost avage violence against his breast.

With great contentment, Delilah surveyed this ardent em- race. Several times she had wondered if she could bring the ing off; but now she had the satisfaction of knowing she'd layed her cards excellently well with these people. Unless he missed her guess, Miss Choice-Pickerell had already de- ided to set her cap at Mr. Dennison, and Delilah imagined hey'd suit very well. "There!" she said aloud, to the enrap- ured Neal. "I'll stake my corset-cover that we'll *all* be happy s grigs!"

EPILOGUE

As matters evolved, Miss Mannering's corset-cover was to
main in her possession. Miss Choice-Pickerell achieved her
nbition of being married in St. George's, Hanover Square;
d though in later years she and Mr. Dennison grew to
sapprove of everything but each other, they did so in per-
ct harmony. Though a similar accolade could not be accorded
e fair Phaedra and her colonel, they did manage to resolve
eir domestic difficulties, or so it must be assumed: Phaedra,
ter her debacle with Lord Knowles, was never seen to pay
arked attention to any gentleman; and it was noted by the
lonel's subalterns that his tolerance had grown. Lord
nowles settled in matrimony with Miss Prunes and Prisms,
d, despite her tendency to laugh at him, achieved the
most felicity; Toby, whose muteness was pronounced in-
rable by the doctors, grew up into a young man of such
lossal charm that he had no need of speech. Edwina Childe,
eed of the anxiety attendant upon living in a household
here everyone was at loggerheads, abandoned her dieting
d achieved a remarkable girth; Caliban, too, grew plump
1 a regime of tasty tidbits snatched from diverse sources,
d sired a large and unlovely progeny.

As for the tinker's lass herself, Miss Mannering formed her
nnection with the gentleman whom she considered most
igible, and shared with him an adoration undiminished by
me. Over their definitely ramshackle household ruled the
ithful Jem, who in return for his loyal services was ele-
ated to the status of butler, and who despite his exalted

standing was never less than eager to join his employers in spree. Sprees there were in plenty: the decorum befitting to lady of breeding Delilah never achieved. But whatever a verse comments might have been made about Lieutena Baskerville's dashing lady—and such comments were occ sionally made, thought not by Mr. and Mrs. Dennison, who pointed silence on the subject was generally considere queer—no one was ever heard to deny Delilah's frequent voiced assertion that she was a damned knowing one indee